How Laura Lewis Met Richard Brown

HOW LAURA LEWIS MET RICHARD BROWN

JOANNE BODEN

Choc Lit

A JOFFE BOOKS COMPANY

Choc Lit
A Joffe Books company
www.choc-lit.com

First published in Great Britain in 2024

Cover art by Jarmila Takač

ISBN: 978-1781898093

In memory of Peter John Scott, 1954–2024.
I am so sorry you didn't get to see this one.

For all the care workers out there.
Thank you.

CHAPTER ONE

Laura Lewis stood in front of Church View Cottage and, despite the biting cold and the persistent drizzle, smiled. It looked just like those cottages she had read about in fairy tales as a young girl. Those country cottages with two matching lattice windows, a central chimney and a bright-yellow door. Church View Cottage had obviously seen better days, but it looked to have been cared for and loved over the years. Laura hovered by the wooden gate, breathing in the fresh country air, so unlike the thick and dust-polluted air back in the city where she had lived and worked.

Entering the village on the local bus had been like stepping back in time. Fairy lights still glistened along the hedges which ran either side of the road and bunting had been hung up advertising that the January coffee morning would be taking place in the village hall. As the bus circled the village square, the Christmas tree still stood tall and proud, although it was now well into January.

Laura had spied a little shop and a pub, and as the bus had continued on its way she passed a small primary school. The children had been running around the playground, wrapped in scarves and with brightly coloured woolly hats on their heads. Church View Cottage was located on the outskirts of the village it seemed, the last stop before it headed back to the local town. She had been the last person off the bus.

As Laura opened the small gate and wheeled her suitcase down the path, she wondered why it was called Church View as she hadn't passed a church. She should have asked the estate agent about the name.

Laura propped the suitcase against the small step leading up towards the front door and unzipped her shoulder bag to locate the keys she had been given. This cottage and the village were to be her new home for the next six months. Had she made the right decision in coming here? She didn't know, not yet, as only time would tell. But she had made the only decision she could. To flee.

There were only two keys on the key ring, so Laura quickly found the one she needed and with a gentle twist, the door groaned open. Stepping into the narrow hallway, she flicked the light switch and was surprised by how bright and welcoming the narrow space was. A picture hung on the wall by the front door, showing the sun beaming down and flowers in full bloom. Laura stepped closer to examine the picture, noticing that it was actually a black-and-white photograph, but there was no date. Below it was a small wooden table and on that sat a telephone, the old-fashioned type with large square digits. She really had stepped back in time. She lifted the receiver and heard a dialling tone, so at least she was connected to the outside world. She wondered if she would get a mobile signal out here. Fumbling in her coat pocket, she retrieved her mobile and noted that there was a weak signal, just one bar, so the landline could come in handy. Laura hadn't thought much about internet connection, another thing she had forgotten to mention to the estate agent. She didn't own a laptop and wasn't on social media, but she would need email and to be able to browse the news on her phone. It didn't look like there was any 4G signal. She would sort all of that out tomorrow. In the scheme of things, it was relatively unimportant.

Laura peered around the door on the left side of the hall-way. She found a small and cosy room, described by the estate agent as the snug. The room was perfect for curling up in with a good book in front of the open fire. She closed the door and headed straight on into the kitchen at the back of the cottage. She had expected to find a small yet functional kitchen, so she couldn't help the smile that spread across her face at the sight of a large scrubbed pine table, and the huge Aga that took up the back wall. She hoped it came with instructions. The cooker in her tiny one-bedroomed flat had been electric. She gazed at the low beams, the worktops free from clutter, and realised that all she could hear was the humming of the fridge. Pure bliss. She would have time to think here. Time to find herself again.

Laura dropped the keys onto the pine table and noticed a handwritten note addressed to her propped up against a large biscuit tin decorated with flowers.

We hope that you enjoy Church View Cottage as much as we did. We've left out the instructions on how to use the Aga for cooking and heating. Both are pretty simple when you get to grips with them. We mainly used the wood burner in the snug, though. Keep the door open and the whole cottage heats up.

    Jenny and Dave xxx

    P.S. We hope you like the biscuits — homemade choc-chip.

Laura picked up the tin — it felt heavy. Prising off the lid, she looked inside to find it full of biscuits. She inhaled the rich chocolate smell. There was no way she could make biscuits like this, although she made a mental note to do the same when it was her time to leave. She could always buy a few packets. Such a simple and kind gesture made all the difference.

She decided to leave her coat on until she'd got the fire going. Hopefully there would be wood. Walking back along the hallway and opening the door to the snug, she found a large basket to the side of the fireplace, and indeed, it was full to the brim with logs and kindling. They must have stocked up before they'd left. She knew that they had only left a week ago. Just before New Year. They were emigrating to New Zealand. The timing could not have been better, seeing as Laura was starting her new job at Cedar House care home in only two days' time. She could hear her mother's voice loud and clear in her head: *Cutting it a bit fine, aren't we, Laura?* Well, yes, she was, but it had all worked out, hadn't it?

Laura dragged her suitcase into the kitchen and made a quick plan in her head. Locate cups, tea bags and milk, start a fire, and then unpack. Opening the fridge, she was glad to find a bottle of milk, eggs and some butter, which the estate agent had provided for her. Apparently, she lived not far away and had popped the provisions in for her last night on her way home from work. Also, presumably to check that the cottage was clean and presentable. Now, all Laura had to do was find the tea bags which she had packed in her suitcase.

* * *

An hour later, Laura had successfully lit the fire, thankful that there were firelighters on the mantelpiece. She'd also explored the kitchen, rummaging in cupboards and finding chunky mugs in a range of pretty colours, and had had two cups of tea. The kitchen was surprisingly well-equipped. There was a fridge freezer, a microwave, every utensil she would ever need, dinner plates, bowls, mixing bowls and even cake tins, although Laura wasn't much of a baker. After her tea she had lugged the suitcase up the narrow rickety stairs. There was only one bedroom, but it was spacious and bright, and the pretty floral duvet cover made her smile. Now kitted out by Jenny and Dave as a holiday let, the house came with bedding and towels, which was a huge bonus. The large window overlooking the back garden meant she wouldn't hear the traffic rumbling by. But, if the past few hours were anything to go by, not much traffic passed through this sleepy Lancashire village.

With all her strength, Laura managed to lift the suitcase onto the double bed and threw back the lid. Her world lay inside the dull, brown interior. A few pairs of jeans, T-shirts, jumpers, pyjamas, underwear, work shoes, a couple of treasured books, her Kindle, phone and Kindle charger, make-up bag and a few photographs — none of which she could look at right now. She just needed them to be with her, to be a part of her new life. Picking up the envelope of photographs, she shoved it into the top drawer of the bedside cabinet. Her pyjamas were placed under the pillow and the rest of her clothes were folded neatly into the awaiting empty drawers. No need to use the wardrobe.

Laura took a step back from the bed and caught her reflection in the dressing-table mirror. Her long dark-blonde hair seemed even duller than usual and her pale complexion was slightly flushed. There was nothing extraordinary about her. She'd never thought herself pretty, just rather average. Average build, average height and even her blue eyes were nothing to write home about, neither dark and mysterious nor light and pretty. With a sigh, she looked at her meagre belongings. She didn't seem to have accumulated a lot from her previous life. She wanted no reminders, needing to shrug off that skin in order to wear this new one.

Of course, Lottie, her younger and highly successful sister with the model family, had laughed when Laura had told her about her plans to move to the countryside. *Running away, more like*, Lottie had said, giving her that annoying knowing look she had perfected over the years. Laura had protested, telling her that she wasn't running away but that she needed to go somewhere new. Somewhere without memories, somewhere where she wasn't reminded of Mark everywhere she went. The restaurant they'd gone to for their first date. The first house they'd lived in, and the last. She couldn't stand it any longer. She'd had to get away. Lottie and their mother, Maureen, just hadn't understood why. They'd told her she had no reason to run away. That the memories would only follow her like long-lost friends. Laura was determined to prove them wrong.

She had come across the sleepy village of Buttermarsh quite by accident one afternoon while browsing the internet, during a rare day off. She'd wondered what it would be like to simply get away. To just up sticks and move to somewhere where no one would know her past, know what had happened. There was only her to consider. Nothing was stopping her, only herself. So, Laura had started to look for villages in Lancashire, having been on holiday there as a child. It was only a short drive away from the outskirts of Liverpool where she had grown up in a two-bed semi with a backyard. It was only when she'd found out that the village had a care home and an open vacancy that she'd begun to make serious plans, thinking that perhaps she could move to the countryside after all. What had started out as a glimmer of an idea had turned into reality. And here she was. Standing in Church View Cottage with no church in sight.

Making her way downstairs for another pot of tea, she halted in her tracks at a persistent knocking on the front door. Laura wasn't sure if she could be seen hovering on the stairs through the door's frosted stained glass, and for a fleeting moment thought about crouching down and ignoring who-ever it was. Another knock made her mind up and she scurried down the stairs to find out who it was.

Laura flung open the door to be greeted by an elderly lady wearing a green Barbour jacket, matching green wellies, and holding the lead that belonged to a black-and-white border collie.

The woman, her white hair scraped severely and neatly into a bun, beamed at Laura. Her cheeks were flushed as if she'd been on a brisk walk.

'Hello, dear. I thought it best to knock and introduce myself. I'm Gwen.'

Laura stood motionless as Gwen thrust out a gloved hand towards her. Slowly, Laura held out her own hand and politely shook it.

Laura forced a smile and then let her hand drop. She had no idea what the country code was for introducing yourself to a complete stranger who knocked on your door. 'I'm Laura. That's a beautiful dog,' she said eventually.

Gwen beamed once more and reached down to pat the dog's head. 'Oh, this is my Benji. He's an old man now.'

Laura wondered whether this woman was one of those people who treated their dog like it was a child.

'He's been with us for such a very long time,' Gwen continued. 'Don't know what we'd do without him.'

'Well, he's very well behaved,' Laura said, as she grew more concerned that she had left this woman and her dog on her doorstep for longer than was necessarily good manners. Should she invite them in for tea and biscuits? It was on the very tip of her tongue to do so when Gwen interrupted her thoughts.

'Well, I'd best be off. I just wanted to say hello. You'll probably see us around. Me and my husband, Bill, we own the Fox and Hound in the village, so be sure to pop in and have a welcome drink on us.'

Laura smiled, thanked her and then waited for the question that never came.

What are you doing here?

With a thankful sigh of relief, she said goodbye and slowly closed the door.

CHAPTER TWO

'Come and get your shoes on, Henry,' Richard yelled. A quick glance at his watch confirmed that they were already running late. He'd have to apologise once again to the preschool staff.

'Henry!'

Richard picked up the bright-red shoes from the wooden rack by the front door, and once his four-year-old son was seated on the bottom step of the stairs, quickly pushed them onto Henry's feet. Thank goodness for Velcro straps.

'What's next, Henry?' Richard asked.

'Coat,' Henry replied, reaching for his blue duffel coat hanging on the peg.

Richard unhooked it for him, and although he knew that his son should learn to put on his own coat, he helped him with the arms and buttoned it up. He could hear Sally's voice in his head telling him off, but he ignored it. They were late and she was no longer here.

Grabbing Henry's Spider-Man lunchbox, Richard slung his work satchel over his shoulder and grabbed the key from the hook on the back of the door.

'Righto, Mister, off we go,' he said.

'Off we go, Daddy,' Henry repeated, followed by a mischievous smile.

Richard ruffled his dark-brown, almost black hair, so like his own, and they headed out the door.

* * *

'I'm so sorry we're late, again,' Richard said, ignoring the sympathetic stares from the manager whose name he still couldn't remember.

'It's not a problem, Richard. We know how busy you are.' She gave him that look he had grown to loathe.

Henry had run off as soon as they'd arrived without so much as a backwards glance. Richard wished he could do the same.

Were the staff like this with all lone parents who were busy? Or was it just the dads? Or possibly the bereaved? He didn't want to be treated any differently. A telling-off would actually make him feel better.

'Right, well, I'd best be off. Tracey will be picking him up tonight,' he said.

'Okay, no problem. She knows that the password has changed for this month, right?' the manager asked.

Richard blinked. Nodded. Had he remembered to tell her? He'd better give her a call later to remind her. He still thought it slightly daft that they used a password at all. It was a small village preschool which only a handful of children attended. But he supposed it was best to be careful, even though Tracey picked Henry up a couple of times each week.

'We will see you in the morning, then?' the manager said, as if dismissing him.

Richard nodded. Coming to the realisation that he was being let out, he quickly retreated through the main entrance and made his bid for freedom.

* * *

Richard Brown was a well-liked and much-respected primary school teacher. The kids adored him, as did the parents. He loved his job. He had known that he'd wanted to teach as soon as he'd met his new teacher, Mr Peters, when he was in Year Six. During that impressionable year when changes were being put in place for the transition to secondary school, Mr Peters had been kind, understanding, fair and fun. He had provided that much-needed male role model in Richard's life. Richard loved his gran, Gertie, like a mother. She had brought him up single-handedly and he would always be eternally grateful to her. But, as a little boy, sometimes all he had wanted was to kick a ball or have a rough-and-tumble or talk about boy things with someone, all things he couldn't do with Gertie.

His mother and father had both been twenty-three years of age when they'd been killed outright by a drunk driver. They had left two-year-old Richard with Gertie for the evening, to enjoy a rare night out at the cinema. They'd never known that it would be the last time they would see their son. They'd never even said goodbye as he'd been asleep in his new toddler bed and they hadn't wanted to wake him. It wouldn't have been fair on Gertie.

Richard had stayed with his gran, his father's mother, ever since that fateful night. She had taken on the responsibility of a full-time mother at the age of forty-two. Although today this would still be considered young, thirty-eight years ago she'd been perceived as an older mother. When it came to school pick-up, the other mothers at the gate wouldn't engage with her. Gertie would stand alone and wait for Richard to run out of the reception-class door, while the other mums stood around in groups, chatting about playdates and sleepovers. Richard hadn't understood what was happening at the time — how could he? He was only a child. But now he saw the older parents, and the grandparents, many of whom stood alone while the younger parents chatted. He had never understood why they didn't congregate together. Perhaps they didn't need to. Not everybody needed to be part of a group. Some people were happy to be alone. Himself included.

Richard now approached the same school, but instead of the school gate he headed towards the staffroom. He knew that Alistair, the head, would already be there, sitting in his usual chair with a freshly brewed cup of coffee in his hand. Alistair lived alone. No ex-wife, no children. He lived for teaching and golf, and at the age of fifty he was here to stay. As expected, when Richard pulled open the creaking staffroom door he was greeted by the smell of coffee and the tapping of keys that radiated from Alistair's laptop.

'Good morning,' Alistair said, raising his eyes from the laptop screen. 'Coffee is ready for you.'

'Thanks.' Richard placed his bag on the floor and reached for his coffee cup that had *World's Best Dad* embossed on either side. 'You have a good weekend?' He sank down into the faded low-slung armchair with his drink. The armrests were now threadbare with age.

'Spent most of Saturday here,' Alistair said with a sigh. 'Easier to catch up with work here than at home.'

Richard nodded. Sipped his coffee. Too many distractions at home, such as television and having a snooze.

'How was your weekend with Henry?' Alistair closed his laptop screen.

'Good and exhausting,' Richard said, but his smile betrayed him. He'd had a busy weekend, but they'd packed so much into their time together. During the week he hardly got to see him. A snatched hour here or there. By the time he picked him up from Tracey's, or Megan's, it was time for a bath and bed. Richard would sit alone, marking homework and planning lessons while his son was safely tucked up in bed. He knew that as Henry grew older, things would become easier. But at this moment in time, he missed him. Preschool, his mother-in-law and sister-in-law were all getting the best of his little boy.

Richard shouldn't grumble. He got every weekend off — many single parents didn't have that luxury — not to mention the long school holidays. He didn't work shifts and he had a good support network. Things could be a lot worse. But, then again, Sally could still be with him. Henry could still have a mum. Life was never fair. You made do with what you

11

got. But, he couldn't help feeling guilty about Henry, the fact that he was motherless. Richard had grown up without knowing who his mother was. He couldn't remember her. His only reminders were those of faded sepia photographs, blurred and distorted with age. Henry, too, had photographs. His were clear, digital copies, but no matter how accurately they captured that moment in time, it was still in the past. There would be no new memories of his mother for him.

'So, all ready for the day, then?' Alistair had placed his cup in the sink and now stood by the door, ready to retreat to the safety of his office.

Richard blinked. Tried to clear the fog from his brain, but knew he'd been rumbled. Knew that Alistair was fully aware that his thoughts were somewhere else entirely.

Richard cleared his throat. 'All good, thanks.'

With a nod of his head, Alistair opened the door. The sound of voices could be heard from the corridor. Time to head to his classroom and get ready for the day ahead.

* * *

Tracey Williams lived on the other side of the village, a good fifteen minutes' walk from the primary school and the pre-school which was located on the other side of the road. It was then a further ten-minute walk to Richard's house on the edge of the village. Richard didn't know how he would manage to juggle it all without the help of his mother-in-law. Although Sally had died nearly three years ago, he still thought of Tracey as his mother-in-law. She was a huge part of his life and always would be. He'd see the concern etched onto her face when he mentioned the name of a female colleague or friend. Those unsettling thoughts that another woman would drag Henry away from her. But Richard had told Tracey that she would always have Henry in her life, no matter what happened in his personal life, and he meant every word. Henry was what mattered.

Before Richard could even knock on the front door it was flung open and he was ushered inside, into the warmth of the kitchen that he knew so well.

'Will you stay for a cuppa?' Tracey poured boiling water into the sturdy brown teapot which always had a place on the wooden mat on the sideboard. 'Henry's happily playing with the trains, so he'll be fine for a bit.' She smiled, reached for the biscuit tin and placed it in front of him as if he was four years old, not nearing forty. 'Stay for tea if you like?' she added.

'That's kind of you, but I need to get back. Loads of paper-work to get through, plus a lesson plan.' Richard leaned against the kitchen counter.

He watched her smile slip and instantly regretted his words. He always felt bad when he refused her food. 'We can make Wednesday, though. We'll have our tea with you and then go straight to the home. It's my non-contact afternoon so I can have the evening off.'

Tracey's smile appeared once more like magic, easing Richard's guilt at having to work such long hours, for not spending enough quality time with his son.

Tracey placed his cup of tea on the table.

'Daddy, Daddy.' Henry ran into the kitchen clutching a miniature Thomas the Tank Engine train.

Richard bent down and scooped him up into a bear hug.

'How was your day?' he asked, pulling out the kitchen chair for Henry to sit on. Richard sat down next to him and sipped his tea.

'I had a good day, Daddy. I did you a painting.' Henry's face broke out into a huge grin as Tracey pulled the painting free from the grip of the fridge magnets and passed it to Richard.

'You want some apple juice, Henry?' Tracey asked, already opening the fridge door. She always had several bottles in the fridge.

'Yes, please, Nana.'

'This is wonderful.' Richard gazed at the brightly coloured painting of a rainbow over a square house with four windows.

13

On the path outside, Henry had painted two stick figures. One taller than the other. Underneath he had written *Daddy* and *Henry*. A sudden lump formed in Richard's throat.

He turned to his son, smiled and uttered one word. 'Perfect.'

* * *

The air had turned colder and so Richard quickened their steps for the short walk home.

'Fish fingers and chips for tea. That okay with you?'

Richard got a beaming smile in return and a quick thumbs up. It was obviously too much effort for Henry to speak and walk at the same time.

Richard chuckled and clutched Henry's hand even tighter to propel him towards home.

They passed the Fox and Hound. Richard could feel the warmth creeping towards him as Gwen opened the pub's door.

He knew that they wouldn't make it past her without a quick hello. She doted on Henry. She and Bill had never had children. He didn't know why, but there was a sad story lurking somewhere in her past.

'Oh, I thought it was you,' Gwen said cheerfully, brandishing a bag of sweets. 'Here you are, Henry.'

'What do you say, Henry?' Richard said.

'Thank you, Mrs Gwen.'

'Oh, you're welcome, love. And how was preschool today?' Her eyes flickered towards the painting. 'Ah, you've been painting, I see.'

'Me and Daddy,' Henry told her proudly. 'We're going to put it on our fridge.'

Gwen looked at Richard and smiled. 'The perfect place,' she said.

'And how are you today, Gwen?' Richard asked.

'I'm fine, love.' Gwen leaned in closer. 'I met the new neighbour today.'

Ah, Richard thought. This was the real reason they'd been stopped. Henry began to jiggle up and down.

'New neighbour?' Richard wasn't aware that anyone new had moved into the village.

'Yes, you know, the cottage on the other side of the village. The cottage that's after mine.'

'Church View Cottage?' He had always thought the name a little strange as there was no church in the village, nor in the viewable vicinity.

'Yes, that's the one. Well, she only moved in today. Not from around here. I didn't get much chance to talk to her, but she seems like the professional type. Well spoken, you know. I invited her here for a drink, so if she turns up I'll find out more info for you.'

'For me?' Richard tried to hide his irritation. He'd briefly toyed with dating again, testing the water, but he didn't need any help from Gwen.

Gwen sighed. 'Yes, you,' she said slowly.

Richard held his hand up. He did not want to have this conversation. Not with Gwen, not with anyone, and especially not in front of his four-year-old son. 'Well, we must be off. Henry's ready for his tea.' Richard wasn't quite able to meet her eye and cursed the fact that he could feel his cheeks turning pink.

Gwen took a step back and nodded. He noticed the knowing smile flicker across her face. She knew she'd touched a nerve.

'Well, see you soon, and enjoy your tea. Anything nice?' Gwen asked.

'Fish fingers and chips,' they said in unison. Then he grabbed Henry's hand once more and they made their way home.

CHAPTER THREE

Laura was glad there wasn't a raincloud in sight as she had no umbrella, but the country puddles and mud were something else. She had shoved her feet into previously unworn yellow wellies — bought five years ago on a whim. Now, as she navigated the narrow lanes towards the care home, she was very glad that she'd brought them with her. Her sturdy work shoes were tucked safely into her shoulder bag, along with sandwiches and a packet of jelly babies. She never went anywhere without them.

Keeping her head down and her pace brisk, Laura prayed that she didn't bump into anyone. Her only visitor had been Gwen a couple of days ago and she'd avoided the local shop for fear of the gossip mill. She just wanted to settle into village life and find her feet. Only then would she be ready to meet the locals.

As Laura crossed over the road, she noticed cars already parked in the village school. Teachers getting a head start on the day, despite it being only just gone seven. She would be far too early for work, but nerves had got the better of her. After her breakfast of toast and jam, and two cups of instant coffee, she couldn't stay in the cottage any longer. She'd buzzed with a restless energy. She needed to get out. Laura's plan had been to walk slowly, just take a leisurely stroll, but her footsteps had matched her racing heartbeat. She glanced at her wristwatch — she was going be half an hour early for her first shift. She would either appear to be too eager or incredibly nervous. She wasn't sure which was the better option.

Laura turned the corner, which housed a small play area, and Cedar House care home came into view. The young and old only divided by a small patch of land. Laura remembered an article she'd read recently about how a care home in Sweden had brought in primary school children to talk to the older residents. It had not only been beneficial for the older people, but it had also been beneficial for the children. Good for everyone. Laura pondered this thought as she passed by the swings on her way towards the main entrance.

The long and winding path cut through a sculpted green landscape with empty flower beds. Laura thought that it must look lovely and full of colour during the summer. She pressed the intercom by the side of the door, and several seconds later she heard a buzzing sound and a loud click as the lock was released. Laura pulled open the door and stepped into the warmth and comfort of the home. The manager's office was to the right of the entranceway and towards the left was a large day room. Just past the office was a large communal reception area, which was where Laura decided to wait until someone greeted her. She didn't want to go to the staffroom because of safeguarding issues. She'd wait until someone came to greet her. She assumed that all the day staff would head towards the staffroom once they came on duty. So, if no one came to find her, she'd follow the first member of staff to walk through the front door. Laura sat down on one of the comfy reception chairs and gazed out of the large panoramic window which offered views of the front lawn and the path she'd just made her way down. She found it a little strange that the member of staff who'd buzzed her in hadn't greeted her, or even checked to verify who she was. This would never have happened on the ward where she used to work, and things shouldn't be any different here, even though it was a care home in the middle of nowhere. For all they knew, she could be an axe-wielding murderer. She could have ransacked the entire place and made a swift exit before anyone noticed what had happened.

Glancing back towards the window, Laura saw a figure walking down the path. Then, as they got closer, she saw that it was an older woman in a care-assistant's uniform, just like her own. Laura watched as the woman pressed the intercom, then, following a click and a buzz, stepped into the entranceway.

The woman quickly removed her bright-blue woolly hat and gloves, and after stamping her feet on the mat, briskly made her way towards Laura.

'Hello, I'm Linda, the senior carer on duty this morning. You must be Laura.' Linda held out her hand and Laura shook it.

Such a formal thing to do, but Laura liked her immediately. The older woman had that brisk, no-nonsense manner that carers often had when they'd been in the job for a long time. Nothing surprised them anymore. They'd seen and heard everything. Laura knew Linda's piercing grey eyes would catch everything. Laura would be sure to make an ally of her.

Laura offered what she hoped was a welcoming smile. 'I wasn't sure where to go so I thought I'd hover and wait for someone to turn up.'

Linda tutted, and for a moment Laura thought she'd said the wrong thing. Should she have made her way to the staffroom after all?

'That bloody woman,' Linda muttered under her breath. 'Hazel, our manager, had to cover a shift last night — she should have answered the door to you.'

Laura thought exactly the same but wasn't going to say so. She didn't know this Hazel — who hadn't been the one to interview her — and Laura didn't know the working dynamics yet. She would soon make her own judgement about the manager and the other staff. 'Well, I understand that this must be a busy time. I didn't mind waiting,' Laura said.

Linda tutted again but decided to say no more on the subject. 'Well, let's get you settled. I'll take you to the staffroom for a quick cup of tea and then we'll head on upstairs. We're working on the upstairs floor today — Pine Floor — but then we'll be down here on Cedar Floor for the rest of the week. You'll be shadowing me.'

'Sounds great.' Laura picked up her bag. Maybe the day wouldn't turn out so badly after all.

* * *

Laura had received handover with the other three members of staff on shift in a cramped side room on the upper floor of the home which was known as Pine Floor. Hazel had rushed through the handover, not even bothering to acknowledge Laura's presence, or wishing her well on her first day. In fact, Laura took an instant dislike to the woman. Her manner during the entire two-minute handover had been utterly unprofessional. Hazel had made snide comments about the residents and hadn't even tried to hide the disgust she'd felt for having to attend to an elderly gentleman who had soiled his bed. Laura was shocked. This was the first time Hazel had met her, yet she hadn't even bothered to put on a show of professionalism or empathy. It had been the deputy manager who had interviewed Laura, and for some reason she was no longer working at the home. It was both unsettling and bizarre that this woman wasn't trying her utmost to present a professional and caring image to her new member of staff.

More worryingly, what was she like with the residents? A cold shiver ran down Laura's spine. She would have to sit back and watch for the time being, and remember to keep quiet about her background as a registered nurse. That type of basic training never left you.

* * *

After a quick tour of the floor, in which Linda showed Laura where the toilets, kitchen and day room were situated, Linda read out the list of residents they needed to help wash and

19

dress ready for breakfast. The other two carers would start at the far end of the corridor so they'd meet in the middle.

Adrian was a young man, filling in time and gaining experience before starting his nursing course in September. He had politely said hello to Laura and had diligently taken notes during handover. The other carer, Cerrie, must have only been in her late teens or early twenties, but Laura had taken an instant shine to her, with her bright-pink hair and infectious smile. She probably brought much life into the home. Laura couldn't help but wonder what her old nursing sister would have made of the young woman.

The working hours passed by in a blur of activity. Laura helped each resident to choose their clothes for the day, and then to wash or have a shower if preferred. When ready to face the world, or the other residents of Cedar House, she helped them navigate the hallway towards the large and airy dining room. A similar dining room was located on the lower floor which had access to a large patio area. Laura enjoyed giving basic nursing care, and with a pang realised how much she'd missed working on her old acute elderly care ward.

As Laura fastened buttons, combed hair and linked arms, she told each resident that she'd recently moved to the village. Every single person had asked her if she was married or if she was courting. They all found it strange that a single woman would choose to move to this village and work in the home.

Laura tried to remember the name of each resident and their room number. Luckily, she'd remembered to pop a small notepad into her tunic pocket and as she left each room, she made a few, brief notes to help her remember. It had been drummed into her as a nursing student to always see the bigger picture, not just the person sitting in the chair or lying on the bed. The photograph outside each room, which showed the resident as they had been in their younger years, was a nice touch. Sepia photographs of days gone by, linking arms with loved ones, smiling at the camera. But it also made Laura feel sad, in the fact that it was also important to remember the now. They were still here. They shouldn't be ignored, but listened to. Laura needed to make the time to listen. That was one of the most important factors of nursing.

Harold had been a pilot and had stacks of photograph albums on his dresser just waiting for someone to enter his world. Lillian was what Laura's mother would call a proper lady with her make-up applied meticulously. She had been a dancer on a cruise ship and told Laura that she had many a story to tell. Laura didn't doubt that for a second. Margaret's room was full to the brim with paintings of flowers, landscape scenery and houses. Margaret had painted her entire life and still enjoyed doing so in the weekly art class she attended at the village hall.

'Here's Harold's porridge,' Adrian said, handing Laura a tray with the bowl, a pot of tea and a small jar of jam. 'He likes to add the jam himself, always strawberry.'

Laura thanked him, took the tray and walked into the dining room. She set the tray down on the dining table before Harold.

'He never forgets my pot of jam.' Harold beamed. 'He's a good 'un, he is.'

Laura smiled as she removed the breakfast items from the tray. She had a feeling she would enjoy working in Cedar House. As long as she could stay away from Hazel.

* * *

Laura's first shift went surprisingly quickly. Breakfast was followed by tidying rooms, chatting to the residents and planning for the week ahead. She'd been given her duty rota for the month and was disappointed Hazel hadn't given her set hours as discussed. Her shift patterns were all over the place. The early one started at seven thirty, and the late finished at eight thirty p.m., which was fine, but there was no observable pattern. Maybe when she'd been here a few months she'd ask again.

21

Before she knew it, it was time for lunch and then when she next looked at her watch it was two o'clock.

Linda made her way towards the staffroom, surprised to see that Laura wasn't following her.

'You not in a rush to get home then, Laura?' she asked.

'I just thought I'd stay on for a bit and fill out the online health-and-safety course, and the other bits that need doing. I still haven't got any Wi-Fi access at home, nor a laptop, so it'll be easier to do here.'

'Oh, you should have said. You could have gone off and done that. You shouldn't be doing it in your own time.'

'I don't mind. I'll just stay back an hour, hour and a half max, and I know it's done.'

Linda looked as if she was about to protest, but she remained tight-lipped and nodded. Laura hoped that she hadn't upset her. Crossed an invisible line.

'If you need any more time, though, you can do some of it tomorrow — we always have a quiet spell after lunch.'

'Thank you.' Maybe she wasn't in Linda's bad books after all.

* * *

Three hours and two cups of coffee later, Laura closed the lid of the laptop and stretched out her arms. A completed health-and-safety certificate and home induction wasn't bad going for a few hours' work.

It had grown dark, so Laura was glad she'd popped a torch in her bag. After gathering her belongings, she decided to say goodbye to the residents sitting in the day room. She was greeted by a chorus of 'bye, love' and 'see you tomorrow', to which she replied that, yes, they would. It was as she was turning away to step back through the doorway that an old lady caught her eye. She was sitting apart from the others, a paperback with yellowing pages open on her lap. But she wasn't reading. Her piercing green eyes, which showed no signs of cloudiness, were fixed pointedly on Laura. Unsure of how to respond, not knowing if the lady approved of the intrusion, Laura simply smiled. To her surprise, the lady smiled back before slowly lowering her head to read once more. Laura shook her head, making a note to talk to this woman tomorrow. Something made her think she'd be interesting to be around. She just didn't know why.

Laura made her way down the stairs and to the office to say goodbye to the carer in charge. Maddie, a young woman in her mid-twenties with bright-red hair, was on the phone but gave Laura a wide smile and wave when she popped her head round the door.

As Laura approached the front door, a man and young boy were waiting to be buzzed in. Laura was unsure if she should open the door for them, but when she heard the man announce his name and who he was visiting, Maddie buzzed them through. Laura stood back to allow them to pass and smiled at the man with the black curly hair as he held the door open for her. He smiled, held her gaze as she passed him.

She blinked, once, twice, then found her voice. 'Thank you,' was Laura's reply. As she stepped outside into the cold evening air, she sucked in a steadying breath, wondering how a simple smile from a handsome man could make her feel like she was sixteen all over again. She rooted her hat out of her bag, pulled it down over her ears and slowly made her way home.

CHAPTER FOUR

Gertie Brown was bored. She had wanted to stay in her room, but Hazel had insisted that she needed to *mingle* and that just sitting and reading in her room all day was not good for her *mental health*. Silly woman. Gertie enjoyed nothing more than dipping in and out of her various novels that were scattered around her room. It was what she enjoyed most in life — reading, immersing herself in other people's lives. After all, what else was there really to enjoy when you were stuck in this place? Gertie knew that there was no alternative and if she could be left alone for most of the time, then she was happy. It was when people tried to interfere for her *own good*, that she became miserable.

That was why she now found herself sitting in the chair by the doorway in the day room. The chair that always got the draught. Gertie was convinced that Hazel had done it on purpose.

Gertie had been seated next to Sadie who, fortunately, didn't talk much as she spent most of the day asleep. At least this meant that Gertie could sit and read her book — which she'd shoved into her handbag without Hazel noticing — in peace. The entire purpose of the day room was for *socialising*, but all Gertie wanted was some peace and quiet. And as for Albert, well, she would keep an eye on him all right. What, with his wandering hands and all. She was so very glad she hadn't come across him as a young girl. Albert Greenway was no gentleman. Thankfully, he was out for the day with his long-suffering daughter. Gertie felt sorry for her.

Gertie opened her book, Thomas Hardy's *Jude the Obscure*. She hadn't read it for some time, and for some strange reason she had felt the need to pick this particular book as she'd scoured her shelves that morning.

Gertie needed to read. She had read and studied books for most of her life, and she wasn't going to stop now. She'd tried to get the staff interested, tried to make them set up a library for the residents, but they hadn't been interested. They'd told her that the one bookshelf in the day room was sufficient. Gertie had been about to protest, as all that housed was large-print romances. There was nothing wrong with that as such — everyone needed romance in their lives — but where was the diversity? The choice? But the look on Hazel's face had said it all. Gertie doubted the woman had ever picked up a book for pleasure in her life.

Gertie wondered if this not wanting a library, or not discussing books, was because Gertie had been an English lecturer for forty years. By Hazel refusing to start a book club or creating a library for the residents, she took away a little piece of Gertie.

Gertie tried to forget about the constant ache in her back and the shortness of breath that had steadily become worse. She told herself there was no use in worrying or moaning, as that wouldn't change anything. But she couldn't help thinking about what had happened in her life, and that very little time was left remaining.

The countdown had begun.

She used to be someone. She *was* still someone.

She was not the smiling fifty-year-old woman in the picture stuck to her door. Gertie found it insulting. Obviously, it had been Hazel's idea. The photographs had only started to appear outside doors after she'd been appointed manager.

Gertie sighed, tried to concentrate on the flowing and descriptive language, but her thoughts kept wandering back to the new girl. When she first saw her, stumbling into the day room, Gertie could see the aura that surrounded her. It was a black one — a sad one. Gertie knew that something bad had happened to this girl to bring her here, to this village, to this home. A black aura signified death and unresolved issues, but then coupled with this was a brown haze, which signified a lack of self-worth, yet a down-to-earth person.

What Gertie knew for sure was that this girl was not like the others. There was something about her, something that she couldn't quite put her finger on, but with time she would know what secrets this girl held. Gertie knew she'd entered her life for a reason. Her turning up here was no coincidence. Gertie knew deep in her bones that somehow fate had played its cards. She would keep an eye on her. Try to read her. Then she would know.

Gertie smiled. Perhaps her days would no longer be so boring.

* * *

'Nana, Nana!' Henry raced towards Gertie, throwing his arms out towards her.

Gertie gently touched his face with the palm of her hand and ruffled his dark curls with the other.

'It's so lovely to see you,' Gertie said, making room on her footstool, which was where Henry liked to sit. 'Right, love. Let me see what I've got in here for you and then you can tell me about your day.'

Gertie began to root around in her large canvas bag which went everywhere with her. She always bought jelly babies, crisps and biscuits from the trolley that did the rounds every morning, so that she would have goodies to give to Henry when he visited.

'Why aren't you in your room?' Richard asked before planting a kiss on Gertie's cheek and taking the chair opposite hers.

'Hazel thinks I need to socialise,' Gertie said, handing Henry a few jelly babies. She looked up from her bag and gave Richard a wide smile. 'Anyway, how are you, love? Busy day?'

Richard leaned back, nodded, rubbed his eyes. 'Just the usual really. They're a good bunch of kids.'

'No gossip then?' Gertie had a twinkle in her eye.

Richard smiled and shook his head. 'Gossip there is plenty of, but as you very well know, I can't share it.' Richard used his index finger to touch his nose and gave an exaggerated wink. He had to stop himself from laughing at the expression Gertie was pulling — that of a sulky toddler.

'But I did bring you this.' Richard held out a battered paperback.

Gertie reached out hungrily to take the book. She gasped in surprise.

In her hands was a limited-edition copy of a collection of poems by Emily Dickinson.

'I know how much you love her poetry and I also know that you don't have a copy. So, I ordered this one online for you.'

Gertie's reaction was all that Richard needed to know that he had chosen the right book.

'Thank you, Richard.' She reached out to take his hand.

Richard held her hand and gave it a gentle squeeze, alarmed that he could now feel the delicate bones underneath her thin skin. He leaned back a little in his chair and took in her features. Had she lost weight? Her cheekbones seemed a little more prominent, but it was difficult to tell. When you saw someone nearly every day it was hard to spot those subtle changes. Her cardigan didn't appear loose fitting, but then she always wore so many layers it was difficult to tell.

'I can see you looking at me, you know,' Gertie said, her tone light but her green eyes accusing.

'I just worry you aren't eating enough. You need to eat and drink properly.'

Gertie shot him a warning look while raising her hand. 'Richard Brown, you may be a teacher, but I know my own mind and my own body. I've been eating and drinking for the past eighty years.'

Richard sighed and decided to drop the subject. Not that he didn't still feel uneasy. He was sure she'd lost weight. He would collar a member of staff in the office before they left, just to have a quick chat, to be on the safe side.

'Are there any more jelly babies, Nana?' Henry asked eagerly.

Gertie looked at Richard.

'Just a few more, little man,' Richard said. 'We had tea at Tracey's.'

'We had chicken nuggets,' Henry said, taking the jelly babies from Gertie's outstretched hand.

'How is Tracey?' Gertie asked.

'She's fine.' Richard shrugged. 'She never changes.'

'She's a remarkable woman. She's had to put up with such a lot these past few years. But sometimes . . .'

Richard waited for Gertie to continue. 'But what?' he asked, when Gertie remained tight-lipped.

'Well, you know that she visits me?' Gertie shifted herself back in her chair and rested her hands in her lap. 'Well, there are some days that all she talks about is Sally. What Sally would be doing now if she was alive . . .'

Richard shook his head and placed a finger to his lips to silence her. He didn't want to talk about Sally in front of Henry.

Gertie clamped a hand to her mouth, her eyes wide. 'I'm so sorry, Richard — I didn't think. I'll tell you another time.'

'It's okay,' Richard told her. 'She's exactly the same with me and I find it hard to stomach sometimes. It's not natural.'

'No, love, it's not. Life, sadly, has to carry on.'

That it does, Richard thought. Life could be so cruel. His gaze landed on Henry, a little boy who no longer had the love of his mother, but who did have Richard and lots of people who loved him. There was Gertie and Tracey, and Sally's brother, Jack, and his wife, Megan. There was a lot to be said for that.

'We can stay for another half hour, but then we'll have to make tracks,' Richard said, changing the subject.

'That's fine. I'm tired anyway, love. I need an early night.'

A sense of unease grew once more in the pit of Richard's stomach. He had a nagging feeling that Gertie was keeping something from him — and his gut instinct was nearly always right.

* * *

Richard hesitated at the office door. Hazel was chatting on the phone and Henry was pulling at his arm to leave. It wasn't Henry's fault. He'd had a long day and just wanted to go home, have supper and go to bed after a bedtime story.

Richard knocked gently on the glass door, hoping to alert Hazel to the fact that he wanted to chat to her.

The office chair spun around so that she faced him, a scowl plastered on her face and a warning finger raised.

Richard felt his pulse quicken as he tried to steady his breathing. This woman annoyed the hell out of him.

Henry tugged once more on his arm, whingeing. 'Daddy, can we go now?'

Richard was about to tell him one more minute when, to his astonishment, Hazel stood and slammed the office door shut. Richard was left standing open-mouthed.

Resisting the urge to yank the door back open and tell her what a rude woman she was, and that actually he wanted to talk about his grandmother who he was worried sick about, he took a deep breath and headed for the main door, pressing hard on the buzzer to be let out. A small smile escaped him, knowing that this small act would annoy her. He would speak to another member of staff during his next visit, but his sense of unease remained.

CHAPTER FIVE

Laura woke up on Saturday morning to the sounds of birds chirping in the trees, despite the early hour and the fact that a layer of frost covered the ground. *Didn't birds fly south for the winter?* She eased herself out of bed, thankful for the fluffy rug by the side of her bed and the sheepskin slippers she'd bought during her visit into town. The cottage consisted of a mixture of wooden and flagstone floors, both of which were too cold for bare feet.

Huddled in her dressing gown and with a blanket covering her shoulders, Laura made her way into the warmth and comfort of the kitchen. How she loved that Aga.

She busied herself making toast and a pot of tea while she listened to the news on Radio Four. She still had no internet access or 4G, and only hoped that when the engineer called on Tuesday it could all be sorted out. She'd tried to arrange an earlier appointment, but the earliest slot they had was Tuesday morning. Luckily, she was working the late shift that day. There was internet access at the home, so the village was obviously on the grid, just not her cottage.

After two cups of tea, a quick tidy of the already immaculately clean kitchen and putting on a machine-load of washing, Laura wondered how she was going to fill in the hours until bedtime. Could she get away with going to bed at eight? Such a thought filled her with sadness — she wasn't an eighty-year-old woman. But wasn't this what she had wished for? An uncomplicated life, away from everyone and everything.

It was still early days, she reminded herself. Her first weekend in the village. She needed to make a plan for the day, seeing that it was her day off. If she kept busy, then the hours would pass more quickly.

Laura opened her bag and pulled out the notebook that she used at work. Ripping off the top piece of paper, she picked up her pen and wrote *Plan for the day* at the top of the page.

What did she need to do?

She didn't need to go shopping — the fridge and kitchen cupboards were already groaning with food. She had done the washing and the cottage had been cleaned.

Laura stared at the blank piece of paper.

Frustrated, she scrunched it into a tight ball and threw it across the room in the direction of the bin. It landed on the floor by the sink.

She should go for a walk. Stretch her legs. Maybe pop into the café — the Cottage Bun. She had walked past it every day to and from Cedar House, but hadn't had the time to go in. At least it would be something to do. She would take a book with her. That way she wouldn't have to talk to anyone if she didn't want to.

A knock on the door as Laura stepped into the hallway made her halt in her tracks. It was too early for the postman. Even in the short time she'd been in the village, she knew that he never delivered the post until at least eleven o'clock.

Laura pulled her dressing gown tighter around herself, feeling embarrassed that she wasn't yet dressed, and hesitated. Perhaps whoever it was would go away. A salesman or Jehovah's Witness?

'Laura, I know you're in there. Let me in.'

What on earth was Lottie doing here?

* * *

Lottie threw her arms around her older sister and told her that she looked tired and had lost weight. Those were her first words before being ushered into the kitchen with the promise of a cup of tea and a chocolate biscuit.

Laura still couldn't believe that her sister had made a two-hour car journey to see her so early on a Saturday morning. It was her only time with her husband, Paul, and their two children, Evan, aged four, and Maisie, who had just turned three, to enjoy the day together. Paul always worked Sundays as he was a chef in the local pub.

'I can't believe you're here,' Laura told her sister.

Lottie tutted, but she couldn't quite hide the start of a smile. 'Well, if you charged your phone then you'd have got the message I sent you last night.' Lottie pointed her finger towards Laura's mobile which was now charging.

Laura huffed. 'Nobody ever phones me and I'm not even sure if I've got a full working signal.' Why did she always feel the need to explain herself to her little sister?

At just three years younger, Lottie had always been the vivacious, talkative and popular sister. Her red curls and petite frame were in direct contrast to Laura's average build and height, and dark-blonde straight hair. Laura had always felt somewhat in the shadows, but this had never bothered her. She wasn't the jealous type, and now, at the age of thirty-five, she knew her own mind and body. Or she'd thought she had, before what had happened to Mark. She was a different person now and still learning to grow into that skin. Lottie showing up on her doorstep, as nice and unexpected as it was, was not part of that plan.

'Well, I don't have your landline number yet.' Lottie made yet another tutting sound.

'Well, I'll give it you and then I will never miss one of your important messages,' Laura said, her tone clipped and sarcastic. She instantly regretted her words as she looked at her sister's crestfallen face. Lottie had done something nice. She had wanted to show her sister some support and Laura had just thrown that back in her face.

'I'm sorry,' she said. 'I don't mean to sound ungrateful. It's just that . . . seeing you here is difficult. I hadn't planned on seeing anyone so soon and it's just thrown me a little to be honest.'

Lottie sighed, reached across the table and gently squeezed Laura's hand. 'I know and that's why I left you a message. I just assumed you'd got it.'

'Can we start again? It *is* nice to see you and I do appreciate you coming all this way. Do you want a tour of the cottage?'

Lottie's face broke into a huge grin. 'I would love that and then you can show me this village of yours.'

* * *

The two sisters linked arms as they strolled from the cottage in the direction of the Cottage Bun. To the casual observer they appeared as friends, not sisters, but anyone who looked closely enough would see the tight bond that they shared and the similar nose and laugh.

Laura noticed that the Christmas tree had finally been taken down, as had the twinkling fairy lights and other Christmas decorations. She felt a little sad at that.

As they stepped through the doorway of the café, Laura heard the old-fashioned tinkle of the bell as the door closed gently behind her. The sound took her right back to her childhood, when she and Lottie would visit the corner shop, full of hope and excitement in their anticipation for chocolate mice and cola bottles.

Laura scanned the room and found an empty corner table with a window view. They headed over and she draped her coat over the back of the chair. Before she had the chance to sit down, a woman came scurrying over, notebook and pen in hand.

'I was hoping you'd call in. I've seen you walk past every day,' the woman said with a wide smile.

Laura wasn't sure if she should feel flattered or like she was being stalked. She went with the former thought. 'I've been meaning to pop in, but I haven't had the time.' A white lie never hurt anyone.

The woman's smile grew even wider. 'Well, I'm Sue and this is my café. I saw you were wearing some kind of nurse's uniform the other day, so I thought you must be the new nurse at the home?'

Laura began to shake her head. 'No, I'm a new care assistant. It's not a nursing home, but a residential care home.'

'Oh,' Sue said, sounding somewhat taken aback. 'Well, I don't know the difference. Sorry about that. My Dobbs always says I jump to conclusions. I just assumed you were all nurses.'

Before Laura could tell her that there was a world of difference, Lottie stepped forward and held out her hand. 'Hello, I'm Lottie and this is my sister, Laura.'

Shaking hands and returning her attention to Laura, Sue said, 'Well, welcome to Buttermarsh.'

* * *

'Why didn't you just agree with her and tell her you were a nurse?' Lottie asked as soon as Sue had scurried away to get their drinks and cakes.

Laura placed the laminated menu back into its plastic holder. 'I told the truth. I'm not working there as a nurse. They don't employ nurses as it's a care home.'

Lottie sighed and raised an eyebrow. 'You know full well what I mean. You are a trained nurse and—'

'I'm not employed as a trained nurse, but as a carer.'

'But the knowledge is still there,' Lottie said, tapping the side of her forehead. 'They can't take that away from you. You did all that training.'

'I know. It's just that here I want to be known as Laura the healthcare assistant, not Laura the nurse from the big city.'

Lottie sat back in her chair and narrowed her eyes. 'Why does it matter so much to you that nobody knows? Surely people will start to guess. You know, the way you talk about medical matters.'

'Nobody will guess.' Laura was irritated at having to explain her actions once more to her sister.

'I still don't get it, though. Just tell people.'

'No.' That was louder than Laura had intended. The couple at the next table turned their heads in her direction.

'It's just simpler this way,' she said in a more hushed tone. 'If they know I'm a nurse then they'll only begin to ask questions. They'll become suspicious. You know what people are like. They will wonder why I am no longer practising. Have I been struck off? Killed someone? And I will feel the need to tell them why, the real reason I am here, and I don't want to do that. I don't want anyone here to know my past. I want them to see me for who I am. Not who I was.'

Lottie bit her bottom lip, but couldn't quite stop the slight quiver and the tremble in her voice as she spoke. 'You're still the same person, Laura. And nobody has the right to judge you about what happened.'

Laura swallowed and tucked her hair behind her ear, stalling for time. The thing was, she was different. What had happened to Mark had changed her and she knew deep down that people would judge her. That they would blame her for what had happened to him if they knew the truth. But she also knew that Lottie would dismiss this version. Lottie had many flaws and annoyances, but she was a devoted sister. She would never see that the way in which Laura had acted, and the choices that she had made, had led to what had happened. Laura opened her mouth to tell her sister that this village was her new start and that she wanted her and their mother to just go along with it, to try to understand, when she was interrupted by Sue returning to their table with their drinks and cakes.

'Here you go, ladies. Two lattes and two carrot cakes.'

Laura said thank you and offered a beaming smile as an apology. She hoped she hadn't come across as aloof. She liked this woman with her warm and open face.

35

'You're most welcome,' Sue said, smiling back and returning to the counter.

'This is divine,' Lottie said through a mouthful of cake. Swallowing, she continued, 'I need to get the recipe. The kids would love this and I'd feel less guilty about giving them cake if it contained a vegetable.'

Laura couldn't help but laugh. Her sister was a hopeless cook and even if she did manage to get her hands on the recipe, it would still end up as a hard biscuit or burnt.

'How are the kids?' Laura picked up her latte.

Lottie's face lit up as it always did when she spoke about her children. 'They're fine. A handful, but I wouldn't have it any other way.'

'And how's Paul?' Laura half wondered if they'd had an argument and that was partly the reason for her sister's visit. So she was relieved when Lottie smiled.

'Busy, but fine. We're fine,' she said.

Laura sipped her coffee, the hot liquid scalding her tongue. She placed the cup back on the table.

'Actually, I was worried about you,' Lottie said. She held her hand up to silence her sister. 'No, let me finish. I was worried. I was worried about you making a huge mistake. The fact that you were moving away from me, from Mum, to the country.' She waved her hands around. 'The thought of you not knowing anyone and having to start again just about broke my heart, Laura. But, now that I'm here, and have seen the cottage and the people who live here . . . well, it's beginning to make a little more sense.' Lottie let out a huge breath and sank back in her chair.

'I still can't believe that you did it, though, you know — that you just upped and left us.'

Laura gritted her teeth. It wasn't as if she'd emigrated. She was only a few hours' drive away.

'Lottie, can't you just be happy for me?'

'Of course, I can.' Lottie nodded. 'I *am* happy for you. I just can't help worrying. It's just the way I am.'

Laura let out a puff of air. 'Please don't worry. I'm going to be happy here and I have my work. Just give me a chance.'

Lottie's voice was barely a whisper. 'I so want this to work out for you. It's just you can't run away from your problems or your past.'

Laura closed her eyes, trying to block out the words. Lottie was right. But it didn't mean she needed to acknowledge that truth.

CHAPTER SIX

Richard closed the classroom door after the last of his Year Six children had run in the direction of the dining room. As soon as the bell struck twelve, they'd jumped up from their seats like they were jack-in-the-boxes.

Richard's stomach grumbled in protest. He'd only eaten a slice of toast for breakfast and had washed it down with three cups of instant coffee. Not at all good for his health or his stomach.

His plan was to pop along to the canteen and see what was on offer. It was Monday, so that usually meant vegetable pie and chips. It was his favourite dish of the week, but although his tummy was rumbling in protest from a lack of food, he had no appetite.

Richard stacked the exercise books from that morning's English lesson into his cardboard box to take home and mark. A doodle of a small flower, created with coloured pencils, caught his eye. It was on the corner of an exercise book and strictly speaking he should tell the child off. He peered at the name: Jessica. But in truth it made him smile. It was something that Sally would have done. As a journalist she'd kept notebooks all over the house and each and every one had been covered in elaborate doodles. So, too, had been her notes.

When Sally died, Richard had gathered all those note-books and placed them into a cardboard box which was now tucked into the bottom of his wardrobe. Although three years had passed since her death, he couldn't bring himself to throw that box out. He told himself that he kept the notebooks to show Henry something of his mother. Something she had created, something that could be seen. In truth, Richard couldn't bear to throw them away, as the physicality of each doodle proved she had been real. She had been flesh and bones. They were a part of Sally.

His fingers brushed the paper, tracing the delicate lines of the flower. A lump formed in his throat. He blinked, cleared his throat. He had no time for this now. If Sally was here, she would tell him off, tell him to pull himself together and that life was for living.

Richard picked up his bag, flung it over his shoulder and made his way to the canteen.

* * *

'Are you all ready for the coffee-and-cake afternoon?' Emma asked, her eyes wide and full of excitement.

Emma and her class always made the bunting and deco-rations for the school events.

Richard didn't really share Emma's enthusiasm. Actually, he wished he could avoid it, but as the Year Six students were taking an active role in proceedings, Richard had to be there. Plus, it was in aid of raising money for new playground equipment.

Richard offered Emma his best sarcastic smile. 'All ready, just need to get them to calm down a little.' He laughed. 'It's the promise of cake that they love. That and a chance to run around.'

Emma laughed too. She had no idea what he really thought. He pushed the remains of his vegetable pie away, half eaten. He couldn't stomach it today. Images of Sally kept creeping into his head. The way she always used to have her

39

nose stuck in a book, her cooking spag bol on a Friday night, the way she had gripped his hand when in the throes of labour, her laugh. God how he missed her laugh.

'You okay, Richard?' Emma asked, touching his arm.

Richard blinked away the memories. Nodded. Without a word he stood and walked back to the classroom.

* * *

Richard noticed how Gertie's eyes lit up when he and Henry entered the day room. He thought her excitement was due to the appearance of her grandson rather than him, but as they approached, Gertie quickly ruffled Henry's hair and then held her hands out to Richard. Taking his hands in hers, she gently squeezed his fingers and asked how he was.

'Busy. It's been a busy day.' Richard wasn't quite able to meet Gertie's eyes. He cleared his throat and slowly removed his hands from hers. 'I'm surprised to find you in here again,' he said. 'I thought you'd be in your room reading.'

'I don't mind it in here so much, especially when I have the room to myself,' Gertie said.

'I made you a painting, Nana Gertie,' Henry said, shoving the piece of paper into Gertie's lap.

Two stick people, one painted in blue, the other in pink, had oversized heads and were standing on a patch of green grass.

Gertie rewarded him with one of her famous grins. 'What a beautiful painting.'

Richard let out a long-held breath and scooped up Henry onto his knee.

'Thank you, love. I'll get one of the carers to pop it on my wardrobe,' Gertie said. She leaned forward and ruffled his hair again. Henry let out a giggle. 'Do you want to see what's in the play box while I talk to Daddy?'

Henry nodded, jumped down and scooted over to where the box was located by the window. It was there for all the children to play with, but Henry viewed it as his own as very few other children came to visit their grandparents.

Gertie fixed Richard with one of her hard stares before she spoke. 'Really, love, how are you?'

Richard averted his gaze. He'd managed to hold it together all day, but one look from Gertie could change all that. He'd picked up Henry from preschool because it was his afternoon off, but the real reason he'd wanted to pick up his son from school was to avoid seeing Tracey. He couldn't face her. Not today. He would phone her later on instead.

The other reason was that he needed to feel that connection once again with Sally, through his son.

'Talk to me, love.'

Richard sighed and met her gaze. 'What is there to say?' he said.

Gertie remained silent.

Richard looked over to where Henry was lying on the floor, completely unaware of the significance of the day. 'I miss her. Today is . . . it's just . . .' He sighed and shook his head.

'I know, love, I know.' She cleared her throat. 'You just need to think about the good things that you had, that you shared together, the good times. It's what she would have wanted. You know that.'

'I know and I do,' Richard replied. He really did. 'It's just so hard sometimes, and today I just can't think straight. My mind is all messed up. I couldn't even keep my mind on the class today. I'm sure the kids picked up on it, that my thoughts were elsewhere and not on them.'

'Sally would have been thirty-five today, wouldn't she.' Gertie said the words gently. It wasn't a question.

'Yes.' He sat up straight in the chair, kicked his long legs out in front of him. 'You're the first person to ask me about her today. No one mentioned her name at school.'

'Perhaps they were afraid of upsetting you, love, and more than likely they didn't know it would have been her birthday.'

'It's only been three years.' Richard heard himself snapping at Gertie and sighed. He hadn't meant to be sharp with

41

her. She was only trying to help. He took a deep breath. 'I'm sorry, I didn't mean that.'

'Yes, you did.' Gertie's eyes were full of pity and understanding. 'But there is something that I need to tell you.'

Richard's head darted from where he'd been watching Henry playing on the floor, surrounded by toy cars, oblivious to the fact that they were talking about his mother, back to his grandmother's piercing gaze. He knew he wouldn't like what she had to say.

'It *has* been three years, love, and I know how much you loved her.' Her tone was gentle, softly spoken.

'I still love her, not *loved*.' Richard's voice was barely audible. 'I will never stop loving her.'

'I know you still love her, but she's not here. You need to *live*, Richard. Love again, be happy.'

Richard felt the sudden urge to escape from the room. He rose to his feet. 'I can't believe you said that. I can't believe you said those words and on today of all days.' His hands shook as he ran them over his face in a bid to calm himself down. He couldn't look at her.

'Henry, we need to go.' He realised he was shouting.

Henry, hearing the anger in his father's voice, sat paralysed, a car clutched tightly in his fist.

'Oh, don't be like that, Richard,' Gertie said pleadingly.

Richard kept his attention on Henry, ignoring her plea.

'Oh, Daddy, I want to stay. You said we could stay and have cake with Nana.'

'Not today.' Richard began to quickly scoop up the cars into the toy box. Pressing the lid firmly into place and dashing any hopes that Henry may have had of staying a little longer, he took his hand and without saying another word, they left the room.

All thoughts of asking the staff about his gran's health had vanished from his mind.

* * *

Laura spent Monday in the cottage, walking aimlessly from room to room, drinking endless cups of tea and trying to listen to the radio. She'd sat for a bit and read her book, made a simple lunch of soup and bread, and had done a few chores. At five p.m., she reheated a bowl of soup, wolfed it down and then got into her uniform. She headed off to the home, even though her shift wasn't due to start until eight. She couldn't stay in the cottage a minute longer. Hazel had phoned that morning as Laura had been eating breakfast and asked if she would be willing to cover a night shift tonight and have the following day off. Even though Laura was meant to be having two weeks of supervised shifts, she'd said yes.

The irony of the situation hadn't escaped her notice. Laura had deliberately chosen the village for its remoteness, in the hope that the sleepy village would give her time to think and reflect about what had happened. But, although she loved the peace and tranquillity, she did miss being surrounded by people and the care home was full of them. It was where she needed to be.

As she rounded the bend, making her way past the playground, then the hedgerows and flower beds, her torch lighting the way, she nearly collided with a tall, dark-haired man who was clutching the hand of a little boy.

Luckily, Laura was watching where she was walking, unlike the man, and she managed to jump to the side, out of harm's way. The man and boy continued on their way while Laura spun on the spot, mouth agape at what had happened.

At first, she was angry and an insult was on the tip of her tongue, but two things stopped her in her tracks.

The first was the little boy. She didn't want to frighten him. The second was the man's profile. The way he walked, hunched over, as if in pain. Perhaps he had just received bad news?

It was while Laura stood there, pondering these thoughts, that she became aware of having seen the pair before, the previous week. He had been the man who'd held the door open for her. Should she call after them? Ask if he was okay? But it was too late. They were too far away.

* * *

'You're a bit eager, aren't you?' Hazel sneered as Laura passed by the office. She stopped and glared at the woman.

'Excuse me?' Laura asked, all innocence.

'You shouldn't be here. Your shift doesn't start for another two hours. Nothing else better to do?'

For the second time that day, Laura swallowed down the words threatening to spill from her mouth. She answered with a tight smile. 'I'll go and see what Linda would like me to do.' She headed off in the direction of the staffroom.

* * *

Laura found Linda in the day room, sitting next to the woman she had spotted the other day. The lady with the piercing green eyes who had been sitting alone reading. The woman was clearly upset. She kept dabbing at her eyes as Linda whispered what appeared to be comforting words into her ear while rubbing her back.

Laura had clearly stumbled upon a private moment. She should go. She didn't know this woman. But before Laura had time to leave the safety of the doorway, Linda shifted position in her chair and caught sight of her standing there. Linda looked surprised to see her but quickly regained her composure. Keeping her hand on Gertie's shoulder, she beckoned Laura over with a wave of her hand.

'Hello, Laura. What are you doing here so early?' Linda asked.

'Oh, I was at a loose end and thought I'd make myself useful,' Laura said.

'Do you want to sit with us?' Linda asked.

Laura hesitated for a moment before she dragged over the stool that was next to Linda's chair and sat down. She smiled and waited for the old woman to speak.

'Hello, Laura. I'm Gertie.'

'Hello, Gertie. What's upset you?' Laura looked at Gertie as she asked the question, but then glanced at Linda.

'She's a bit upset after what happened with her grandson,' Linda explained.

'Richard won't listen to me. He won't listen to anyone,' Gertie said, dabbing at her eyes with a damp tissue. 'I just want him to be happy.'

Laura nodded. She had no idea what Gertie was going on about, but it was evident that the woman needed to vent her feelings. Then Laura put two and two together. The man who had very nearly bumped into her outside must be her grandson. At least Laura now had a name for the man who had looked equally as upset as his grandmother. Should she tell Gertie this detail? Laura decided to say nothing and instead listened as she nodded sympathetically, allowing Gertie to speak.

Linda leaned forward and held Gertie's hand. 'I just need to check everything is okay in the kitchen.' She turned her attention to Laura and raised an eyebrow.

Laura nodded and asked Gertie if she was happy for her to stay.

Gertie removed the crumpled tissue from her face. Those piercing green eyes met Laura's once more.

'My dear,' she said, ever so quietly. 'I have so much to tell you.'

CHAPTER SEVEN

Gertie held Laura's hand and closed her eyes. It was nice to sit and feel another person's touch, their warmth, their skin. That's what she missed living in this home. Although hands and fingers and arms touched her on a daily basis in the rigmarole of helping her to put her stockings on, to wash her hair and to help her navigate her way from bathroom to bedroom to day room, that touch was merely a practical one. Needs must and all that. There was just something more personal about someone holding your hand. Simply sitting and thinking, not having to talk. That was the problem with Cedar House. Too many people who liked the sound of their own voices but not others'. They spoke *at* you, not *to* you, and Gertie knew that there was something different about this girl. She wasn't like the others with their inane chatter and who were permanently glued to their phones.

Gertie squeezed her eyes tight and tried to get a read on this young woman. That black aura still hovered around her body, and this troubled Gertie. Perhaps this girl needed to hold Gertie's hand. Perhaps she needed this connection with another human being just as much as Gertie did.

Then the spell was broken.

'How can I help, Gertie?' Laura asked. 'Do you want to talk about what happened? Would that help?'

What would help, Gertie thought, was going back in time, so that Sally was still alive. But that could never happen. So, instead, she began. 'It's my grandson, Richard — you haven't met him yet. He has a little boy. Henry.' Gertie felt her heart swell as she said her great-grandson's name.

'I bumped into them on my way in,' Laura said. 'Well, I didn't know it was them at the time. The man was tall, rugged-looking with dark curly hair, and the little boy had black hair.'

Gertie nodded, the corners of her mouth lifting as she attempted to smile. 'That's my boys. I think the world of them — and now he hates me.' On the last word, Gertie began to sob once more.

'Oh, don't think that way, Gertie.' Laura rubbed the old woman's back in a comforting way. 'I just think you're both very upset, that's all.'

'Richard was upset? In what way?' The words rushed out of Gertie's mouth, her hands twisting in her lap.

Laura opened her mouth to speak, then closed it again. Her eyes flickered upwards to the ceiling before focusing on Gertie once more. 'He seemed preoccupied. He nearly bumped into me.' Laura gave a chuckle.

Gertie saw through Laura's white lie. Her grandson had been upset and he had obviously caused Laura some distress.

'He apologised?' Gertie asked. 'For nearly mowing you over, I hope!'

'Yes, yes, of course he did,' Laura replied quickly. 'It was a near miss. I wasn't looking where I was going either. No harm done.' Laura said all this with a shrug of her shoulders.

After a beat, Gertie nodded. 'So, he looked preoccupied then?'

'Yes, as if he had a lot on his mind.'

'It's all my fault. I shouldn't have said anything.' Gertie shook her head.

'Gertie, what happened between the two of you?' Laura asked. Her tone was gentle, as if teasing the words from Gertie's mouth.

Gertie felt Laura's eyes on her, probing but kind. She took a deep breath. 'I told him that he needs to be happy, to move on with his life.'

Gertie watched the puzzled expression play across Laura's face. She knew that she had to make this young woman understand. To understand that her grandson was desperately unhappy because he was living in the past. No one else in this home would listen to her. Gertie took a deep breath in before she finally spoke. 'His wife died three years ago and today would have been her thirty-fifth birthday.'

A gasp escaped before Laura clamped her hand to her mouth. 'Thirty-five. The same age as me.'

'It was cancer, the aggressive kind. It took her quickly. Too quick. Henry was just a baby.' Gertie shook her head.

'No wonder he was so upset today.'

'He was upset, but that's not the real reason.' Gertie took a ragged breath. 'He was upset because I more or less told him that it was time to move on.'

'Oh.'

Gertie could see the accusation in this young woman's eyes. 'You think I was too harsh?' Gertie asked. 'That I should just let him wallow in self-pity and grief?'

Laura pressed her lips together. She said nothing.

Gertie knew that this young woman, with her perceptive stare and clear blue eyes, had a lot she wanted to say. And probably none of which Gertie wanted to hear. 'That's why I'm so upset,' Gertie continued. 'I shouldn't have told him that it was time to move on. He's clearly still not ready. But the truth is that I think he needs help. Some kind of counselling.'

Laura's features softened, transforming her entire face. She gave Gertie a brief smile, but not before Gertie noticed a flicker of emotion in her eyes that she wasn't quite able to place.

'I think that he probably knows you're right, but hearing these thoughts is often different to thinking them. The change needs to come from within him,' Laura said gently.

'He's always so sad, and it breaks my heart.'

'That must be hard for you,' Laura said. 'For you to see him like that. Must be hard for any grandmother.'

Gertie squeezed Laura's hand once more. 'Did you know I brought him up?'

Laura shook her head. 'No, I didn't know that.'

'Richard's mother died when he was a baby. It was a car accident.'

'Oh, that's awful. What was your daughter's name?' Laura asked. She knew that asking the name was important.

'Her name was Joanna and she was my daughter-in-law. She was with her husband, Thomas, my son, when the car was hit by a drunk driver. They didn't stand a chance.' Gertie watched as Laura raised her hand to cover her mouth for the second time that evening.

'Oh, Gertie, I don't know what to say.'

'No one ever does, love,' Gertie said, followed by a huff of air.

'It must have been such a difficult time for you.'

'It was. I'd done my time changing nappies and doing the school run, but he was my flesh and blood so what else could I do?' Gertie smiled, a smile that contained all the memories of the past. Of happier times. A contented smile.

'You've had a remarkable life,' Laura said.

'I'm still having one,' Gertie replied quickly. 'What I want is to make my grandson happy.'

Laura opened her mouth to speak, but before she could reply she was distracted by a commotion outside the day room. Gertie sat up straight and leaned her head towards the door.

What on earth was going on?

Laura jumped out of her seat when she heard a loud crash and the sound of a walking stick repeatedly hitting the drinks trolley.

'I need to get out of here. I have a plane to fly. My men are depending upon me.'

Harold's voice was growing louder and more insistent with every word. If Laura didn't interfere soon then someone was bound to get hurt.

Scurrying out of the room, she entered the hallway to a scene of absolute pandemonium.

Cerrie had been pushed up against the wall, hands raised in the air as if she'd been arrested by the police. Looming over her was Harold Biggins, a former RAF pilot who was clutching his walking stick as if for dear life. However, instead of it being firmly planted on the floor to help with his stability, he was waving it in front of Cerrie's face.

Laura took a moment to process all this information. Experience while working in Accident and Emergency had taught her that confronting an individual who was already anxious and ready to strike was not a good idea. So, instead, she took the soft approach.

'Hello, Harold,' she said.

Harold turned around to look at the newcomer, alerted to the fact that this woman might be able to help him. He lowered the walking stick. Laura watched Cerrie deflate as she stepped to the side, out of harm's way.

'Can I help in any way?' Laura asked, taking a step towards him.

'I need to get to my plane. My men are waiting for me,' Harold yelled, his face now resembling a ripe tomato.

'I've told him no—'

Laura's hand shot out, palm facing forward, to stop Cerrie as she began to shout.

'I've just had a phone call from your commanding officer. He's told you to stand down. No flights are planned for today.'

Laura watched as Harold's face lost its determined look. His eyes flickered from where Laura stood, over to Cerrie, and then lost focus.

Laura's stomach twisted. It was fight or flight.

'Well, I might as well go and have a rest then,' Harold said eventually. 'So I'm ready for the next time they call me up.'

Laura nodded. 'Thank you, sir.' With an inward sigh of relief, she watched the frail, old man, who still had a steely glint in his eye, walk down the corridor towards his room. She couldn't help but feel a pang of sympathy towards him.

Now that the situation was over, she turned her attention back to Cerrie, now fidgeting with her hands, a flushed expression on her face.

'Thanks for that,' Cerrie mumbled, not quite able to meet Laura's gaze.

Laura took a step towards her and offered a smile. She remembered what it was like to be a nursing student and being faced with challenging circumstances.

'Thank you,' Laura said, taking the girl by surprise. 'You handled that well. You stayed calm. Tried not to confront him. Just remember that sometimes it's kinder to play along if it's in the best interest of the patient.'

Cerrie nodded vigorously and said that she would.

'I don't know about you, but I could do with a cuppa after that,' Laura said, giving Cerrie a flash of a smile.

Cerrie smiled back. 'I'll go make us one.'

'Me, too, dear, if you don' t mind.'

Laura turned around to see a smiling Gertie standing by the door to the day room.

'Poor man. Makes you think, doesn't it,' Gertie said with a shake of her head.

Laura and Cerrie nodded in unison.

'I'll go and make us that tea,' Cerrie said.

'And biscuits.' Gertie shouted this at Cerrie's retreating back before her face suddenly turned serious. 'I'll have to introduce you to him, you know,' she muttered.

'Harold?' Laura asked. 'I've met him a few times. He's a nice man.'

'No, not Harold!' Gertie said impatiently. 'Richard, my grandson. You're going to love him.'

CHAPTER EIGHT

Laura closed the front door and breathed out a deep sigh of relief. The engineer had been friendly, efficient, and, more importantly, had got her back online.

She quickly filled the kettle and placed it on the Aga. She was dying for a cup of tea. Barry, the engineer, had declined her offer of tea. He'd laughed, saying that he'd already had five cups and that it wasn't yet ten o'clock. He'd checked that everything was working by asking Laura to log into her emails. She now clicked on her last email to Lottie and began to compose a new message.

Back online. So, email me whenever you like. It was really lovely seeing you the other day. And I do miss you and Mum and the kids. But I need this time alone. I'll be fine. I'll be happy again. Trust me. Write soon.

She sent it before she could change her mind.

As she went through the comforting rituals of making a pot of tea, Laura wondered what she was going to do with the rest of her day. She now wished that she'd put her name down for overtime, but perhaps that wasn't such a good idea. She needed the time to figure out this new life of hers and she needed time away from work to rest. She could only care for others if she looked after herself and that meant enjoying her days off. What she couldn't do was go to bed, even for a few hours, not with having worked the nightshift last night. Doing so would completely mess up her body clock. She would go to bed a little earlier, catch up on sleep that way. She just needed to keep herself busy and stay awake until at least eight o'clock.

Laura hadn't been on the bus since arriving in the village. Perhaps it would be a good idea to jump on one and head into the city for the day. Window shop, go to the bookshop and grab a coffee. The more she thought about it, the more she liked the idea. Yes, a bus trip would do her good.

* * *

The bus was crowded and almost every seat was taken when Laura stepped aboard, greeted by heating cranked up to the max against the January chill. She found a seat towards the back of the bus, by the window, unwrapped her scarf and removed her hat as soon as she sat down. She had assumed the bus would be empty, as she'd been the last passenger off when she'd arrived in the village, but obviously this bus had travelled a different route.

The window was steamed up, and even when Laura wiped the glass with her sleeve, it quickly steamed up again.

She wished she'd brought her Kindle. In her hurry she had left it charging in the kitchen. She had her smartphone and it was loaded with podcasts, but she had no earphones. She'd have to buy some.

She had been late leaving the house because of Maureen's phone call. As Laura gazed out of the misted bus window, she replayed the conversation in her mind. How she had reassured her mother that she was fine, that she had settled in and was off out soon with a friend from work. A white lie to make her mother feel better, but even at the age of thirty-five she felt guilty for the lie that had tripped so easily from her tongue.

Maureen was a born worrier and Laura knew that her mother worried even more now that she was all those miles away from home. Maureen refused to believe in Laura's need to get away.

Laura tore her gaze away from the window. She couldn't see anything other than the streak of greens and the odd car that passed by.

She turned her attention to the other passengers.

None of them looked familiar and no one had tried to catch her eye or say hello. Then again, she hadn't really been looking. She wanted a quiet day, time alone with her thoughts. No chatter. No need to listen to anyone else. She only wanted to hear the voice in her head, the one that told her everything really would be all right.

* * *

Laura kicked off her shoes and dumped several shopping bags onto the kitchen table. She now had more than enough food for the week, a stack of library books to work through and had treated herself to a new pair of jeans that she'd spotted on sale. She had ignored the brightly coloured dress reduced to less than half price. There was no point in buying a dress that she would never wear. The jeans were practical, skinny and made her feel good.

She carried the books into the snug and placed them on the coffee table by the little lamp. One of the books was on nursing patients with dementia. Laura planned to take it into work to show Cerrie. *Just for a quick read. It will give you some ideas*, she'd tell her. Cedar House was a care home, not a nursing home, meaning people with dementia were nursed in more suitable environments, such as a nursing home that specialised in dementia care. However, Laura felt it important that carers knew what signs to look out for, in the best interest of their residents, and could liaise with local GPs and other specialist services, ensuring residents got the best care. Laura knew that she should discuss her concerns with Hazel, but she didn't want to draw attention to herself. She'd keep quiet for now. Maybe she should talk to Linda? Perhaps she would be prepared to talk to Hazel?

Laura returned to the kitchen and began to unpack the shopping. She removed a ready meal — chicken in a sweet-and-sour sauce — from its plastic sleeve, pierced the film with a fork and placed it in the microwave.

By the time the microwave pinged, Laura had put all the shopping away. Grabbing a tea towel, she scooped the tray up and out of the microwave and popped it on a plate, although she would eat it out of the tray. Less washing up.

She carried the plate into the snug, put it on the coffee table and sat down in the cosy armchair. It was then that it hit her. The fact that she was alone with a ready meal and a pile of books. But this was what she wanted. Time alone. A kind of penance for what had happened. But she was alone, even when surrounded by people on a busy bus, in the library, at work.

She still craved to be near people. To feel that connection. To listen in to conversations. To hear their stories. To feel life, even though she felt that her life had been put on hold. That she could feel nothing.

Laura pushed the plate away. No longer hungry. She'd put it in the fridge for later.

Without knowing why, she picked up the library book on the top of the pile — a psychological thriller that everyone was talking about — and headed back into the kitchen. She dropped the book into her shopping bag, found the bag of jelly babies and popped an orange one in her mouth. Then, having shoved her feet into her work shoes, she picked up her house key and opened the front door. She needed a drink.

* * *

Richard picked up his pint and took a well-earned gulp. It had been one of those days.

He closed his eyes and tilted his head back. He'd been in a bad mood ever since his run-in with Gertie. He should have called round tonight to see her, but the staff meeting had gone on far too long. It had only finished half an hour ago and when he'd gone to pick up Henry from Auntie Megan and Uncle Jack's house, Henry had been having such a fun time that when Jack had suggested a quick pint at the Fox and Hound, Richard had jumped at the opportunity.

'Looks like you needed that.' Jack grinned at his brother-in-law.

Richard grinned back, wiping his mouth with the back of his hand.

'Want to tell me what's on your mind?' Jack's piercing blue eyes, so like Sally's, gave him that knowing look. He wasn't going to take no for an answer.

'I had an argument with Gertie, a stupid argument, and I need to apologise to her,' Richard said.

'What about?' Jack asked before shoving a salt-and-vine-gar crisp into his mouth.

Richard clutched his pint glass. He wasn't sure how Jack would feel about Gertie's comments. He cleared his throat. 'She told me it was time to move on. That I was living in the past, that . . .'

Richard stopped mid-sentence. His face now flushed at the thought of how he'd reacted. How he had spoken to his gran.

'Just tell her you're sorry. That you were upset. She'll understand,' Jack said, his mouth still full of crisps.

'The thing is, she hasn't been looking well these past few weeks. I'm worried about her. And I was going to have a chat with one of the staff, but I just stormed out, dragging Henry with me.'

'Oh, mate.' Jack patted Richard's arm. 'I think you need another pint.'

* * *

Half an hour later, Richard was on his second drink, this time a cola, and had told the entire story to Jack. The truth was,

Gertie had touched a nerve. He should move on with his life, not just for him, but for Henry. He just wasn't sure how.

'These things take time, though, Richard. You and Sally were together a long time.'

'We were, and you can't undo that, can you?' Richard's voice shook. 'You can't just *unfeel* everything, stash it in a box and hope for the best. That's just asking for trouble, that is.'

Jack nodded, sipping his pint.

'I still think she's going to walk through that door.' Richard laughed, but there was no humour to it. 'You must think I'm mad.'

'Of course I don't. You're just a man who still loves his wife. There's no shame in that.' Jack stared at his pint.

'No shame perhaps, but it's not healthy.'

Jack shook his head. 'There's nothing wrong in remembering Sally. I think about her every day — she was my sister. But . . .' Jack hesitated, picked up his pint glass and drained it before speaking. 'But what I do know is that she'd want you to be happy again. I just know she would feel that way.'

Richard knew Jack was right. Sally had told him during those last months that she wanted him to be happy. That she wanted him to find someone else to share his life with. And that that someone might become a mother figure for Henry. She had wanted Richard to live. But he knew that he wasn't ready and trying to voice exactly how he felt was impossible. There were no words.

So, he said nothing.

* * *

Laura took a deep breath before pulling open the heavy oak door belonging to the Fox and Hound.

Her heart hammered in her chest. Not because she was walking into a pub alone. She had done the same thing many times before. She was nervous because she was unsure of how people would react to her. The *new* girl. Buttermarsh was such a small village. Everyone knew each other.

The warmth enveloped Laura as she made her way towards the bar past the small wooden tables. She strode quickly, with purpose, eyes forward, refusing to meet the gaze of the locals. She could feel eyes burning into her back. It was then she remembered Gwen, the older lady who'd called round the day she'd moved in — she remembered Gwen saying she owned the pub with Bill.

A big, burly man stood behind the bar. With rippling muscles and a tattoo of what appeared to be a German shepherd dog on his arm. He smiled at Laura as she approached.

Was this Bill? She couldn't quite see Gwen with him. For starters, he seemed a lot younger than her. But then again, appearances could be deceptive.

'What you drinking, love?'

Laura scanned the bar's optics and bottles.

'Just a coffee, please,' she said while she rooted in her bag for her purse. She had to remove her library book and bag of jelly babies to find it.

She looked up to see the barman smirking at her. 'You must be Laura?'

Laura nodded.

'I'll get you that coffee. First drink is on the house.'

'Thank you,' Laura said to his retreating back. She hadn't expected that, no matter what Gwen had said.

She put her book and sweets back into her bag, and when she looked up again, the cup of coffee had been placed in front of her on the bar.

The barman smiled once more. Stuck out his hand. 'I'm Bill, by the way. Gwen said she'd met you.'

Laura shook his hand and peered over his shoulder, half expecting Gwen to jump out from behind him.

'Nice to meet you,' Laura said, picking up her cup. She needed to find a quiet table.

'You too,' Bill said before turning his attention to an elderly man waiting to be served.

Laura scanned the room for an empty table. She spotted one by the fire. A small table for two which had just been vacated. She walked slowly so as not to spill her coffee. As she sat down, she caught the eye of the man sitting at the next table, chatting to a younger man with blond hair.

Where had she seen him before?

And then it struck her. It was Richard. Gertie's grandson.

Laura watched him pick up his glass of cola. His eyes met hers over the rim of the glass.

They were a dazzling blue.

Blinking, she quickly pulled her bag towards her and pulled out her book.

She wasn't sure if Richard knew who she was. The woman he had nearly bumped into outside the home.

But, then, why would he remember her?

Laura picked up her book and began to read.

CHAPTER NINE

Gertie pulled the colourful crocheted blanket up towards her chin and adjusted the reading lamp. Her cup of tea was sitting on top of her pile of books — the perfect height for her to lean across and pick it up with ease. These things were important as you got older.

She had planned an early night in bed, sipping tea and reading her book, but her eyes were heavy and her heart sad.

Richard hadn't called in to see her. He hadn't even left a message with reception. She knew he had a staff meeting and that it would finish late, but she'd hoped he might pop in. She wanted the opportunity to say sorry to him. The words were no longer stuck in her throat.

Gertie closed her eyes, rested her head back on the soft pillow that was covered with images of tiny birds and flowers. A Mother's Day gift from Richard last year. He was probably still angry with her, wanting to teach the silly old woman a lesson.

But no. Gertie shook her head. He wasn't like that. He didn't have a bad bone in his body. It was the pain that was tainting everything. Casting an unwanted shadow over her thoughts and words.

Gertie shifted position under the covers, pushing herself back up against the pillow. She winced at the sudden stabbing pain in her lower back.

She was able to hide her discomfort during the day. Nobody paid her much attention and she was pretty much left to her own devices. It was only Hazel who tried to make her socialise. To engage with others. To get her out of her room. Gertie liked her room. It was where her memories lived. But the pain was worse at night. At least there was no one to see her wince or groan as she tossed and turned in bed, unable to get comfy.

The nights were long. Only a quick check at midnight to see if she needed anything. Other than that, the staff would pop their heads in every couple of hours, but she knew most nights they left her alone.

Gertie knew she should tell Hazel about the pain, even though she didn't trust the woman as far as she could throw her. Hazel could arrange a doctor's appointment. But what was the point in that? All that would lead to was blood tests, and prodding and probing and a conversation that Gertie didn't want to have. She didn't need a doctor to tell her what was wrong. She already knew.

The loss of appetite, the gradual weight loss and the pain in her stomach that made her bend over. Took her breath away. The Big C. That's what it was. There was nothing they could do. She was eighty years of age. When the time came, when the pain was too much, then she'd be able to get pain relief. If she needed it. Here, in the place she now called home. There was no way she was going to end her days trapped in a hospital bed. She'd seen enough hospitals to last her a lifetime.

She wasn't worried about herself. She wasn't afraid of dying. She worried about Richard. He had watched his wife suffer for months near the end. There was no such thing as dignity in death. Gertie couldn't put him through that again. She wouldn't put him through it again.

When the end came, she wanted it to be quick. It was best for everyone.

Gertie needed to put her plan in motion. She couldn't leave things as they were. She couldn't leave this world knowing that Richard was all alone.

Gertie needed to know more about Laura. Her past. She was the key.

* * *

It took Laura a few moments to get her bearings after she'd left the pub. She'd forgotten there were no streetlights in the village and the darkness of the January night caught her by surprise, in its direct contrast to the brightly lit pub.

Clutching her torch for dear life, she began to make her way back home along the narrow lane.

Her steps were quick, cheeks puffed out as she picked up her pace. After a few minutes she no longer felt the cold.

The evening hadn't been as restful as she'd intended. She had drunk her coffee too quickly and had found it hard to concentrate on her book. The pub had been lively, music playing on a jukebox, which had taken her by surprise. She had wrongly assumed that she would be surrounded by muffled conversations and old men drinking pints.

Laura had caught bits of conversation from those sitting around her, particularly Richard and his friend. She hadn't caught his name. From what she had heard, Richard was feeling sorry for the way he had behaved towards Gertie and planned to visit her tomorrow. Laura hoped to see him at the home, as she had been put on the rota for the upper floor and she was working a double shift. She would keep an eye on Gertie. She hoped that the two would reconcile their differences.

Laura's thoughts returned to the haunted look on Richard's face. The hunched shoulders. She felt so sorry for this man she had never spoken to, never properly met. A single father whose wife had died too young. From what Gertie had told her, and the snippets of conversation she had overheard in the pub, it was abundantly clear that Richard was a good man. A kind man. A devoted dad who still loved his wife. Was that such a bad thing? To have loved someone so much, so deeply, that you could never let them go? Never stop loving them? Laura felt a lump rising in her throat. A heavy feeling formed a knot in her chest. She had never experienced that type of love with Mark. Not even in those heady early days. Of course, she'd loved him, even when everything had turned sour and her whole world had changed. But the love she felt for Mark would fade over time. It was not a love that would be forever cherished. Not like the love Richard still had for his dead wife. Laura shuddered and quickened her pace. Perhaps it was morbid to think that way.

In the distance, Laura heard the dull throb of a car engine as it gradually grew louder. She stopped and pressed her back into the hedge. She would let the car pass before continuing on her way. But in doing so, she stumbled on the uneven road and dropped her handbag, scattering its contents everywhere. Muttering a curse, she swung the torch, illuminating where her bag had landed, and crouched down to scoop up her belongings.

Laura heard the car slow down. At first she thought this was because the driver was being careful, but when the car crawled to a stop, just inches from where she crouched in the road, she felt an uneasy feeling grow in the pit of her stomach. She plucked up her keys, then her purse.

'Hello, do you need some help?' the man shouted from the car. 'I'm Richard Brown, Gertie's grandson.'

Laura shifted her gaze towards the car that had pulled up beside her and the dark-haired man she'd seen in the pub — Richard. Not a threat at all. She smiled. 'Hello, nice to meet you. Sorry, I dropped my bag.'

Richard opened the door, climbed out. 'Here, let me help you,' he said.

'Hello,' Richard said again, crouching down beside her. He handed her her book, and then a small box of tampons.

Laura felt her cheeks heat as she shoved them in her bag. 'Thank you.'

'Think that's everything,' Richard said, before adding, 'Are you Laura? I don't think we've met?'

'Yes, I'm Laura Lewis. I look after your gran,' Laura said, standing up, trying her best to regain her composure. For some reason, this man flustered her. 'In fact, you nearly bumped into me on your way out yesterday.' Laura could have sworn she saw Richard blush, but it was too dark to tell.

Richard lowered his head. 'Yeah, sorry about that. Yesterday wasn't a good day.'

'No harm done,' she said, followed by a shrug.

'Anyway, do you need a lift?' Richard asked. He inclined his head towards the car, the engine still running. 'I'm with my brother-in-law.'

Laura shook her head. She knew that he was perfectly safe, but there was no need for a lift. 'I live just up there.' Laura gestured a few metres up the road.

'Ah, yes, I'd forgotten — you're the new tenant in Church View Cottage.'

'That's me,' Laura said.

'I have no idea why they called it Church View,' Richard said after a beat.

Laura laughed. 'Because there isn't one? I thought exactly the same.' She shifted the bag on her shoulder as she looked down the lane towards the cottage.

Richard cleared his throat. Took a step back. 'Well, I'll let you get home, then.' Another step towards the car. He opened the door, slowly lowering his long body in. After shutting the door, the engine revved to life. But before the car indicated and pulled away from the side of the road, the window slowly wound down and Richard's head popped out.

'Take care then. I'll probably see you at the home.'

'Yes, you will,' Laura said, followed by a wave.

A quick beep of the horn and the car slowly drove away.

Laura stood for a few moments before fixing the torch on the road ahead. She looked forward to seeing Richard again, and although she wasn't entirely sure why, she hoped it was soon.

CHAPTER TEN

Gertie sat with one eye on the doorway and another on Harold who was sitting next to her in the day room. At barely seven o'clock in the morning, most of the other residents were either asleep or in bed. There was no need to rush about here. Gertie had made sure that she'd been awake and sitting up in bed when the night staff had done their rounds just gone six. Luckily, that young carer had been on duty, the one with the bright-pink hair. Gertie had seen the look of disdain on Hazel's face as she'd spoken to this young girl, who Gertie thought was called Cassie. Or was it Holly? Her mind wasn't what it used to be. Gertie liked the girl. A student who just wanted to earn a little bit of extra money. A clever girl. Reading English literature. They chatted about poetry and books while the girl brushed her hair and applied make-up. Too good for this place, Gertie thought. Such a shame that she wasn't going to be a nurse. She'd make a good one.

Once washed and dressed, the girl had escorted Gertie to the day room, where she'd been left with her book and a cup of tea. The tea had now grown cold and her book remained unread. But it didn't matter. She would soon be getting a hot cup of tea and her book was merely a prop. She was waiting for Laura. She needed to speak to her.

* * *

Laura quickened her pace, refusing to run, but knowing that if she didn't hurry, she would be late for her morning shift and would suffer the wrath of Hazel. She cursed her stupidity at forgetting to set the alarm and popped an orange jelly baby into her mouth, hoping the sugar rush would give her a pulse of energy. She couldn't believe she had slept so late. She hadn't done that in years. Most mornings she woke long before the alarm. Mark had always joked about it when she'd woken him up every morning with a cup of coffee. A sudden stab of pain made her catch her breath as she stumbled to the side of the road, blindly catching the branches of the hedge. She squeezed her eyes shut. Focused on her breathing. Now was not the time to think about Mark. She needed to keep going. Get to work on time. She rooted in her bag for another jelly baby, popped it in her mouth and carried on along the road. Laura had no idea how she would survive the morning without having eaten breakfast. She hadn't had time to make toast or even grab a hot drink, so she'd simply gulped water from the tap. It was either food or a shower, and she'd chosen to be clean. She just hoped Hazel wasn't on the warpath.

* * *

Gertie had a clear view of the front door from her seat in the day room. She could watch all the day staff walking through reception and heading towards the staffroom. Two minutes before half past and still no sign of Laura. She was usually here early. At least fifteen minutes before her shift. Perhaps she was sick? Or maybe she'd grown tired of the village and working in this home? Perhaps she'd gone back to the city? Gertie's guts twisted. That would change everything. She was meant to stay here, in the village, with Richard. Gertie's hands twisted in her lap. She picked up her book for something to do, something to occupy her hands. Half past seven. Where was she? Just as Gertie was convincing herself that she wouldn't see Laura today, the woman herself pushed open the door and ran towards the staffroom. Gertie smiled. Today would go to plan after all.

* * *

Laura pushed the tea trolley into the day room and took a deep breath. Hazel was nowhere to be seen. Linda had greeted her in the staffroom with a big cup of coffee and an even bigger smile. Hazel had booked the morning off to catch up on her admin, whatever that meant.

'Drink that quick while you set up the tea trolley,' Linda said. 'I'll meet you in the day room with the breakfast trolley.'

Laura smiled in thanks, taking the cup. 'I overslept.' She noted the raised eyebrow and the knowing look that Linda gave in reply. Her cheeks grew warm.

Linda winked.

Laura had to put a stop to Linda's train of thought. 'Oh, no, it's not what you think. I did oversleep but it's not, well . . .'

'You just slept through your alarm? You having trouble sleeping?' Linda asked.

'No, the opposite in fact,' Laura said after blowing on her drink. 'I think it's all this fresh air,' she continued with a smile.

'Well, never mind why. Best get to it.' Linda gently squeezed Laura's arm.

Laura glanced up at the staffroom clock. Yes, time to start the day.

* * *

As soon as Laura pushed the tea trolley into the day room, she spotted Gertie sitting in the armchair right next to the door.

67

Laura smiled as she passed by. The old lady smiled back before dipping her head back towards the paperback she was reading.

Laura set to work pouring cups of tea, while Linda buttered toast and poured milk over bowls of cornflakes and Weetabix. The next hour passed by in a blur. Laura helped to feed residents and wipe down tables. She assisted with toileting duties and then it was on to cleaning and daily checks.

The morning shifted slowly into afternoon. Laura helped residents to navigate the hallways to their room or bathroom, feeling Gertie's eyes on her, watching her every move. Laura wondered what the attraction was? Why was she being observed so closely? When Laura had a quiet moment, or perhaps when she was on her break, she'd go and sit with Gertie, see what was on her mind. Although Laura already had a feeling she knew what Gertie would want to talk about — Richard.

Finally, it was time for Laura to grab her fifteen-minute break. She walked quickly to the staffroom, made a cup of coffee for herself and a tea for Gertie. She then headed back towards the day room.

* * *

'Isn't it your break, love?' Gertie asked after gratefully accepting the mug of tea.

'Well, yes, it is, but I thought I'd take my break sitting with you.' Laura settled into the armchair directly opposite Gertie. 'I saw Richard last night.' Laura watched the old woman's eyes widen in surprise.

'You saw Richard? Where?' Gertie asked. Her knuckles turned white as she gripped the handle of the mug.

'I went to the pub in the village and I saw him. He was with a man, having a pint.' Laura cradled her cup as she spoke, and thought carefully about what to tell Gertie. She didn't want to upset her. 'I left early to walk home, and anyway, I dropped my handbag and as I hadn't zipped it up properly the contents went everywhere, so he stopped to help me.'

'That's my Richard—' Gertie beamed — 'always the gentleman.'

Laura smiled. 'Yes, he was very polite.'

Gertie took a slurp of tea before placing it back down on the coffee table.

'So, how did he seem to you?' Gertie asked, her eyes still firmly locked on her cup.

Laura sighed, knowing that she was only going to disappoint her. 'I barely spoke to him and it was dark.' Laura thought for a moment. 'He seemed tired, I suppose.'

Gertie nodded, saying nothing.

'Have you heard from him today?' Laura asked.

'Not yet, no, but it's early and he'll be at school.' Gertie finally looked up. 'He'll call in later on to see me. He usually does.'

'I'm sure he will and you'll be able to clear the air. You just wait and see.' Laura reached over and patted Gertie's hand.

Gertie nodded, picked up her tea and slurped once more before turning her sharp green eyes on Laura. 'Could you spare me another ten minutes? There's something I need to show you.'

'Sure,' Laura said, suddenly intrigued.

Gertie slowly stood and leaned on her stick for support. 'Right then, let's go to my room.'

* * *

Laura had never been in Gertie's room before and couldn't help but gasp when she saw the floor-to-ceiling bookshelves crammed full of books. There was no available wall space to hang a picture or a wall clock. The old woman offered Laura a grin, knowing that she'd impressed the younger woman.

'Oh my,' Laura said, entering the room and heading to the bookshelves. She stroked the books, taking in their musty smell. 'You like to read?' she asked, her attention still on the books, and no doubt stating the obvious.

'I love to read, yes. I was a lecturer in English literature.'

Laura spun on her heel, unable to hide her surprised expression. Gertie was full of surprises, it seemed.

'But they—' Gertie gestured towards the bookcase — 'are not why I asked you here.' Gertie lowered herself into the armchair located in the corner of the room and placed the stick on the floor.

'This is about Richard and *not* about Richard,' Gertie said.

Laura had a sinking feeling that this conversation was going to be all about Richard, and Gertie's desire to matchmake.

'He's a good-looking man, a kind man,' Gertie said. 'I could set you up on a date with him if you like.'

Laura felt her cheeks grow hot. She needed to make her excuses. Get out of the room. She didn't like the direction of this conversation, or its speed. 'I-I don't think that would be appropriate. Not under the circumstances.' She didn't want to get involved with any man — she was still reinventing herself. She hardly knew who *she* was.

'Oh, I don't mean *now* of course. It's far too soon. But in the future. Now isn't the right time for you, dear.'

Laura stared, open-mouthed.

'As I said, this isn't all about Richard.' Gertie tutted. 'I want to show you something.'

Laura took a deep breath and told herself to go along with whatever Gertie wanted to show her. Make the old woman happy.

Gertie shifted forward in her seat and pointed towards the wardrobe. 'You'll find a cardboard box on the floor, pushed to the back. Be a dear and bring it to me.'

Laura did as she was told, found the box in the bottom of the wardrobe and placed it on the bed. The box was large and smelled musty. Laura thought that whatever it contained must be very old. She stepped back from the bed and awaited permission to open it.

'You can open it, dear. I want you to pass me the bundle of letters,' Gertie said.

Letters? That was the last thing Laura had expected to find. Maybe the box had old photographs or ornaments in it too?

Gertie patted the bed for Laura to sit down.

'I want you to read them,' Gertie said, her words slow and measured. 'They are from the man I lost. Then you will understand that you and me are more alike than you think.'

CHAPTER ELEVEN

Richard placed the palm of his hand against Henry's forehead. He didn't have a temperature but the fact that his son had refused to eat his chocolate-encrusted cereal concerned him. A dreaded stomach bug was doing the rounds in the village. Richard hoped his son hadn't caught it and that he was just having an off day. He'd keep him off nursery, just to be on the safe side.

He gave Henry a stack of old comics and set the television to the children's channel.

He'd have to phone Megan as Tracey was out all day on a shopping trip with the Mothers' Union. He knew that his former mother-in-law would cancel the trip to look after Henry, but it was unfair to ask her. Richard just hoped that Megan could cover. Hopefully, she didn't have any meetings. It was at times like this that he was eternally grateful that his sister-in-law was a freelancer, usually able to fit in easily around his childcare emergencies.

After phoning preschool to inform them he was keeping Henry at home today, Richard phoned Megan and prayed that she'd pick up.

She did so on the second ring.

'I'm happy to look after him. I'll just bring my laptop with me. We can snuggle up together on the couch.'

Richard honestly didn't know what he'd do without her, or Tracey in his life.

* * *

Half an hour later, Megan was sitting at one end of the couch, her laptop on the coffee table and cup of tea in hand, while Henry curled up on the other side, asleep.

'Don't you worry about him,' Megan said, giving Richard one of her sympathetic, yet no-nonsense looks that she had perfected over the years.

Richard gave his son's hair a gentle ruffle. He had to go but wanted to stay.

'Really, we'll be fine,' Megan said, her tone soft, gentle, coaxing.

'I know,' he said. 'It's me. I always feel guilty when I have to leave him.' He swallowed. 'I shouldn't have left him last night. I should have known he was brewing something.'

'Richard,' Megan said, sitting up straighter and placing her tea on the coffee table. 'He was fine last night.'

Richard looked at his sleeping son and a tiny bit of guilt edged away. But he found it hard to leave Henry at home, especially as he saw so very little of him during the week.

'I know he's in good hands,' Richard said, a resigned look on his face. 'Take no notice of me. Just tired, that's all.'

Megan pressed her mouth into a hard line and nodded, clearly repressing the urge to say whatever was on her mind.

Richard leaned over the couch and placed a gentle kiss on Henry's forehead.

He straightened up, picked up his satchel and dropped his mobile into his jacket pocket. 'I'll give you a call at lunchtime.'

'I know,' Megan said with a smile before waving him off.

* * *

Laura wheeled the food trolley into the dining room and began to dish out the meals, trying her hardest to listen carefully to the orders that Linda shouted out to her. She needed to concentrate on the task at hand, especially as Hazel had questioned Linda about her whereabouts. Hazel didn't class sitting and chatting to residents as work.

So, Laura dished out the meals and assisted those who needed a little help, but Gertie's words, or rather the words in those letters, kept creeping into her subconscious. They were so very raw, personal, private, and Gertie had allowed her to read them. She had wanted Laura to take them home with her for 'safekeeping' but there was no way that Laura could do that. She had told Gertie that she should keep them and then hand them over to Richard, but Gertie shook her head at the thought of doing so, while muttering that her grandson would never understand what those letters meant to her.

Laura didn't believe this to be true, not with what Gertie had already told her about Richard, but it wasn't her place to pass comment. She had found the letters deeply moving — who wouldn't be moved by reading the dying words of a man proclaiming his love and trust? But what had moved Laura the most was that Gertie had shared this secret with her. That she had been betrothed to another man before her husband, that she had loved this man with all her heart. The words *undying love* rang in Laura's ears. Gertie had told Laura that nobody deserved to die alone and that everyone deserved a second chance. As she'd spoken, it had almost seemed that the old woman could read her mind, delve into her past, that she knew things about Laura that she couldn't possibly know. Laura had never mentioned Mark, nor the cause of his death. Gertie had no idea why Laura had moved to Buttermarsh to start a new life. But the way in which she'd spoken to and looked at Laura made her think that the old woman did know things. And this brought up the question of how?

'Earth to Laura,' Linda said with a gentle prod on the shoulder. 'Lillian would like the chicken casserole with peas and carrots.'

Laura obediently scooped the peas and carrots onto the plate, beside the chicken, and then poured over a generous glug of gravy.

Linda took the plate, her eyebrows raised, clearly waiting for Laura to explain why she was away with the fairies. But Laura shook her head. She would talk to Linda later on. Not now. Not with Hazel back on the premises. Of course, she wasn't here in the dining room, helping with lunch. She was safety cocooned in her office, *working*. Hazel wouldn't know hard work if it bit her on the bum. The nursing sister where Laura had worked had taken one day a week for office-related stuff, and the rest of her shifts were done pacing the wards, doing real work. Hands-on work. Hazel didn't really have a clue about what went on in the home as she was cooped up in her goldfish bowl of an office all day. She was lucky she had good staff.

Laura dished out the last meal. 'We'll chat later,' she said. She could tell Linda what Gertie had said without breaking a confidence. She just wanted someone else to keep an eye on Gertie. The way the old lady had spoken to her had rung a warning bell of sorts. She couldn't quite put her finger on what was wrong, but Laura felt it was almost as if she was preparing for something. That she knew she was about to die. That's what had unsettled her. Laura remembered reading Gertie's file and couldn't remember seeing any unusual blood results or a diagnosis of any kind. If Hazel was a more approachable manager, then Laura would chat to her, but that simply wasn't the case so she would chat to Linda instead. She'd worked at the home for a very long time and knew Gertie well.

It was while Laura was clearing away the plates and putting them in the trolley that she felt Hazel's presence in the room.

Without a hello or even greeting the residents, Hazel tapped Laura on the shoulder and told her to stop what she was doing and follow her.

Laura fought the urge to stick her tongue out like a naughty schoolgirl. She was a grown woman. She shouldn't let Hazel talk to her this way. But she needed the job, for now at least, so that she could stay in the village, rebuild her life. She had to play the role of a care assistant who was afraid of those in charge. Nothing could be further from the truth. She had once run a busy medical ward. But not now.

Laura spun on her heel, forced a tight smile and said nothing. She merely followed Hazel back to the office.

'Shut the door.' Hazel barked the order as she lowered herself down into the chair behind her desk

Laura gritted her teeth and did as she was told. With her hand on the visitor's chair, she waited for Hazel to tell her to sit down.

Hazel made no such offer.

Laura knew this was all about control. Why did this woman dislike her so much?

'Right then, I just want to know where you were this morning when you should have been on the floor working?'

Laura's first thought was, *how on earth does she know that she wasn't on the floor? Who told her? Not Linda? Hazel must have spies everywhere.*

'I was with Gertie, chatting,' Laura said. 'She was worried and—'

'I know all this,' Hazel interrupted with a scowl. 'But why weren't you on the floor working?'

'Why? I've already told you. Gertie wanted a chat.'

'We are not here to *chat*. We are here to *work*. And hiding in a resident's room could be viewed by some as trying to get out of working.'

Laura opened her mouth to protest, wanting to shout out that sitting and talking to a resident was just as important as feeding and washing, but she pressed her lips together. What was the point? Hazel wouldn't listen to her. More importantly, Laura couldn't get angry. Perhaps that was Hazel's goal? To goad her. Give a reason to sack her. Well, Laura had been around the block, too, and knew how to play the game.

So, she said nothing. Silence was her best weapon with people like Hazel.

Hazel sat rigid, waiting for Laura to say something.

Laura stared back. She wasn't going to apologise for talking to Gertie on her break and she wasn't going to share why Gertie wanted to talk to her. Hazel had no right to know.

'Well, please don't let anything like this happen again. You can chat to residents in your own time, not mine.'

Laura bristled at Hazel's choice of words and cool tone. The woman couldn't even refer to this particular resident by name.

Laura took a breath, wondering if she could escape, when the telephone rang. Hazel picked up and waved her hand in Laura's general direction. Dismissing her.

It was as Laura's hand touched the door handle that she heard Hazel say, 'Hello, Richard. How can I help you?'

Richard? Was Hazel talking to Gertie's Richard?

Closing the door as quietly as she could, Laura continued to listen to the conversation.

'Gertie is absolutely fine.'

So, it *was* Richard.

'There really is nothing to worry about. She's been fine this morning. Her usual happy self.'

Laura fought the urge to open the door, storm into the office and snatch the phone from Hazel's claw, to tell Richard that Hazel had no idea how his grandmother was as she hadn't been near her, or any other resident, all day.

Instead, she took a deep breath and walked back to the dining room.

Richard was worried about Gertie.

She needed to find a way to talk to him.

* * *

'You didn't have to cook tea,' Richard said, shovelling a huge forkful of lasagne into his mouth.

'Oh, I don't mind. I had a rummage in the cupboards and fridge to see what I could rustle up.'

77

'Well, thank you. It's delicious, and to be honest, I'd have had beans on toast.'

Megan laughed. 'That's why I cooked. There's loads left as well, so you can just reheat it tomorrow. Henry had a small amount with garlic bread, so whatever he has, it isn't the dreaded sickness bug.'

Richard looked over to the couch where Henry was leafing through a large pop-up book.

'Thank goodness for that, but I'll keep him off tomorrow, as I learned today most of the kids have caught it. Best to play it safe. I'll ask Tracey if she can look after him.'

Megan's fork hovered mid-air. 'There's no reason for that. I'm still working on this big project and, to be honest, I got a lot of work done today, so can take tomorrow off. It's no problem.'

Richard mulled this over in his mind. He had to be careful here. He didn't want to upset Tracey by not asking her, but then, at the same time, he didn't want to upset Megan either. So, he said yes.

Megan beamed back at him. 'Do you hear that, Henry? Me and you again tomorrow.'

Henry looked up from his book and along with a grin, gave her a thumbs up.

Yes, Richard thought. There was nothing wrong with Henry at all.

CHAPTER TWELVE

'Do you want a chocolate milkshake, Henry?' Megan asked, although she already knew the answer.

Henry's face lit up with pure joy. 'Yes, please, Auntie Megan.'

Megan smiled, rooting in her bag for the colouring-in book and felt tips she had brought with them to the Cottage Bun. She placed them on the table in front of him.

'Right then. I'll just go and order. Won't be a minute.'

'What are you two doing here today?' Sue asked, her eyes twinkling and a smile playing at the corner of her mouth.

Megan glanced over her shoulder to where Henry was sitting, hunched over his colouring book, absorbed in colouring in a butterfly and snail. 'There's a tummy bug going round so Richard thought it best to keep him off today. He's fine, though,' she added, not wanting Sue to think Henry was contagious.

Megan watched Sue visibly relax. She could almost read her thoughts.

Not contagious.

'Well, that's good to hear,' Sue said. 'Horrible when little ones are poorly. So, what would you like, dear?'

'Henry would like a slice of toast with honey, a banana and a chocolate milkshake, please.'

Sue wrote it all down on her pad before looking up. 'And for you?'

'Just a slice of toast and a black coffee, please.'

Sue narrowed her eyes at the younger woman. 'That all?'

Megan stifled a laugh. It was always the same remark, ever since she was a teenager. Sue had forever been on a mission to fatten her up. 'Yep,' she said with a grin.

'Okay, dear, I'll bring them over in a minute for you. Not exactly rushed off my feet today.'

Apart from Megan and Henry, the only other customer was an elderly gentleman who frequented the café every morning to read his newspaper — the café's newspaper — and to drink a pot of tea.

'Won't be long, Henry,' Megan said, sitting back down.

'Okay.' His eyes didn't leave his colouring book.

Megan watched him concentrating on his simple, yet important task. The way he held his mouth, his raised eyebrow. He looked just like his mum and it was at moments like this that she could cry for his loss. The least she could do was help out with childcare. She just wished she could do so much more than buying him milkshakes and babysitting when needed.

'Here we go.'

Megan looked up to see Sue with a tray.

'Henry, give me your colouring book while you eat your toast. We don't want sticky fingerprints over your lovely colouring in.'

Henry obediently picked up his book and felt tips and gave them to Megan.

Sue placed the tray on the table.

'Thanks, Sue,' Megan said.

'No problem, loves. Let me know if you need anything else.'

Twenty minutes later, all that remained were the toast crusts, a banana peel and the dregs of a chocolate milkshake.

Megan was nursing another mug of coffee and Henry was drinking an apple juice.

Megan was pondering what to do next with Henry. Should they go to the park or sit out in the garden? She didn't want to overdo things. Her thoughts were interrupted by the tinkling of the café bell, signalling the arrival of an attractive woman pushing open the door.

The woman was of average build, her blonde hair was pulled back into a tight ponytail and she was wearing bright-yellow wellington boots. A large shopping bag with a pretty floral print hung over her shoulder and her hands were plunged deep into her green Barbour jacket.

Megan noticed her immediately because she didn't *fit* into this tiny claustrophobic village.

Megan forced herself to turn away, picked up her coffee, took a sip and tried to tune in to what the woman was saying to Sue.

'Lovely to see you in here again, Laura. The usual, is it?' Sue asked.

'Please.'

'Take a seat and I'll bring it over.'

Megan watched as the woman's eyes scanned the room before walking over to the table by the window. She placed her bag on the table and pulled out a huge paperback. Megan couldn't see the title from where she was sitting, but recognised the cover. It had only just been published.

Before Megan could look away, the woman caught her eye and then after a quick glance at Henry, she smiled.

Megan smiled back.

* * *

Laura tried to concentrate on her book, but her eyes kept drifting over to where the little boy was sitting with a woman she didn't recognise. She was positive that the little boy was Richard's son. She picked up her book and looked over the top, squinting to see if it was really him.

81

'You finished, Henry?'

So, it *was* Henry.

Should she go over and say hello? Introduce herself? But she had no idea who this woman was. It would all look a bit odd.

Shaking her head, Laura placed her book back down and rooted in her bag for her diary and pen. She needed to make a shopping list.

It was as she was placing the diary back into her bag that the dark-haired woman approached her, clutching Henry's hand.

'Hi, I thought I'd come over and say hello. I'm Megan and this is Henry.'

Laura stood up and shook the woman's hand. 'Hi, I'm Laura.'

She could smell a delicate floral fragrance and she noticed a tiny tattoo on Megan's wrist when her sleeve hitched up. She thought it was a flower.

'I've met Henry already, at the home, haven't I, Henry?' Laura said.

Henry nodded. 'When I was with Daddy.'

'Oh, so you've met Richard?' Megan's eyes grew wide with an expression that Laura couldn't quite read.

'Yes, but only briefly, walking home from the pub.'

'From the pub?' Megan asked.

Laura thought Megan's eyes were going to pop out of her head.

She laughed. 'I was walking home when he passed by in his car and I dropped my bag. He stopped to help me.'

'Ah, ever the gentleman,' Megan said with a knowing smile.

Laura smiled at Megan once more and wondered again who this woman was.

'So, you'll know Gertie, then — Richard's gran?' Megan asked, followed by her hand quickly covering her mouth. 'Oh, I'm so sorry. I'm assuming that you work there. You could have been visiting someone.'

'No, I mean, I do work there. I've just started as a new care assistant and, yes, I do know Gertie.' Laura smiled to put the younger woman at her ease.

Megan relaxed and shot Laura a smile. Something changed in the other woman's expression yet again. Laura thought it was some kind of approval. 'Do you want to come to the park with us? To be honest, I could do with some female company.'

'Erm,' Laura looked down at her almost full coffee cup.

'Oh, I'm sorry, you're still drinking your coffee.'

'No, it's fine,' Laura found herself saying. 'I'd love to come to the park with you. I'll just take my coffee to go.' She smiled, thinking she might have just made a new friend in the village.

* * *

The playground was only a short walk away from the Cottage Bun. It was smaller than the one near Cedar House. Henry led the way, skipping along in his haste to get there.

Laura found Megan incredibly easy to talk to. They spoke about the village and the fact that everyone knew each other's business. How Megan was incredibly lucky to have a free-lance writing career that paid well and gave her the scope to do exactly what she wanted, including spending time with Henry.

Laura listened to what this young and vibrant woman had to say as she sipped her coffee. Sue had kindly poured it into a takeout cup.

If Megan thought that Laura was evading any personal questions, then she didn't acknowledge those thoughts.

Megan guided Laura over to a vacant bench and watched as Henry ran off towards the swings, his arms pumping in the air with excitement.

'Such a lovely age,' Laura said.

'Yes, it is.' Megan tried to look at Laura more closely. 'You've not got kids of your own?'

Laura shook her head. 'No.' She wasn't prepared to say any more.

Megan looked away towards Henry.

Laura hoped that she'd got the message.

'So,' Megan said after a few minutes of silence, 'Gertie, eh. She must be a handful.'

Laura couldn't help but mirror Megan's grin.

'She is a character, for sure.' But Laura's smile slipped a little. Should she tell Megan about their last conversation, that she was worried about the old lady? Something wasn't right. She wanted to share her concerns, but she didn't really know Megan, and then there was patient confidentiality. She'd just be vague, give no details.

'Something wrong?' Megan asked.

'Well, it's probably nothing. More of a gut feeling, really.'

'Oh, I believe in gut feelings. Always go with your gut.'

'I'm just a little concerned about her weight. She seems a little thin to me. Linda, one of the senior carers, has told me she has lost weight. But when I mentioned my concerns to Hazel, or rather tried to tell her about them, she just dismissed me.'

'She's a cow. Sorry, I know she's your boss, but she really is.' Megan pulled a face.

'I've been meaning to tell Richard, but I haven't seen him. You see, I overheard Hazel talking to Richard on the telephone and she told him everything was fine.'

Megan let out a huff of breath and shook her head. 'I knew something wasn't quite right when I last visited, but didn't want to worry Richard.'

Laura nodded. She understood.

'I'll have a word with him when he picks Henry up after school.' Megan reached for Laura's hand and gently squeezed her fingers. 'Thank you for telling me.'

'I'll have a word with Richard, too, if you like. When I next see him.'

'Thank you, that would be lovely.'

Megan let go of Laura's hand. Her gaze fell on Henry who was now running around the playground following another little boy.

The two women sat in silence for a little while. Only the shrieks and cries of the children as they played could be heard.

'We'll have to go soon. I don't want him to get too tired,' Megan said.

Standing, she shouted over to where Henry was playing. 'Five minutes, Henry. Then we need to go.'

'That's fine. I need to do a bit of shopping anyway,' Laura said.

Megan turned to look at Laura, opened her mouth to say something and then quickly pressed her lips together and looked away.

'You do know that she's psychic?' Megan eventually whispered.

Why she was whispering Laura didn't quite know. 'Who is?'

'Gertie.'

'Really?' Laura said in surprise. Although nothing about this remarkable old woman should surprise her.

'She predicted that Richard would meet and marry Sally, that I would become a writer and that Sally would . . .' Megan looked down at her lap and let out a sigh. 'You don't believe me, do you?'

'No, I'm not sure what I believe. But there is more to Gertie than meets the eye, that's for sure.'

Megan chuckled, her eyes twinkling once more. 'Just wait till you spend more time with her. I'm surprised she hasn't tried to set you up with Richard yet.'

Laura remained silent. She'd keep that her little secret for now.

* * *

Richard slipped his phone back into his pocket and passed the office on the way to Gertie's room. He had told Megan that he'd be another half hour as he needed to call in to see Gertie.

He'd been surprised when Megan told him that she'd met Laura and they'd discussed their concerns over Gertie's health. Megan had sounded worried, even though she'd tried to conceal the fact. He could hear it in her careful choice of words. Her hesitation. Her tone, which was forced, was too cheerful.

Now he really *was* worried. He would speak to Gertie and then have another conversation with Hazel. He knew better than to mention Laura's name. He didn't want to get her into trouble.

The faint murmur of Radio Four could be heard through the gap in the open door. Richard took a deep breath and knocked.

Gertie was sitting in her armchair by the bed, a stack of books on the bed and by her feet.

Richard moved over towards her, bent down and kissed her lightly on the cheek.

'Hello, Gran.' He moved the books that were on the bed to the bedside table and sat down. He took a moment to properly look at her, while she was distracted putting her book and reading glasses away.

Megan was right, Gertie had lost weight. He could see that for sure now, even though she was wearing a bulky cardigan. It hung off her thin frame.

Richard cleared his throat.

'So, how are you, Gran?' he asked, leaning towards her. He wanted her to look at him. *Really* look at him, so that he would hear the truth.

Gertie dropped her gaze. 'I'm an old lady, love. Just tired. That's all.' She took a breath. 'I'm sorry about the other day. I shouldn't have said those things. I shouldn't interfere. I just worry, that's all.'

'I know you do. I shouldn't have got mad. It's just, it's still difficult. You know . . .'

Gertie reached forward and took his hand. 'I'll say no more about it, eh.'

Richard nodded. Smiled. But all he could think about was how frail she now seemed and why he hadn't seen it — really seen it — before.

* * *

It was just before six when Richard approached the manager's office. He could see Hazel at her desk, hunched over her laptop.

He knocked on the glass.

Hazel carried on typing while shouting for him to come in.

Richard closed the door behind him and took a seat.

Several seconds passed before Hazel finished typing, and then she swivelled around to face him.

'How can I help?' she asked, her voice weary and lacking any compassion.

Richard got straight to the point. 'I'm worried about Gertie. And I know you said I had nothing to worry about, but I am worried. She's lost so much weight and just appears tired all the time.' He stopped to draw breath.

Hazel cut straight in, seizing the opportunity.

'She's an old lady, Richard,' she said, rolling her eyes. 'She'll get tired. She'll lose weight.'

Richard bristled at her tone. Dismissive. All knowing. She wasn't hearing him.

'Has she seen a doctor?' Richard asked.

'She doesn't need a doctor.'

Richard could feel his pulse quickening. He took a steadying breath and asked again if his gran had seen a doctor.

'No, she hasn't,' came Hazel's curt reply.

Richard sat forward and placed his palms on the table. 'I want my grandmother to see a doctor.' He pointed towards the desk diary. 'This is what you're going to do. You're going to make the appointment tomorrow morning and then you will phone me to let me know when it is.'

Hazel's eyes widened in shock, but without a word, she opened the diary and began to write.

CHAPTER THIRTEEN

Cedar House care home took on a more relaxed and leisurely atmosphere on a Saturday morning. Laura pushed the clothes skip along the corridor with Cerrie trailing behind her. The young girl hadn't stopped talking all morning. Laura now knew who she had met last night, where they had gone, what they'd had to drink and that they would be meeting up again tonight. Cerrie had told her that she hadn't got home until 3 a.m., so how on earth she looked so refreshed and able to work, Laura had no idea. She'd never been one to stay out until the early hours when she had an early shift. But it wasn't her place to say anything.

'Right, next up is Gertie,' Laura said, parking the skip outside the room. 'Let's see how she's doing today.'

Cerrie nodded as Laura knocked and pushed the door open. Cerrie followed her into the room.

Gertie was propped up against several pillows. Her eyes flickered towards Laura and she smiled. 'I had a feeling I would see you this morning, Laura.'

Laura made her way across the room and sat on the edge of the bed. She took the old lady's hand in her own. It felt cold. 'How are you, Gertie? Did you sleep well?'

'Not too bad, love.'

Laura said nothing. She was studying Gertie's face. Her breathing. Her colour. She placed her index finger on Gertie's thin wrist and checked her pulse. It was thready. A little too fast.

Gertie was in pain.

Laura turned to Cerrie who was busy tidying the dresser and pulling out clothes ready for the day ahead.

'Cerrie, could you go and grab me the blood-pressure kit, please, from the office and see if Hazel has arrived?'

Cerrie glanced at Gertie and then at Laura, suddenly taking in the gravity of the situation. She nodded and left the room.

Laura turned her full attention back to Gertie.

'How are you, really?' Laura asked.

'Just tired, love, and a little achy. That's all.'

Laura shook her head and leaned in closer to say, gently, 'You can tell me, you know that.'

Gertie sighed and closed her eyes. 'Can I tell you something?' she asked. Her eyes remained closed.

An uneasy feeling settled in the pit of Laura's stomach.

She squeezed Gertie's hand. 'Of course, you can tell me anything.'

Laura held her breath and told herself not to react to whatever Gertie had to tell her. She needed to remain professional.

Gertie turned her face towards Laura. Her green eyes were wide and pleading. She opened her mouth to—

The bedroom door banged open and Hazel charged in. In her arms she clutched the blood-pressure machine and cuff. Cerrie trailed behind her.

'What's going on in here?' Hazel stormed over to the bed. 'What's wrong, Gertie?'

Although the question was directed towards Gertie, Hazel stared at Laura.

'I'm just tired,' Gertie said.

'Her pulse is high and thready. I wanted to check her BP,' Laura said.

'You're not doing anything,' Hazel said sharply. 'You've not had training.'

Laura winced and bit her tongue as she watched Hazel place the blood-pressure cuff onto Gertie's right arm. The sensor in the cuff wasn't aligned with the brachial artery.

She fought the urge to say something.

The cuff deflated and the machine beeped with the reading.

'It's fine, Gertie,' Hazel said, placing the machine on the bedside table. 'I'll check it again once you're up, but there's nothing to worry about. A good day's rest will help.'

Hazel stood and stomped over to the door.

'Cerrie, can I borrow you for five minutes?' Hazel asked. Cerrie jumped to her feet from where she had been sitting near the door. 'Let me know when Gertie is up and dressed, and I'll come back to check her pressure,' Hazel said before exiting the room.

Laura listened to the retreating footsteps. She leaned over the bed and grabbed the blood-pressure machine.

'I'd just like to check your pressure again. That okay with you?' she asked.

'Of course, love.'

Laura wrapped the cuff around Gertie's left arm, ensuring the arrow was over the brachial artery. She pressed the start button. She much preferred the manual machines with a stethoscope.

'She never does it right, that one. She doesn't have a clue,' Gertie said.

Laura stifled her smile and concentrated on the task at hand.

The cuff deflated. A reading appeared on screen.

It was a little high. If Gertie had been on Laura's ward, she would have been monitored. Laura wrote the reading down in her notebook. 'It's a little high, so we'll keep an eye on you.'

'I'm fine, love. Just getting old,' Gertie said.

'Are you in pain?'

Gertie shook her head. 'Never mind that. I need to ask you something. While we're alone.'

'Okay,' Laura said. Had Gertie been about to tell her this before Hazel had burst in on them? She held her breath.

'Promise me you'll look after them. They need you.'

Laura blinked, then simply stared at Gertie. This wasn't what she had been expecting to hear. 'Who do you mean by *them*?' she asked.

'Richard and Henry, of course.' Gertie tutted.

Laura opened her mouth but had no idea what to say. *Look after them — how?* Why did they need looking after? Most chilling of all was the realisation that Gertie wasn't expecting to be around much longer. Did she mean if she had to go into hospital?

'If you need to go to hospital then I'll keep in touch with them for you. Of course, I will.'

Gertie shook her head several times. 'No, no, you don't understand. I mean when I'm no longer here. When I'm gone for good. Buried in the ground. He will need you. They both will.' Gertie took hold of Laura's hand and placed it against her cheek.

Laura's throat closed up. She tried to swallow.

'Promise me,' Gertie said again.

This was a promise that Laura could never keep. How could she? She barely knew Richard. But she said yes. What else could she say?

* * *

On Saturday afternoon Richard stood under the colourful bunting hung across the school hall. He watched Henry as he chased a red-haired girl around the cake stall, narrowly missing Sandra, a fellow teacher, who was carrying a cup of tea in one hand and a slice of chocolate cake in the other.

'Slow down, Henry,' he shouted. 'Keep away from the stalls.'

Henry ran over to his dad and the little girl ran off towards two women on the opposite side of the hall. All thoughts of playing with her new friend now forgotten.

Richard took his son's hand. 'Come on, let's get a cake and drink, eh?'

Henry grinned and together they made their way to the drink-and-cake stall. The older children had done a wonderful job of setting up tables. Some of the kids were serving cups of juice and others were on rubbish duty.

Parents from the PTA and two Year Six students were running the cake-and-coffee stall, and they all greeted Richard and Henry with wide smiles.

'Ooh, now what cake would you like, Henry?' Mavis asked. Her twins were in Richard's class.

'Chocolate cake, please,' Henry said.

'I'll have a slice too, please, plus a coffee and apple juice.'

'Righto, take a seat and I'll bring them over.'

Richard handed over a few pound coins and then led Henry over to an empty table.

He scanned the crowd for Megan's face. She'd told him she would pop along. Jack was working so she said she'd be at a loose end. Plus, she could never refuse a gathering that included cake. And it was for a good cause, raising money for valuable school funds.

Mavis placed the tray on the table. 'Here we go,' she said.

'Thank you,' Henry and Richard said in unison.

They tucked into their chocolate cake, and it was when Richard picked up his coffee cup that he spotted Megan making her way towards them.

Richard put his cup down and waved.

Megan waved back.

'Look who's here, Henry,' Richard said.

Henry turned his attention towards where Megan was, and he, too, waved. If he hadn't been eating his cake, then he probably would have run towards her. 'Auntie Megan!' Megan walked towards Henry and offered him a high five.

Richard stood and kissed her cheek.

'Chocolate cake?' he asked.

Megan grinned. 'As if you need to ask.'

An hour later they were still drinking coffee and eating cake. There appeared to be an endless supply of both. Henry played with some of the younger children in a corner of the hall set up with books, toys and colouring books, while the adults chatted.

'So, did Hazel make that doctor's appointment then?' Megan asked, her eyebrows raised. She had obviously had doubts that Hazel would follow through on her promise.

'Yes, she did. An appointment's been made for Monday morning. I spoke to Hazel this morning.'

'And how is Gertie?'

'Still very tired. They were going to try to see if she'd sit downstairs for a little while. Have a change of scene. I'll feel better when she's seen the doctor on Monday.'

Megan nodded. 'When I spoke to Laura yesterday, she told me she'd keep an eye on her today. She's on the early shift.'

'What do you make of her?' Richard asked.

Megan's eyes widened. 'What exactly do you mean by that?' she asked around a mouthful of chocolate cake.

Richard's cheeks reddened slightly. He tripped over his words. 'I just meant, well, to me she seems pretty confident, trustworthy. Is that the impression you got?' He said all this without taking his eyes off Henry.

Megan studied his profile for a moment, failing to hide her smile.

'I like her, if that's what you're asking. And, yes, she's good at her job. I'm sure she'll let you know if she has any concerns.'

Richard nodded several times in acknowledgement. 'Good, that's good.'

Megan laughed and thumped his arm. 'Shall we get another slice of cake?'

* * *

Laura hadn't planned on attending the coffee-and-cake event at the school. She was tired after her early shift and her thoughts kept drifting back to Gertie. Her words, the way she'd looked at Laura, pleading with her eyes to be believed.

Laura hadn't asked for any of this. Her retreat to this sleepy village had been based upon the need for solitude. To get away from it all. To become invisible. But, slowly, Laura was becoming immersed in village life, in the workings of the home and in Gertie's personal life. It hadn't been the route she'd planned but she wasn't sure how to stop it. Now, to make matters worse, she was standing at the entrance to the school hall, underneath the brightly coloured bunting, wondering if she should quickly pop in. It finished at four, so most people would have been and gone. But they'd be selling cake and she needed cheering up. So, she headed towards the stalls in search of a cup of coffee and cake.

To her surprise there were lots of people milling about.

When she was a few metres from the cake stall, she spotted Megan sitting at a table with little Henry. They were both laughing, sharing a joke. Laura felt instantly at ease. She could sit with them.

She slowly made her way towards them, but, as she got closer to the table, she noticed Richard was also walking towards them, carrying a tray laden with slices of cake and drinks.

Laura froze mid-stride.

Megan and Henry had seen her. They were now waving at her. She was committed. She couldn't suddenly turn around and walk away. That would appear rude.

So, after a deep breath, she carried on walking towards them.

'Hello,' Megan said. 'I didn't think I'd see you here today.'

'Well, to be honest, I was on my way home and as I had to walk past, I thought I'd pop in.'

Richard had now placed the tray on the table. 'Would you like some cake? A cup of coffee?' he asked.

'I was just on my way over,' Laura said, seeing her chance to escape. She couldn't look at him. Gertie's words kept replaying over and over in her mind. Her heart thumped in her chest.

'Please let me,' Richard said. 'There's only coffee cake left, though, I'm afraid.'

His eyes flickered over her face.

Laura dipped her head and started to fumble in her bag.

'Don't worry. I popped a note in earlier to cover our expenses. They owe me cake.' He chuckled.

'Thank you,' Laura said, sinking down into the chair next to Megan.

Within minutes Richard was back, placing cake and coffee in front of her.

'Thank you.'

Richard smiled as he sat down opposite her. Henry asked if he could play with his friend and Richard nodded, watching his son rush off before looking at Laura and clearing his throat. 'So, how is Gertie today? I know she has a GP appointment for Monday.'

'Well, I looked after her this morning. She seemed tired. I got her out of bed for a little bit, but we put her back in after lunch. She seemed more comfortable propped up in bed surrounded by her books.' Laura had to be careful in what she told him.

Richard nodded. He held her gaze.

'I'll keep an eye on her. Linda will too. She's on this afternoon,' Laura added.

'Ah, that's good to know. I like her. She's been there a few years now, I think,' Richard said.

Laura pressed her lips together. Should she mention her concerns? That Gertie wasn't telling the whole truth? That she was hiding something? That she had her own concerns about his gran's health?

Richard put down his cup and tilted his head to the left. 'What aren't you telling me?'

Laura sighed. She had to tell him. To hell with the consequences. 'I just get the feeling that she's hiding something. She seems to be in pain but won't tell me. I don't know. I don't really know her that well. Maybe she'll tell you.'

Richard shook his head. 'I am the last person she would tell. She never complains. Never has and she won't start now. But I think she'll tell you.' He had a sip of his coffee. 'She hasn't stopped talking about you.'

Laura felt a flush of heat in her cheeks. 'I'll try to talk to her again,' she said.

'Thank you,' Richard said with a nod of his head.

Henry ran back to the table, shrieking. 'Daddy, I need the toilet.'

'Okay, let's go.' Richard stood up and guided Henry around the tables and into the corridor.

'You okay?' Megan asked Laura once Richard was a safe distance away.

'Me? Yes, I'm fine.'

Megan offered a slow smile and raised an eyebrow.

Laura picked up her coffee. Whatever Megan was thinking, she was completely wrong. Completely and utterly wrong.

CHAPTER FOURTEEN

Sunday was usually Richard's favourite day of the week. A time to lounge around the house with Henry. Eating toast, drinking coffee and reading a good book. When the weather was nice, he'd take Henry off to the playground or for a walk to the Cottage Bun.

Today was a different kind of Sunday.

The weather had turned colder and the persistent rain battered against the windows. The weather very much reflected his mood. He'd wanted to spend Sunday alone with Henry and his thoughts. He hadn't had much time to think about Sally all week. He felt guilty that she'd been pushed to the back of his mind. He wanted to sit at the kitchen table, surrounded by her notebooks, old photographs and his memories.

But he could do none of these things as they were not alone.

While he stood in the kitchen making a pot of tea and buttering slices of toast, he could hear the low murmur of voices coming from the living room. He could hear Tracey chatting to Henry, and Megan joining in, although he couldn't hear the words.

Richard placed the teapot on the tray and added cups, the set that Sally had chosen with the vouchers they'd received as a wedding present. Brightly coloured patterns of blue, yellow and orange danced before his eyes. Sally had loved them, saying they made her feel happy, brighter.

Richard swallowed down the memory, adding the stack of toast and a glass of juice for Henry.

'Need a hand?' Jack asked, popping his head around the kitchen door.

Richard lifted the now full tray. 'No, I'm fine. Although you can bring in some biscuits if you like. They're in the cupboard above the kettle.'

Jack sauntered into the kitchen, around Richard, and found the biscuits. He followed Richard back into the living room and sank down onto the couch, clutching the two packets of chocolate-chip cookies.

'Are they for me?' Henry asked, his eyes wide at the thought of eating all those biscuits.

'You can have two, but only after a slice of toast,' Richard told him.

'Here, let me do that for you,' Tracey said, taking the pile of side plates from Richard. 'I'll be Mother.'

Richard squeezed in next to Henry on the two-seater couch and gave him a slice of toast.

'Well, this is nice, isn't it?' Tracey said, passing Richard a cup of tea.

'It is, Tracey,' Megan said. 'All of us together. It's a good thing.'

Richard couldn't help but notice that Megan was glaring at him while she said this.

He sipped his tea.

He hadn't invited them round. He'd got up early to go and visit Gertie. Megan had offered to sit with Henry while he was gone, but when he returned, Tracey opened the door and Jack was playing on the Xbox with Henry.

Tracey had said that they needed *family* time. To talk about Sally.

Richard just wanted to put his feet up and have a snooze with Henry snuggled by his side. To remember Sally in his own way. The whole situation was forced. Plus, he was worried about Gertie. She still looked tired. Was still in bed. He'd feel better when she'd seen the doctor tomorrow.

'You okay, love?' Tracey asked. 'You look lost in thought.'

'Is it Gertie?' Megan asked.

Richard nodded. 'She just seems so small, lying in bed, like she's almost fading away.'

'It'll just be a winter bug, that's all,' Tracey said. 'She'll soon bounce back.'

'I'm not so sure.' Richard placed his cup on the coffee table. 'I think she's slowly going downhill. There's something not right. She's lost so much weight.'

'Henry, do you want to show me your new dinosaur?' Megan asked.

Henry jumped up in delight and ran out of the room.

'I'll let you talk,' she whispered and followed Henry upstairs.

Jack shifted uncomfortably on his seat, as if preparing to bolt from the room, but Richard noticed the look that Tracey gave him. Silently telling her son to stay put.

Richard suddenly felt uneasy. What did she want to talk about? He sighed. 'I'm worried, of course I am, but she's in the best place and I know that Laura and Linda will keep a close eye on her.'

'Of course they will. I'll try to pop in and see her myself tomorrow as well,' Tracey said gently.

'She'd love to see you,' Richard said.

The two women had remained firm friends after Sally's death. Tracey tried to visit at least a couple of times a week, usually when Richard was working late at the school.

Tracey shifted forward on her chair.

Jack coughed and wriggled around some more before shooting Richard a warning glance.

Richard reached for the remote control on the table and turned the stereo off. Tracey clearly had something important to share with him.

Maybe she was no longer able to look after Henry for him? Maybe she wanted more free time for herself? He couldn't blame her. He'd relied on Tracey's good nature for far too long.

'I need to say something and then when it's said, well, it's been said, and if you want to forget all about it then that's fine. But it's been on my mind and I don't feel right in keeping my thoughts a secret.'

Richard just stared, wide-eyed. What on earth was she going to tell him? Whatever it was, it was serious. He opened his mouth to speak, but Tracey silenced him with a *shh* and a wave of the hand.

'I need to say this while I have the courage, because if I don't say it now I never will.'

Richard closed his mouth. He looked at Jack who shook his head slightly, warning him to simply listen.

Tracey spoke. Her voice calm and steady, and her words slow.

'Sally would want you to be happy, you know. She wouldn't want you stuck in the past.' Tracey sighed and her shoulders slumped. 'By God, I miss her every day. She was my only daughter, but life goes on. *We* go on. And I know she would want you to be happy.'

Richard fought the urge to stand up and walk into the kitchen. Away from her words.

Her look of pity.

'I really don't think you're coping, Richard. And I don't think I've helped matters. It's been a difficult time for me too. Sometimes I've been selfish. Wanting to grab on to the past. To never let it go. But it's not healthy. Not for any of us.'

Richard nodded. Absorbing her words.

'Listen, Richard, don't take this the wrong way, okay. I love you as a son. And I think you need help. Professional help. Perhaps it's time to see a counsellor?'

Richard shook his head, dismissing her. He knew he needed to seek help. Talk to someone. Gertie's words had drummed that into him. But he didn't want to tell Tracey that she was right.

Tracey sat back in her chair and let out a slow, deep breath. 'Well, I've said my piece. I'll say no more about it.'

Richard nodded. 'I'll make us another pot of tea.'

'I'll help you.' Tracey began to gather the cups and place them on the tray.

Richard put his hand on hers, moving it gently away from the tray. 'I'm fine. I'll do it.'

Tracey nodded and sat back down.

'Have you met the new care assistant?' she asked after a few beats.

Richard halted in his tracks to the kitchen.

'Yes,' he said without hesitation. 'We've spoken a few times now.'

'Gertie can't stop talking about her, apparently. She seems like a nice woman.'

'I don't really know her,' Richard said, now desperately wanting to escape to the safety of the kitchen.

'You should invite her out for a drink,' Tracey said.

Richard didn't reply. He carried on walking towards the kitchen.

* * *

Jack passed the pint over to Richard. 'Here you go.'

The two men were sitting in the snug of the Fox and Hound, having made a break for it while Tracey and Megan took Henry to the playground and then for a snack at the café.

Richard had breathed a sigh of blessed relief. After Tracey had made her speech and basically told him that he needed to start dating again, and that Laura would be the perfect woman for him, he had felt the need to get the hell out of his own house and away from her.

Why did she feel the need to interfere in his life? He was happy with Henry. He didn't need to be pushed into a relationship he wasn't ready to commit to. He didn't even know this Laura woman. For all he knew she had a husband or partner somewhere, and even if she didn't, she'd have no intention at all of dating him. They had to stop interfering in her life too.

'What a day, eh?' Jack said, after sipping half his pint in seemingly one breath.

'Yep, what a day.' Richard took a generous gulp of his own pint.

'I forgot crisps. You want crisps?' Jack asked.

'No. I just want to sit for a little while, you know. Enjoy the quiet.'

Jack chuckled. 'I know exactly what you mean. No problem, mate. I need some quiet, too, to be honest.'

The two men sat side by side. Sipping beer. Each lost in their own thoughts.

CHAPTER FIFTEEN

Gertie loved Sunday afternoons in Cedar House. For starters, there was no Hazel as she had every Sunday off. That woman never worked the weekend if she could help it.

Gertie had managed to grab a few hours of sleep during the night and had spent the morning in bed, propped up, surrounded by her books. She'd been so happy to see Richard, who'd popped in for an hour. He'd looked worried — which she didn't like — and kept asking her if she was in pain. Of course, she'd denied being in pain. Instead, she had successfully deflected his questions and asked her own. She'd asked him about the coffee-and-cake fundraiser, asked if Henry had had fun and then she'd asked if he'd chatted to Laura.

It had been at this point that Richard had clamped his lips together and merely nodded. He'd said that they had chatted for a little bit, while eating cake and drinking coffee, but that she'd then gone home, tired after her shift.

Gertie knew Richard didn't want to talk about Laura. She'd seen the discomfort so clearly evident in his eyes, so she had let it go, but she had taken great satisfaction in getting any reaction at all from him.

Now, Gertie glanced at the wall clock. The afternoon shift would be here soon and she knew Laura would be working on her floor today, along with that nice young man who was going to train as a nurse.

It would be a good afternoon of intelligent conversation. She just needed to get Laura by herself. She had so much to tell her.

* * *

'Hello, Gertie. I thought I'd pop my head round and say hello. I'm on shift this afternoon with Adrian.'

Gertie pushed herself up higher in the bed. She grinned and beckoned Laura into the room with a wave of her hand.

'Will you have time to call in for a chat at some point?' Gertie asked.

'Yes, of course I will,' Laura said, and smiled.

Gertie reached forward and held Laura's hand. She closed her eyes. That black-and-brown aura that signified sadness still surrounded the young woman, but there were also pinks and greens, representing love and a soothing energy. There was still hope that things could change. Gertie wasn't about to give up.

She let go of Laura's hand and reached up to cup her cheek.

'I'll see you later then, love.'

Laura left the room with a promise she'd be back, and an hour later, she returned with two cups of tea and a packet of custard-cream biscuits poking out of her tunic pocket.

Gertie told her to move the pile of books on the bedside table and to place the cups there.

Laura did as she was told, sat on the edge of the bed and ripped open the packet of biscuits with her teeth.

Gertie took one and bit off a large chunk. Custard creams were her favourite. When Richard was a little boy, all the kids had called her the biscuit lady as her biscuit tin was always filled to the brim with Jammy Dodgers, chocolate biscuits and, of course, custard creams.

Gertie finished eating the biscuit, then picked up the mug of tea which Laura had made for her. She smiled at this small gesture of kindness. Laura had made the tea in a mug from the staff kitchen, not in one of the tiny residents' cups. Cradling the mug with both hands, she began to speak.

She looked into Laura's eyes unwaveringly, showing her that what she had to say was very serious and that she meant every word.

Laura lowered her own mug of tea. She nodded, encouraging Gertie to tell her story.

'I've not got long left, love,' Gertie said slowly. 'And before you tell me that I'm wrong and that the doctor will see me tomorrow and tell me that I have an infection or am just run down, you're wrong.' Gertie took a deep breath. 'I'm dying. The big C. Don't need no doctor to tell me that. I've been around the dying for far too long not to know. I nursed Jim during his final days. But that's not what I need to tell you.'

Laura shook her head.

Gertie noticed that she had grown quite pale.

'That's not what you wanted to tell me?' Laura asked, eyes wide, unblinking.

Gertie waited a beat, waited for the young woman to ask what was really on her mind. What did she want to tell her?

But Laura remained silent.

'You remember I showed you that box of letters and cards. The ones from Jim.'

'Yes,' Laura said.

'I wanted to show you them because even though I loved Jim with my heart and soul, he died, and life goes on. I met Robbie. We got married. We were happy.'

Laura nodded. She remained quiet.

'You need to know that life goes on. That you cannot stay in the past. That what happened to your husband wasn't your fault and that you should move on with your life.'

Gertie watched the young woman's face drain of all colour. Watched the mug that was half full of tea fall to the ground, bouncing to a halt on the plush carpet, the brown liquid slowly seeping into the fibres.

'How?' Laura's voice came out in a croak. 'What do you know about my husband?' She shook her head and dashed into the bathroom for paper towels, then scurried back into the bedroom and placed them over the cooling tea. The white paper slowly turned a pale brown like old treasure maps.

Gertie spoke softly. She would have to tread carefully here. This girl was still a non-believer.

'All I know is that something bad happened to him. Something very bad. And he died. And that you blame yourself for what happened.'

'But how do you know?' Laura asked. Her eyes darted round the room, as if searching for answers.

'I just do, love. Can't explain it. Call it a feeling. A second sight. It's just who I am. Listen,' Gertie said. 'I need to tell you something else — then you may begin to understand that we really are very alike. That I understand what you're going through.'

Laura picked up the now empty mug and placed it on the dresser.

She sat once more on the side of the bed.

Gertie began to tell her a story.

* * *

Laura sat on the edge of the bed, hands on her lap, and listened to what Gertie had to say.

She now understood what Gertie meant when she said that they were alike.

Because although somewhat strange, they were alike.

It all made perfect sense.

Laura remained quiet. She didn't interrupt. She gave Gertie the time to formulate her words. She was fully aware

107

that the old lady needed to tell this story, as much as Laura needed to hear it.

'Robbie found it hard to cope after the train crash. That terrible day haunted him for the rest of his life. The other passengers who were killed or injured. He blamed himself for not being able to save the passenger in his carriage, an elderly woman. She'd died in his arms before the emergency services got there. He found it so very difficult to live with what he'd seen, what he'd heard. I know now it was post-traumatic stress disorder. He tried to hide it from me for such a long time.' Gertie's bottom lip trembled as she spoke. 'But I knew the truth. Knew how much he was hurting. But he wouldn't let me in.'

Laura placed her hand gently on top of Gertie's hand. 'What happened, Gertie?' Laura asked. 'What happened to Robbie?'

Gertie pressed her lips together. Swallowed. 'It's easier if I show you,' she said. 'Can you grab the box of letters from the wardrobe for me?'

Laura obediently did as she was told, although she wondered what the letters from her first love, Jim, had to do with her husband's problems following the accident.

Laura gave the shoebox to Gertie who then prised off the lid and began to empty the letters onto the bed.

Gertie went carefully through the pile until she found the letter she'd been searching for, and held it out towards Laura.

'I'd like you to read this. It'll explain what happened.'

Laura hesitated for a fraction of a second before taking the letter. The first thing she noticed was that this handwriting was different. It wasn't from Jim.

Laura began to read out loud.

Dearest Gertie,

These past few months have been so hard. When I sleep, when I work, when I make a cup of tea or go for a walk with you, all I see are images of the past. Images that are best forgotten. I can't even write them on this paper to make you understand.

I just can't go on anymore in this life. I just can't.

Just know that none of this is your fault. It's just that
I am no longer prepared to live a life.
I love you always.
Robbie.

Laura held the letter in her hand. Her gaze flickered towards Gertie, who was dabbing at her eyes with tissue paper.

'I am so sorry, Gertie,' Laura said, her words barely audible.

Gertie offered a wobbly smile. 'Doesn't get any easier. No matter how many years have passed,' she said.

Laura slowly nodded. Unsure of what to say. Of how best to formulate her feelings. This was private and Gertie had shared it with her for a reason.

Laura now felt that she had to tell Gertie the truth about what had happened to Mark. After all, although it completely baffled Laura, Gertie seemed to already know half the story.

Laura inhaled, then exhaled to try to steady her nerves.

'Mark took his own life. And it's all my fault.'

'What do you mean, it was your fault?' Gertie asked. 'My husband took his own life when I was two months pregnant. Not once did I ever think that it was my fault. I wish I could have helped him. That he could have talked to me about his feelings, but it was different back then. We just got on with things. Bottled everything up.' Gertie took a breath. Shifted position. 'But I know it wasn't my fault and you're not to blame for your husband's death.'

Laura shook her head. 'No, Gertie, you don't understand. You had nothing to do with your husband's death, but I had a part to play in why Mark took his own life.'

Gertie's piercing green eyes softened as she spoke. 'I don't believe that, but why don't you tell me what happened?'

'It's a long story and I really need to be getting on with the rounds.' Laura stood up and retrieved the two mugs from the dresser.

'Okay, well, tell you what, why don't you pop back in when your shift is finished? We can chat then.'

Laura nodded. 'I'd like that. I actually think it'll do me good to talk about it.'

'I do too,' Gertie said. 'I do too.'

* * *

Laura tried not to think about what had happened in Gertie's room as she worked. She pushed the words she had read in Robbie's final letter to the back of her mind and buried them with her own thoughts.

She really did want to tell Gertie about what had happened. Not because she sought forgiveness or understanding, but simply because Gertie wanted to know. She was interested in what Laura had to say and what had happened to her. Laura knew that she wouldn't be judged and that gave her courage that she would be able to share her story.

'You okay, Laura?' Adrian asked as they tidied the lounge area, sweeping up magazines and plumping cushions. 'You just seem a little preoccupied. You had bad news or something?'

Laura thought, not for the first time, that Adrian was very attentive. He noticed things. He'd make an excellent nurse. 'I suppose I do have a few things on my mind, but nothing for you to worry about,' she said.

'Okay, but, you know, if you need someone to talk to, you know you can, well, with no one else . . .' Adrian's words trailed off. He shrugged.

'Thanks, that's kind of you, but I'm really okay.'

Buttermarsh was slowly digging its grip into her and she wasn't quite sure how she felt about that yet.

* * *

The rest of the shift whizzed by, and after waving goodbye to the staff, with the pretence of just checking up on Gertie, she made her way upstairs to the older woman's room.

After a quick knock, Gertie ushered her in. 'Come on in, love.' Her grin was matched with wide and expectant eyes. 'I knew you'd come back.'

'Did you now?' Laura said teasingly, followed by a small chuckle.

'Right then, you'd better start from the beginning,' Gertie said.

Laura sat once again on the edge of the bed, exactly as she had done a few hours before.

'So, the beginning,' Gertie said. 'That's always a good place to start.'

Laura fidgeted with her hands, not sure of what to do with them — her palms were sticky with sweat. She placed her hands on her knees and leaned towards Gertie. She hadn't spoken about what had happened in such a long time. She spoke quietly and slowly.

'It was a normal Tuesday morning. I was on an early shift, so I got up at five, had a shower, made a pot of coffee. The usual morning routine. Well, the new morning routine for me. I was still getting to grips with living alone. We'd only been separated for three months. I'd moved out of our home and into a small flat. It was near the hospital. It suited me. Anyway, just as I was about to leave to walk to work, I got a text. He never texted me. He preferred to phone. He was old school. But the fact is that I hadn't heard from him for several weeks and when he did call it was never so early in the morning. I should have known then that something was wrong. It was a warning sign.'

'What did the text say?' Gertie asked.

Laura opened her mouth to speak. Then closed it again. She took a breath. *'I love you.'*

'Go on,' Gertie said, her voice now low, soothing, encouraging Laura to tell her story.

'He hadn't told me that in such a long time. What happened between us . . . well, it was messy. It was something we could never get over. He had an affair. I couldn't forgive him. So, we, no, *I* decided that we needed to separate.'

'I can understand that, love,' Gertie said. 'There's nothing to feel guilty about.'

'But I was so angry, Gertie. So angry with him. I wanted him to suffer. We'd been married fifteen years and he betrayed me. Had an affair with a twenty-year-old. I was so angry and humiliated. He begged me to take him back but I said no, and because of that, his life just spiralled out of control.'

'In what way?'

'He started to drink. Turned up at the flat drunk, shouting, swearing. Saying he wanted me back. It got to the point where this happened most nights and in the end I had to get a restraining order. I hated myself for doing that, but I did it for him. I thought it would help him, but all it did was drive him further into drink and depression.'

Laura put her head in her hands. 'I should have known. I was a nurse. I should have seen the warning signs. That he was vulnerable, that he was depressed.'

Gertie raised an eyebrow. 'What happened?'

'Ten minutes after sending that text he jumped from a railway bridge. I learned what had happened when I got to work.'

The two women sat silently, Laura trying desperately to stop the tears threatening to spill down her cheeks.

'You can't tell anyone about this,' Laura eventually said. 'I don't want people to know. Especially Richard.'

'But you've both come through a loss,' Gertie said. 'You could help each other.'

'No,' Laura said, followed by a shake of her head. 'What happened to his wife was completely different to what happened to Mark. I don't want him or anyone else knowing. I moved here because people wouldn't know my past. I don't want to see his look of pity. Or be told that if only I'd been kinder, then it wouldn't have happened.'

'Oh, love, why would anyone think that?' Gertie asked.

'Because that is exactly what Mark's mother accused me of,' Laura said, before bursting into tears.

CHAPTER SIXTEEN

The Cottage Bun was surprisingly busy, even for a Monday lunchtime. Laura peered through the window and wondered if she should give it a miss and just have a quick sandwich at home before walking to the home to start her shift. Spotting an empty table in the far corner of the room, she spun on her heels and pushed open the café door. As usual she was greeted by the tinkling bell and the smell of freshly brewed coffee.

Laura headed to the counter and looked at the chalkboard which displayed the lunchtime menu. She wanted something hot because she wouldn't be cooking anything when she got home, gone ten that night. A bowl of cornflakes and a cup of tea would be all she'd rustle up before bed.

'Hello, there,' Sue said with a welcoming smile. 'Didn't expect to see you in here today. Aren't you working today?'

Laura wondered how Sue knew what shift she was on. It was true what they said about small village life — everyone knew your business.

'I'm not starting until two today, so thought I'd eat out of the house. Make a change.'

'Well, I like the sound of that,' Sue said, wiping down the counter.

'I'll have a pot of tea and the homemade soup, I think, with a white roll.'

Sue nodded and gestured over towards the only empty table. 'Well, grab a seat and I'll bring over a pot of tea in a minute.'

'I'll carry it over if you like,' Laura said.

'No, go and rest your feet. You won't get chance later on.'

Laura smiled and did as she was told. She unbuttoned her coat and hung it over the back of the chair. She then opened her bag and took out the paperback she'd been trying to read for the past week. She still hadn't managed to read the first hundred pages.

All around her, people were huddled over cups of tea and coffee, tucking into toasted sandwiches and engrossed in conversation. A melodic hum enveloped her. As she cast a furtive glance around her, she realised what was so different about this café, as opposed to the coffee shops in the city. No one was glued to a smartphone, tablet or laptop. That's what was different. Not one single person was staring at a screen.

It was like she'd stepped back in time and she liked it.

Laura's mother had told her from a young age that she should have been born a hundred years earlier, that she was an old soul.

Laura chuckled at the memory.

Maureen had been right.

'Here you are then,' Sue said, placing the pot of tea on the table along with a sturdy brown mug.

'Thank you.' Laura moved her book to the side.

'Ooh, what are you reading?' Sue asked. 'Anything good?'

Laura picked up the book to show Sue the cover. 'It's good, but I haven't got very far yet. I picked it up from the library. They have a very good selection.'

Sue nodded. 'Tell you who you should visit — Gertie in the home. She was an *English lecturer*. Her house used to be full of books. I'm sure she took most of them with her.'

Laura couldn't help laughing as she remembered the first time she'd seen Gertie's room with the walls covered from floor to ceiling with books. 'I've been caring for Gertie,' Laura said with a smile. 'And I think you're right. She has her own library right there in her room. Perhaps I should talk to her about setting up a mini library in the home.'

'Ooh, that sounds like a lovely idea,' Sue said, placing the book down on the table.

Laura nodded. Yes, it really was. She wondered why Gertie hadn't already thought of it.

'Right, I'll be back in five minutes with your soup and bread,' Sue said, scurrying off to the counter where a customer was waiting to pay.

Laura poured the tea and then picked up her book.

* * *

Laura didn't hear the tinkle of the bell when the door was pulled open, nor did she see the man who walked through it with a brown satchel slung over his shoulder. He wore a thick woollen coat and a woolly hat pulled down low over his ears.

She didn't see the man place his order at the counter, or make his way over to her table. Which was why she nearly dropped her book when he spoke.

'Do you mind if I sit with you?' Richard asked.

He held a mug of coffee, his satchel slung around his chest.

'Of course,' Laura said, moving the pot of tea closer to her. Her hands trembled slightly. She wasn't entirely sure why she felt a little nervous around this man.

'Thanks,' Richard said. He put his mug of coffee down, removed his satchel, placing it on the floor by the table leg, unbuttoned his coat and pulled off his hat. Short black curls suddenly sprang to life.

Laura had the sudden urge to smooth them down.

She wasn't sure if she should carry on reading, giving Richard his own space in pretty much the same way she would have done when sharing a table in a crowded city-centre coffee shop. Or was the etiquette different here? She suspected that it was. She didn't want to appear rude so she closed the book and placed it back in her bag.

'Oh, you don't have to stop reading,' Richard said, leaning back, the cup of coffee warming his hands.

'No, it's fine. I'm not sure if I'm enjoying it to be honest.'

Richard nodded and sipped his coffee.

A whole minute passed without either of them saying a word.

'So, the school not feeding you then?' Laura asked with a small smile.

Richard laughed. 'They do, actually, but I just wanted a change of scene.'

'Me too,' Laura said.

'Are you not working today then?' Richard asked.

'I'm on the late shift. I'll be heading off once I've had lunch.'

Richard was about to reply but was interrupted by Sue arriving at the table.

'Right. Here we go. Vegetable soup for you, Laura, and a ham-and-cheese panini for you, Richard. Now, can I get you two anything else?'

Richard shook his head.

'No, thank you,' Laura said.

'Well, then, I'll let you enjoy your meal together.'

Sue stepped back and Laura could have sworn she winked at them. Or perhaps she had a twitch?

'I won't be long actually. A quick lunch and then back to it,' Richard said.

Laura said nothing. Just ate her soup.

Did he not want to sit with her? Stupid question really, as he would have sat by himself if another table had been free.

'Gertie was seeing the doctor this morning, wasn't she?' Laura asked. She didn't like the silence between them.

'Yes, she did. I'm going to the home later on to see her. Find out how she got on. That's if she tells me,' he said. He

116

stared at the untouched panini on his plate. He pushed it away, then carried on staring at it.

Laura put her spoon down. 'I can chat to her if you like. Find out what was said.'

Richard looked up at her. 'I'd be very grateful if you could. I just know that she won't tell me the whole truth and I really don't want to talk to Hazel. It's only really you and Linda who keep me informed.'

'It's a tricky one, you know, because of confidentiality,' Laura said gently. 'Gertie is of sound mind. She's able to make her own decisions. To withhold information from you. But I can chat to her. Tell her you're worried. Perhaps then she'll talk to you.'

'Thank you.' Richard offered her a half-smile that lit up his blue eyes.

Laura thought, not for the first time, that he was an incredibly attractive man.

Richard cleared his throat and twisted the white serviette in his hand.

Laura noticed that he couldn't quite meet her eye. 'I, erm, well, I hope you don't mind me asking, but could we swap numbers?'

Laura stared at him, eyes wide. Was he about to ask her out? No, surely not. They'd only ever talked about Gertie. She didn't really know him at all.

'It's just, it would be good to be in contact with you, seeing how close you've grown to Gertie. It would make me feel a lot better. If I need to know anything or you need to update me, then it will be easier if we have each other's number.'

Laura puffed out her cheeks and let out a small giggle. She rooted in her bag for her phone. 'Of course. No problem. Tell me your number.'

Richard reeled off his number from memory and Laura typed it into her phone contacts before sending him a quick text.

'Got it.' He grinned, showing her his phone screen.

Laura didn't quite understand the twinge of regret she felt at not being asked out. She didn't want to go on a date with Richard Brown. Yes, he was an attractive man, and he would be good company, but she wasn't ready for any type of relationship just yet. But at the same time, she craved friendship. And she felt it in her bones — Richard Brown would be a good friend.

Richard glanced at his phone screen once more before putting it back into his pocket. 'I'd better be off.' In one swift movement he shrugged on his coat, slung the satchel over his shoulder and shoved his hat back on.

'Maybe see you later then?' he said.

'Yes, maybe,' Laura said.

He smiled. 'Bye, Laura.'

'Bye, Richard.'

Laura watched him walk through the café door, her eyes fixed on the door as it swung shut behind him.

Then she watched him through the window as he made his way back to school.

CHAPTER SEVENTEEN

Laura woke long before the alarm. The weak January sun had yet to make its appearance. This was Laura's favourite time of the day.

She swept the duvet back with a flourish, forced herself out of bed before she could change her mind, and, shoving her feet into her slippers, padded over to the bedroom door. She grabbed her dressing gown from the hook and wrapped it tightly around her waist.

Time for tea

Laura filled the kettle and set it on the Aga.

Laura had the day off so she made a plan in her head. First tea, then she'd strip the bed, put a wash on, do a quick hoover, and then she'd have a shower. She would immerse herself in these everyday chores. Switch off from worrying about Gertie and the feelings of guilt building in her gut because she had yet to phone her mum. She just couldn't do it. Laura had told Maureen that she'd phone when she was settled, when she felt stronger. The sound of Maureen's voice would send her spiralling back to the woman who had been Mark's wife. The woman who had let him down in the most horrendous way. Maureen and Lottie were part of that past and Laura could not go back there. She had to rebuild her life. She had to feel strong again. To be happy in her own skin. She had started on this journey. She felt she was doing well, but there was still a long way to go.

The kettle was steaming so she filled up the teapot and switched on her phone to check the news headlines. Thirty minutes, then she'd make a start.

* * *

The village bus had one passenger on the back row when Laura stepped on board. She made her way to a seat in the middle and sat down, bag on her knee. She removed her pink bobble hat and loosened her scarf.

The morning had been spent cleaning and tidying, and she'd finished every task on her list by eleven. Then she'd decided to get dressed and to take the bus into town.

She needed to register with the GP and then find an NHS dentist — two things she'd been putting off. Laura had never liked going to the dentist. She always got a telling-off about not brushing her teeth properly. As for the GP, well, in usual circumstance she wouldn't think twice about registering, but they would want to see her. Do the usual checks and inevitably they'd probe into her mental health. Ask about Mark. They would know what had happened. It would be in her notes. She needed to prepare for this.

Laura was glad that she'd spoken to Gertie. It was as if a weight had been lifted. But Gertie's words also troubled her. The fact that the old woman had suggested she see a counsellor. Was that such a good idea? Wasn't it best to leave the past buried? What good could there be in telling a stranger that her estranged husband had killed himself because she refused to speak to him. To forgive him. They wouldn't understand her guilt. Just as Gertie hadn't been able to understand it. No, she would think about counselling at a later date.

Now wasn't the right time.

The bus made its way slowly along the village lanes. Nobody else got on. Laura delved into her bag and found the jelly babies. She popped a red one into her mouth and savoured the tangy strawberry taste. At this rate she was heading for type-two diabetes. She would buy some peanuts or crackers to keep in her bag. Before she knew it, she'd be forty and fat. She needed to take better care of herself.

Laura felt her phone vibrate through the fabric of the bag. Her fingers were still cold, despite the warmth from the blowers on the bus, and she fumbled with the inside pocket of her bag, retrieving the phone. She read the message on the lock screen.

It was from Lottie.

She had half expected it to be from Richard and she felt a confusing pang of disappointment.

Pushing this thought aside, she smiled as she read her sister's words.

Just checking in. Hope you're okay? Just text back so we know you're alive. If you need to talk, I'm always here.

Laura felt a sudden stab of affection for her younger sister. Mark's death had brought them closer together, but ultimately, Laura had pushed her away. She just hoped that, with time, they would be able to have their old relationship back. That they could return to how things were before the tragedy that had rocked her world.

Laura replied with a quick: *All good, on the bus. Don't worry.*

She switched the phone off.

Her thoughts drifted back to Gertie. Laura couldn't help worrying about her. The GP had wanted to run tests, but Gertie had refused. So, all they could do was monitor her. Make sure she was comfortable. During handover, Hazel had explained what had gone on and that Richard had been informed.

Laura wanted to phone him but knew she had no reason to. There was nothing to update him with and the only reason he'd given her his number was to be kept up to date about his grandmother. She had no reason to phone him. But her fingers itched to do so.

The bus ground to a halt in the bus station.

Laura stood and made her way down the aisle.

She would go to the library first. Take back her books and look for some more. Cerrie had found the book about dementia very interesting. Laura would try to find some more about nursing older people.

She stepped off the bus and disappeared into the moving crowd.

* * *

Richard leaned back in his chair, put his feet up on the stool and turned on the TV to watch the news headlines.

He hadn't stopped all day.

A day of teaching, followed by meetings and then a trip to Tracey's to pick up a very tired Henry. He had only just finished marking his Year Six maths homework, and although his eyes were scratchy with tiredness, his brain wouldn't switch off just yet. He needed to unwind with his cup of tea, a few digestive biscuits and the news. Then he could think about sleep.

He sipped his tea, watching the screen as an image of a young woman filled the screen. Only just turned twenty, she had been missing for nearly a week. Richard felt terrible for her poor parents.

He muted the sound and thought of his own little boy, safe and asleep in his bed upstairs.

Sometimes Richard didn't want his little boy to grow up. It was a cruel and dangerous world out there. He pushed himself further back in the armchair, adjusted his head on the cushion and closed his eyes. An image of Laura popped into his mind. How she had looked at him in the café.

She had looked so sad.

He had fought the urge to ask her what was wrong. To ask if he could help? It wasn't his place to ask such questions.

He thought about the way she had reluctantly agreed to let him sit with her. He had felt awkward, stupid. A grown man who didn't know the right words. He'd muttered under his breath the entire walk back to school, cursing his inability to talk to anyone like a normal human being.

He had no idea what she actually thought of him.

He had seen the way she agreed to have his mobile number. Like she didn't really want it. But she obviously cared about Gertie enough to keep him up to date.

Richard told himself that was all that mattered.

It shouldn't really matter what she thought about him.

She was a woman caring for his grandmother.

That was all.

The trouble was that she was incredibly intriguing. In the few fleeting times that she had spoken with her, he'd had a sense that he wasn't talking to the real Laura. It was almost as if there was a protective shell around her. He could sense it in the way she spoke, and the things that she didn't say.

He'd given Laura his number so that she could keep him informed about Gertie. But, on a deeper level, he also knew there was another reason.

Richard hadn't seen Laura at the home yesterday. She hadn't been working on Gertie's floor. He'd spoken to his grandmother about her appointment with the GP. She'd tried to brush it off with a wave of her hand, but in the end, he'd got the truth out of her. That she didn't want any tests or intervention. So, they'd agreed to monitor her condition. Although Richard hadn't been happy with this decision, he knew there was nothing he could do about it.

He'd spoken to Gertie tonight on the phone. Only for five minutes, but it was reassuring to hear her voice. Luckily, Linda had been on shift and had used her mobile. Strictly, this wasn't allowed, but he wasn't going to say anything. He'd also heard the mischievous edge to Gertie's voice as she spoke, knowing that it was forbidden.

Richard picked up his now cooling tea and drained the cup. He rubbed his eyes.

He'd head up to bed soon. The living room had grown cold now that the fire had died down. He kicked the footstool to one side and pushed himself up from the chair.

He took his cup and plate into the kitchen and dumped them into the sink. Leaning against the draining board, he looked out into the shadows of the garden.

He chuckled at the memory of how Gertie had perked up when asking him about Laura. About how their lunch date had gone.

Richard hadn't told her that he'd had lunch with Laura in the café, so at first he'd wondered how his grandmother knew. But, of course, she had extracted this information from Laura. Gertie had proudly told him that Laura had told her all about it when she'd gone up to see her before heading home.

Richard wished Laura had kept this to herself as he knew Gertie would read too much into the situation. After all, she had called it a *date*.

'Ask her out,' Gertie had told him. 'She doesn't know anyone here in Buttermarsh.'

But Richard had remained quiet at the suggestion. He had no intention of asking Laura out. She wasn't even a friend. He barely knew her.

But there was something about her. She was hiding something. He just didn't know what it was.

CHAPTER EIGHTEEN

Gertie had slept well and felt fully rested and a lot better than she had during recent days. She was sitting in the day room because she wanted a change of scene. As long as she could sit and read her books, without being forced to talk to anybody, then she was happy.

But Gertie had another reason for wanting to sit in the day room. She wanted to keep an eye on the office and see what Hazel was up to. and more importantly, she needed to talk to Laura.

The day room buzzed with chatter and activity — residents being helped into seats, cups of tea being served and the constant chatter that accompanied it all.

Harold was sitting by the window reading the paper and Albert was chatting to Margaret about art and how art today wasn't how it used to be.

Gertie shook her head. *Stupid man. Of course art isn't what it used to be. It evolves. Becomes something new. That's the way of things.* She clamped her mouth shut and picked up her book. She wasn't even part of their conversation. Best leave them to it.

She looked up at the large wall clock. Not long ago she would have complained about being patronised, but now she was glad of the large clock face, what with her failing eyesight. Nearly two. Laura would be here soon.

Gertie turned her attention towards the office. Hazel wasn't sat there in her chair, in the goldfish bowl of an office. She averted her gaze to the main entrance.

She really needed to speak to Laura. She would know what to do. Gertie smiled as she watched Laura push open the main door and stumble her way into the home, scurrying down the corridor, unbuttoning her coat as she went.

* * *

Friday was laundry day at Cedar House care home. Laura enjoyed ripping the sheets from the beds, unpopping the duvet covers and plumping up pillows after removing the pillowcases. She threw all the bedding into the laundry skip as she made her away quickly along the corridor.

She wheeled the skip down to the laundry room and returned to the floor with a trolley stacked high with freshly washed and ironed sheets, duvet covers and pillowcases.

Laura loved that smell of freshly pressed sheets, that floral aroma. It reminded her of her childhood, of how, together with Lottie, she would help their mother with the weekly wash, sorting the whites and delicates. They were happy memories, those days before her father had left them to embark on a new life with a younger woman. Laura hadn't seen nor heard from him since. She had no idea if he was dead or alive. Perhaps she should try to find him, but she had a feeling that he'd be difficult to find, if he could be found at all. Laura didn't think she had it in her to unearth the past, just to find out how her father had changed. He had a new life. A whole new family. She didn't need him, nor did her mother. Laura shook her head to clear her thoughts. She needed to concentrate on the task ahead of her — she was in for a busy shift.

She was only supposed to make the beds. That was the task printed on her list of chores for the day. Make the beds — tick

— then on to the next task, but Laura went one step further by adding a single chocolate and a small handmade soap to each pillow. Just like you would find in a five-star hotel.

On her last trip into town, she had found a shop tucked away down one of the side streets. She'd assumed that the shop would be small, but it had been like an Aladdin's cave inside, with floor-to-ceiling shelves groaning with soaps, potions and lotions of every imaginable colour and fragrance.

She'd been spoiled for choice.

After spending half an hour browsing the vast display of handmade soaps, she'd bought a box for the residents of the home on impulse.

Cerrie approached the linen trolley. 'Ooh, something smells nice. Is that soap?' she asked, eyebrows raised as she pointed to the box which was partly hidden on the lower shelf by a stack of pillowcases.

Laura smiled and shrugged. She didn't want to make a big deal about it.

'Can I have a look?' Cerrie peered at the cardboard box.

'Course you can.' Laura picked up the box and placed it on top of the folded sheets.

Cerrie opened the box and was hit by the floral scent of lavender, jasmine and rose.

'Oh, they are so pretty,' Cerrie said. 'Did you buy them from that new shop in town?'

'Yes, I did, but I didn't realise it was a new shop.'

'Yup, only opened a few weeks back. Years ago it was a newsagent's, but when old Mr Johanson died, nobody wanted to take it over so it remained an empty shell. It was such a shame. It's wonderful to know that the shop is loved once more.' Cerrie closed the lid. 'This is such a lovely idea, giving everyone a soap.'

'It's just a little thing. It's just, well, I know that some residents don't see anyone all week. They don't get any gifts.' Laura shrugged and placed the box back on the lower shelf of the trolley.

'Well, I think it's lovely,' Cerrie said.

'Let's go make these beds then.' Laura pushed the trolley as they made their way along the corridor.

* * *

After all the beds had been made, Laura entered the day room.

Gertie dropped her book into the large, open floral bag by her feet, the one that went everywhere with her. She sat up straight and beckoned Laura over with a wave of her hand.

'Hello, Gertie,' Laura said. She dragged a stool over and sat down next to her. 'How are you?' She tilted her head to one side and smiled. 'You look a lot brighter today.'

'I feel much brighter, and rested,' Gertie said. 'But listen.' She leaned forward in her chair to whisper in Laura's ear. 'There's something I need to tell you.'

Laura nodded.

'Well, the thing is, the morning staff kindly helped to bring my books down here to the day room. I needed to get out of my room. Been cooped up in there too long. But once I was settled, I realised I'd left my bag behind with the book I'm currently reading. I put it in my bag last night, before bed.' Gertie looked down at her bag to prove her point. 'Never go anywhere without it.'

Laura smiled, encouraging the older lady to carry on. She had no idea where she was going with this story, but it was obviously important to her.

'There was nobody around to ask to fetch it for me. Everyone was far too busy and I felt awkward asking. They'd already been good enough to help me. So, I thought I'd go and fetch it myself.' Gertie took a deep breath, then lowered her voice even more. 'That's when I saw her.'

'Saw who?' Laura asked.

'Hazel,' Gertie said in an exaggerated whisper.

'Hazel? She was in your room?'

Gertie nodded.

'Well, it is Friday, laundry day, but . . .'

'But what?' Gertie asked.

'Well, I was going to say that she was probably stripping the bed, but when I checked your room, it hadn't been done.'

'Exactly. So, what was she doing in my room?'

Laura thought for a moment, then shook her head. 'I don't know.'

'She told me she was cleaning.' Gertie had a look of disbelief on her face. 'She was lying.'

'How do you know she was lying?' Laura asked.

Gertie gave Laura a stern look and sighed. 'When have you known Hazel to clean? Plus, she had no cleaning stuff with her. No furniture polish or even a duster.'

'Oh,' Laura said.

'Oh, indeed,' Gertie said.

'So, what was she really doing in your room, then?'

'Snooping is what she was doing,' Gertie said. 'Caught her looking at my books. And before you say anything, I know there's no crime in that, but she shouldn't have been in there without a reason.'

'You're right,' Laura said. 'What would you like me to do about it?'

'Nothing, love.'

'Nothing?' Laura had expected the older woman to have a checklist of what they needed to do. 'I can report her to senior management.'

'Ha.' Gertie shook her head. 'What good would that do? What would you tell them? That I saw her in my room reading a book? Hardly criminal behaviour.'

'But it's still wrong,' Laura said.

'I know, love. That's why I need more evidence.' She touched the side of her nose with her index finger. Her green eyes shone with renewed energy. 'That's why I'm sitting here. I'm on surveillance, gaining evidence. Information.'

Laura let out a short laugh. 'I love the sound of that. I'll keep an eye on her too.'

'Good,' Gertie said. Then she dropped her voice even lower.

'Now, tell me again all about that date in the café with Richard. I need cheering up.'

Laura sighed but began to retell the story.

CHAPTER NINETEEN

Richard pushed open the door to Cedar House care home after being buzzed in by Hazel who was sitting in her goldfish bowl, ear glued to the phone.

No change there then.

He was surprised to see her on a Sunday. Someone must have phoned in sick.

Hazel didn't look at Richard or even smile at Henry as they passed by.

Clutching Henry's hand, Richard strode along the corridor and stopped abruptly outside the day room, wondering if his grandmother was in there, engrossed in a book.

His eyes quickly swept the room.

No sign of her.

She must be in her room.

Richard's heart sank a little. He'd hoped she was feeling a little bit better. That she would be up, dressed and annoying the other residents.

He wondered what version of Gertie would greet them today. Perhaps he should have left Henry with Tracey, as she'd suggested? But Richard had refused, telling her over the phone that Henry really needed to spend time with Gertie. Who knew what the future would bring? But right now, he had an uneasy feeling that was proving difficult to quash. Maybe this wasn't such a good idea after all.

Too late now.

Richard turned away from the day room and made his way towards Gertie's room.

They bumped into Linda as they rounded the corner.

'Hello, Richard, and hello, Henry.' Linda cooed at Henry as she bent down to ruffle his hair.

'Hello, Mrs Linda.' Henry rewarded her with a wide smile.

'Hello, Linda. How's things?' Richard asked. His usual greeting.

Linda offered her usual reply. 'Oh, you know, we keep plodding on.'

But Richard could tell she was happy in her job. Her quick smile and perceptive eyes returned the question to him.

'I'm fine. It's Gertie who's got me worried,' he said.

Linda nodded. Touching his arm, she spoke quietly. 'Come find me after you've visited her, then we can have a quick chat if you like.'

'I'll do that,' Richard said, before adding, 'So, no Laura today? She's not on shift?'

Linda narrowed her gaze, a small smile playing at the corner of her mouth, keeping it in check.

Richard wondered why she found this so amusing. He was only wondering if she'd be looking after Gertie too.

'It's her day off,' Linda said. 'She's back in tomorrow.'

'Okay, thanks. I just thought that I might bump into her.'

'You're not the only one who asks after her,' Linda said with a wry smile. 'She has plenty of admirers.'

Richard felt his face beginning to warm. He shifted his gaze towards his son and cleared his throat before speaking. 'I was only asking after her in a purely professional way, nothing more,' he said.

As soon as the words were out of his mouth, he regretted saying them. How long had he known Linda? She would see straight through that comment. He hadn't meant to sound so harsh.

'It wasn't a criticism at all. Just a heads-up, that's all.' She looked over at Henry, pulling on Richard's arm, having grown bored of this adult conversation. 'I'll let you get on, but come find me later on if you like.'

'Thanks, Linda.' Richard was grateful for the chance to escape to the comfort of Gertie's room. 'See you later then.'

Henry gave a quick wave and followed his dad down the corridor.

Linda called after him. 'Richard.'

Richard stopped and turned around. 'Yes?'

'It would really be a good thing, you know,' Linda said, with a huge grin. Chuckling under her breath, she strode away in the opposite direction.

* * *

Although Gertie was in bed, she was sitting up with the help of several plump pillows. Richard thought she looked fairly comfortable and not in any visible pain. But then his grandmother was good at hiding how she really felt. She never wanted him to worry.

'How are you really feeling? Are you in any pain?' Richard asked for the second time.

Gertie tutted and silenced him with a wave of her hand, just as she'd done when he was a little boy.

'I'm fine. Stop fretting. I don't want to talk about me. I want to talk about you and this little one.' She cuddled Henry closer to her and kissed the top of his head.

'Nana Gertie, do you have biscuits in your room?'

Gertie smiled. 'Of course I do. I've always got my secret stash, especially when a certain someone forgets to bring me any.' This was said with a pointed look in Richard's direction.

'I'm sorry, been so busy. I did buy some packets but left them on the kitchen table.'

'Oh, I'm only joking with you. I've got enough to last me through a zombie apocalypse.' She laughed.

'What are zombies?' Henry asked, having squirmed his way out of Gertie's grasp.

'Oh, never mind that. You need to find the biscuits,' Gertie said. 'Go look in the bottom drawer over there, Henry.'

Henry leaped off the bed and within seconds had opened the drawer and retrieved the biscuit tin.

'Why is it in there?' Richard asked.

'Why is what in where?' Gertie asked, not quite meeting his eye.

'The biscuit tin. You usually keep it on the dresser.'

'I moved it,' Gertie said. 'For safekeeping.'

'Safekeeping?' Richard asked. Was this a symptom of her illness? Forgetfulness, memory loss? But no, it couldn't be. Gertie was still as sharp as she had ever been. She'd put the biscuit tin in the chest of drawers for another reason. A simpler one. She wanted to keep it safe. But from whom?

'Bring it over here, love.' Gertie gestured Henry over to the bed.

'Is everything really okay?' Richard asked, watching Gertie open the lid. 'Anything you want to tell me?'

'Not really, it's just a hunch I have — no proof, so I can't tell you at the moment.' She looked up at him. 'Oh, don't look at me like that.' She tutted. 'I'm not going crazy. It's just something that me and Laura are working on, that's all.'

Now, Richard was even more confused. 'What are you two working on?'

Gertie shook her head and handed Henry two custard creams.

'Thank you,' Henry said after he'd taken a bite.

'Oh, Richard, don't look so worried. Laura isn't really helping me. I just told her my plan and what I was going to do, that's all. Nothing for you to worry about.'

Richard very much doubted that, but he decided to let it go.

'I think there are some colouring things in the basket over in the corner, Henry. Would you like to draw me a picture?' Gertie asked.

Henry's eyes lit up. He ran over to the wooden basket and started to pull out sheets of coloured paper and colouring pencils.

Settling himself on the floor, he began to draw.

'Would you like a biscuit, love?' Gertie asked.

Richard shook his head. 'No, thanks.' He had to think about his slowly expanding waistline.

Gertie put the lid back on the tin. 'So, what's going on with you, then? Any news? Nothing exciting ever happens here.'

Richard gave Gertie a knowing look. She was always in the thick of any gossip that happened in Cedar House. In fact, she was the one who often created it.

'Nothing new really,' Richard said. 'Just work. It'll soon be half term, though. It'll be nice to spend some quality time with Henry.'

'Oh, yes, that'll be nice. You should go somewhere for the half term. Book a holiday cottage or something.'

Richard kept quiet. He had no intention of doing any such thing. He wanted to stay here in Buttermarsh and keep a close eye on Gertie.

'What's been happening here then?' he asked. 'You always have some gossip to share with me.' He winked.

Gertie laughed. 'Well. Laura told me all about your date. She told me things that you didn't tell me.' Gertie wagged her finger playfully at him.

'What things?' Richard couldn't believe she was going on about this fictitious date again. What on earth had Laura told her? Had she made stuff up?

'Oh, don't look at me like that, Richard Brown. She just told me that it was nice chatting to you and that she was looking forward to your second date.'

'Laura said *that*?' Richard's voice squeaked. 'Really?'

'Well, no, not exactly. But I could read between the lines.'

'Gran,' Richard said, unable to hide his exasperation. 'What happened was that there were no free tables. The only available seat was at Laura's table, so I asked if I could join her.'

'To share a meal,' Gertie added.

'W-well, yes, I suppose so.'

'And sitting and sharing a meal together is the definition of a date,' Gertie said.

Richard almost shrieked. 'It wasn't a date.'

Gertie sighed as she slowly shook her head. 'Well, whatever it was, it sounded lovely. You really must do it again.'

'No, no, you don't. I know exactly what you're doing with this whole matchmaking business of yours, and I just won't fall for it.'

'So, when are you going to ask her out on a proper date then?' Gertie asked, ignoring him, unable to hide her look of mischief.

Richard clamped his lips together. He wasn't going to play this game.

Time to change the subject.

'Let me fill you in on what Henry's been up to.'

* * *

After saying goodbye to Gertie, Richard and Henry took a detour to buy some sweets, bread and milk from the village shop on their way home. As they left the shop, Richard spotted Laura crossing the road towards them.

Her large canvas bag was slung over her shoulder. Richard could see a French stick poking out of the top, like a Roman sword.

Despite the fact that the weather was dry, Laura was wearing bright-yellow wellington boots. He didn't think he'd seen her wearing them before. They suited her. She stepped onto the pavement.

'Hello,' Richard said. 'Been shopping?' He directed the question to the shopping bag and then felt instantly foolish. What was it about this woman that made him so nervous?

Laura answered with a smile and a small chuckle. 'Yep, bought some supplies for my tea. Been anywhere nice?' Laura looked down at Henry.

'We went to see Nana Gertie in the home. She gave me biscuits and I made her a picture.'

'Oh, that sounds lovely.' Laura bent down so that she could see him properly. 'I'm sure that Nana Gertie will show it to me when I see her tomorrow.'

Laura stood back up and looked at Richard. 'How was she? Causing trouble in the day room?'

'No, no, she was in her room, in bed. She'd been reading.' Richard was unsure if he should mention that Gertie had spoken about working with Laura on something. After a few seconds he decided that he might as well tell her.

'She was fine, well, tired-looking, but normal Gertie if you know what I mean. I still can't get any truth out of her about how she's really feeling, but I spoke to Linda after our visit and she told me that all is as expected and not to worry. So, I'm not worried about that, but there was something that she said which seemed a little unusual.' Richard stopped to draw breath. It actually felt good to say these thoughts out loud.

He felt Henry, now restless, pull on his arm, wanting to go home.

Richard pulled out a bag of sweets and handed them to his son. 'You can eat three sweets while I have a quick chat with Laura.'

Henry grabbed the bag.

'What did she say?' Laura asked, now frowning.

'She told me that you were working on something together, that she had a hunch. She had hidden her biscuit tin in a drawer.'

'Oh,' Laura said. 'I know what this is about. Didn't she tell you about finding Hazel in her room?'

Richard shook his head and his jaw clenched. 'No, she didn't tell me that. What was Hazel doing in her room? Cleaning?'

'No, she wasn't cleaning. Gertie found her looking through her books. She thinks she was snooping.'

'Was she? She'd better not have been.'

'I think she was snooping too. Gertie obviously doesn't trust her and I trust Gertie, so she's on surveillance. Keeping tabs on what she gets up to. She'll tell me if she finds anything out.'

Richard looked at Laura more closely. She believed his grandmother. Believed in what she had seen. Others would have rejected what she'd said as pure fantasy. The ramblings of an old woman.

Laura was proving to be a woman who was good at her job and at reading people, but Richard still couldn't shake off the feeling that there was a hidden side to her.

'I don't trust Hazel and I believe my grandmother. You'll let me know if she uncovers something?' Richard asked.

Laura nodded. 'Of course I will.'

Richard looked down at Henry, whose mouth was full of chewy sweets. He took the bag from his son's tiny hand, knowing that Henry had eaten more than three sweets as it felt much lighter.

'Well, I'd better let you get on,' Laura said.

Richard nodded. 'Yes, better get this little one home.'

He noticed the flash of disappointment that crossed Laura's face before it was replaced with a too-wide smile that didn't quite reach the eyes.

'Well, I'll probably see you at the home on your next visit,' she said.

'Yes, you will.' Richard turned to Henry. 'Come on then. Let's get you home. Say goodbye to Laura.'

Henry shot Laura his cutest smile before saying, 'Bye, Laura. My nana Gertie is psychic.'

Richard froze. How did Henry know that?

He watched Laura as she tried her best to suppress a smile.

'Yes, I have been told about Gertie's psychic abilities,' Laura said, turning her gaze to Richard and offering him a shrug.

Richard had no idea what to say, so he just shrugged back. He shook his head as if to say *the things kids hear*.

Richard was surprised that she laughed in good humour. She didn't seem shocked at the thought. What had Gertie told her?

'Bye, then,' Laura said.

'Bye, Laura,' Richard replied. He opened his mouth to say more but stopped himself. Instead, he stood there, gripping Henry's hand as he watched her walk away, her yellow wellington boots fading into the distance.

It had been on the tip of his tongue to ask her out for a drink.

Gertie's words rang in his head with the fact that Laura was all alone, going home to an empty house.

But the moment had passed.

CHAPTER TWENTY

Laura was so happy when she saw Gertie sitting in the day room. As usual she was surrounded by a stack of books and a cup of what was presumably tea. She clutched the cup in her hand.

Laura stood quietly in the doorway, observing the older woman. She seemed happy, almost peaceful, immersed in the power of words. She hoped that Gertie wasn't in any pain. She knew that the old lady was good at hiding her feelings, but the way she sat made Laura think she was comfortable. This tied in with the handover she'd just been given. She had just wanted to check for herself.

Knowing that she couldn't stand in the doorway all day, Laura made her way over to Gertie and took a seat next to her.

Gertie looked up. A smile slowly spread across her face. She used a scrap piece of paper as a bookmark and closed the book. 'Oh, it is so lovely to see you. I forgot you were working today.'

'Did you now?' Laura said, followed by a smirk. She knew only too well that Gertie hadn't forgotten. 'How are you feeling today?'

'I feel much better than I did yesterday. I had a good rest, you see.' Gertie paused before adding, 'And I saw Richard and little Henry. That always cheers me up.'

'He's a lovely little boy and so kind,' Laura said. 'He told me he'd drawn you a picture.'

'Oh, yes, he did,' Gertie said, clapping her hands together. 'I must show it to you later on.'

'I'd like that.' Laura smiled and stretched out her legs. Her feet were aching this morning.

'Did Henry tell you about the picture when you bumped into them outside the village shop?' Gertie asked.

Laura narrowed her eyes. How did Gertie know that?

'I did bump into them outside the shop. They were on their way home from visiting you.'

'He told me all about it. You two meeting quite by accident. Said he enjoyed your little chat.' Gertie grinned at Laura, her green eyes twinkling.

Laura was acutely aware that Richard had said no such thing.

'It was just a chat,' Laura said, her voice rising an octave.

'If you say so,' Gertie said. 'Anyway, I'd like to go and sit outside for a little while. I want to look at the sky. Not sure how long I have left. Got to make the most of this weather.'

Laura was about to protest, thinking that it was far too cold to be sitting outside, but then she thought what did it matter if they went and sat outside for a little while? The weather was dry. She'd just be sure to wrap Gertie in a blanket. What Laura didn't like was all this talk about not having long left. It unsettled her. Did Gertie know that she was dying? She would try to talk to her about this once they were settled outside.

'I'll just go and grab our hats and coats and a couple of blankets. I'll get Cerrie to make you a cup of tea.'

'Thank you,' Gertie said.

Laura wasn't sure if her thanks were because of the promise of tea, the chance to sit out in the fresh air, or the fact that the two women would be alone.

* * *

Gertie accepted the cup of tea from Cerrie with a smile and a thanks.

'Such a lovely young girl. I love her pink hair, but I do wish she wouldn't tell me about all the boys she meets on her nights out on the town.' Gertie tutted. 'It wasn't like that back in my day.'

All of this was said once Cerrie had stepped through the conservatory door.

Laura had taken Gertie onto the patio area which led out from the day room. Wooden benches and round patio tables had been placed around the edge of the garden, with the central space being home to a water fountain and fragrant flowers during the summer months.

None were to be seen in the depths of winter, although there was still a silent beauty and tranquillity to the space.

Laura had positioned herself next to Gertie on one of the benches. She watched as the old lady turned her face upwards towards the sky and closed her eyes. After a few seconds, Gertie lowered her gaze, opened her eyes and lifted the teacup to her lips.

Laura felt her guts twist. Something wasn't right. She had the feeling that Gertie needed to tell her something. That she was trying to find the right words. So, she sat quietly and allowed Gertie to take the lead.

Gertie sipped her tea.

Laura watched the robin which had found its way into the garden.

No one spoke for several minutes.

It was Gertie who spoke first, having finished her cup of tea.

She cradled the empty cup.

'You need to tell him about your past,' she said, her eyes closed. 'It will be good for you both.'

All Laura could do was stare. What was she on about now? Tell who exactly? 'You mean I should tell Richard?' Laura asked. Why on earth would she tell Richard about her past? She'd moved to Buttermarsh to start a new life. The last thing she wanted was to relive her past by talking about it. At the time she had felt a great catharsis when sharing her story with Gertie. It had felt as if a burden had been lifted from her. That perhaps everything would eventually work itself out. That she would come through the other side. That she could have a new life. That she was deserving of a new life. But now, hearing Gertie's words, pleading with her to tell Richard, she was regretting her decision to share her past.

She should have kept her mouth shut.

Laura turned to face Gertie, but the old lady refused to turn to meet her gaze. She remained still, her face turned upwards, eyes closed.

'Gertie,' Laura said pleadingly. She needed Gertie to look at her, so that she could tell her face to face that she had no intention of telling her grandson anything about her past.

But Gertie continued to ignore her. Instead, she squeezed her eyes shut even tighter. She gripped the teacup tighter, her knuckles turning white.

Laura began to feel more uneasy by the second. How was she going to say no to this woman without offending her?

'He needs to know,' Gertie said, her words barely audible in the quiet of the garden. She shifted on her seat and angled her body so that she could look at Laura.

'That decision is mine to make. Not yours,' Laura said. She could feel a pulse throbbing in her temple. She clenched her jaw.

'You need to tell him, love,' Gertie said. She reached over to place her hand on Laura's.

Laura felt some of the tension ebb away at her touch, but she still felt uncomfortable. She didn't know Richard. She would not share her past with him. She let out a long-held breath. 'Why does he need to know?' she asked eventually.

To Laura's great surprise, Gertie clamped her mouth shut.

She needed to take a moment to think how best to answer this question. The last thing she wanted to do was to frighten the young woman, but if she didn't act soon then it would be far too late and all her hard work would have been for nothing.

She had to tell her. She just needed to be careful with her words.

'Laura,' Gertie said. 'Do you trust me?'

Laura's eyes widened in surprise. 'Of course I trust you,' she said.

'Then you know that I would never lie to you.' It was a statement. Not a question.

Laura nodded, her face echoing the same solemn look. 'Yes, I know you would never lie to me.'

'Then you have to believe me when I tell you that Richard needs to know about your past.' Gertie paused to catch her breath. 'If you hide your past about what happened to your husband, then it will destroy your relationship.' She emphasised the last three words.

'What relationship?' Laura asked, her face a mask of confusion.

'Your relationship with Richard.'

'What? My *relationship* with Richard? We're not *in* a relationship.'

'But you will be,' Gertie said. 'Not so far into the future you will be. I've told you I can see into the future and you two belong together. That's my prophecy. If he finds out the truth, that you lied to him, it will hurt you both, and I can't have that on my conscience.'

Laura opened her mouth, then closed it again.

Several minutes passed.

'So, let me get this straight then,' Laura said, having regained her composure. 'I need to tell Richard what happened to Mark, because if I don't, when we begin a relationship it will end badly. Have I got that right?'

Gertie cursed her bluntness. She had gone about this all wrong. Laura didn't believe her. 'You said that you believed me, that I would never lie to you.'

'I did,' Laura said. 'But this is on a whole other level. I want to believe you, I really do, but even you have to admit that you can't really predict the future. You may have feelings, or what you believe to be premonitions, but none of us know what the future holds. Not really.'

Gertie shook her head. That's where this young woman was completely wrong. 'The future can change, I'll admit that, but I know that you and Richard will be together and I can't stand the thought of either of you being hurt just because you kept your past hidden, and for what? I know my grandson. He wouldn't pass judgement. He would understand.'

'I barely know him, Gertie. I can't just blurt out to him that my husband killed himself.'

'I know that,' Gertie said impatiently. 'That's why you need to get to know him. Then you'll see. You can tell him anything. He'll make you happy.'

Laura sucked in a deep breath and counted to ten. This was getting ridiculous. Did Gertie actually believe in happy ever afters? This wasn't some romantic movie she was living in. Laura felt as if she'd been transported back a century. She did not need Richard Brown to make her happy. She did not need any man.

'Things happen in their own good time, Gertie. You can't rush these things,' Laura said eventually. 'We need to get to know each other.'

Laura was rewarded with a smug smile plastered on the old woman's face.

'I'm not even sure if Richard likes me,' Laura added.

'Oh, he likes you. He's just cautious because of what happened to Sally. You two are so alike.'

Laura sighed, wondering if Gertie had meant that she was like Sally, or Richard. 'I am not making any promises, Gertie. We'll have to see how things go. Give it time.'

'But that's one thing we don't have,' Gertie said, looking Laura directly in the eye.

Startled, Laura reached out and touched her arm. 'What do you mean?'

'Time. There's not much time left. I have cancer.'

* * *

Richard stood by the open door and watched his class grab their coats and bags from the hooks in the cloakroom.

Bags and coats littered the floor, alongside PE kits which had been picked up by accident and then discarded on the floor. He really needed to chat with the children about this. Again. The lack of respect that they had for others' belongings saddened and infuriated him in equal measure. But now was not the time. Half the class had already left the building and those who were still here would be too eager to leave school to listen to him.

He would talk to Year Six in the morning.

Once the last child had walked outside, Richard ventured into the cloakroom and picked up the various PE bags and discarded hats and scarves, and attempted to hang them onto the relevant pegs. Some of the items were missing names, so he took them into the classroom. The kids could pick them up tomorrow in class.

Richard sat down behind his desk and rubbed his eyes.

What a day.

The whole class had seemed restless and unable to concentrate. They had been hard to settle, even those children who were usually quiet and got down to their work. Richard wondered if something was in the air. Something he didn't know about.

Then there was the issue with Gertie. She had been on his mind all day. He was still worried about her. Even though she'd seemed better yesterday, had appeared to sparkle when talking about Laura, he still had that unsettled feeling in his stomach. His grandmother wasn't well, but she was putting on a good show of everything being well in the world.

Then there was the issue of Hazel. Why had she been snooping in Gertie's room? What had she been looking for? If it wasn't for the excellent care staff who worked there, and the fact that Gertie would refuse to go anywhere else, then he would be looking for another home right now. He didn't like Hazel, and what was even worse was that he suspected that Hazel didn't like his grandmother.

Richard pushed himself up from his chair and made his way around the room, picking up chairs and placing them on the tables ready for when the cleaner arrived in around an hour's time. He didn't need to do this, but he knew it saved Dave time. He had to clean every classroom and he only had a few hours to do so.

Richard had a stack of marking to do before tomorrow and although he could take them home to mark after Henry was in bed, he decided to get the work done before picking him up from Tracey's. They'd arranged for Henry to have tea there, Richard too if he liked, but he still felt a little uncomfortable after that particular conversation.

He'd do his marking then go pick his son up, making a quick getaway. He knew that he was a coward, but he didn't want to hear any more about Laura Lewis and how he should be asking her out.

Hearing it from Gertie was bad enough.

He had no intention of asking her out on a date.

He was a single father and far too busy for the dating world.

He wasn't ready for a relationship with anyone. Perhaps they could be friends? But he would have to get to know her better. Find out exactly what she was hiding.

He picked up the exercise book from the top of the pile and found the page he was looking for. Located his stickers, and black and red pens.

This wouldn't take too long.

The mobile phone began to buzz on his desk, slowly making its way across the surface.

Richard picked it up and read the text on the lock screen.

It was from Laura.

Gertie is in better form today. Sat out in the garden this morning. No new news.

Richard read the text. Then read it again.

Short and to the point.

He was surprised she'd sent him a text.

How should he reply?

A simple thanks, or should he ask how she was? Would that seem a little forward?

He pondered the problem for a few seconds before tapping out his reply.

Thanks for letting me know.

He would keep it short and simple too. Professional.

He hit send, not expecting a reply, which was why he jumped when his phone rang several minutes later.

Scooping it up from the desk, he felt a twinge of disappointment in seeing Megan's name on the screen.

'Hello, Richard,' Megan said. 'You good to talk?'

'Just marking. You okay?' he asked. Megan very rarely called him at this time of day.

'I'm fine. I just thought I'd give you a call as I'm taking Laura out tonight to the pub. Do you want to join us? Thought I'd ask before I phone her.'

'You haven't asked her yet? Haven't asked if she wants to go to the pub with you?' Richard said. Had he got this completely wrong?

'No, not yet,' Megan said.

'How do you know she'll say yes?'

'I just do,' Megan said, not quite hiding her irritation.

'Oh, so you're psychic now then, too?' Richard said.

'Oh, don't be like that. She could do with a friend and you could do with getting out more.'

Richard knew what was going on here. First Gertie. Then Tracey. And now Megan.

He took a deep breath. 'I don't want to go out tonight.' He ended the call.

CHAPTER TWENTY-ONE

As soon as Laura returned home to Church View Cottage after her early shift, she had a quick shower, changed into her favourite pair of tartan, fleecy pyjamas and wolfed down a bowl of cornflakes drenched in milk. She felt rather smug, as she used semi-skimmed milk and added no sugar.

She then scrubbed the kitchen clean, although there wasn't much dirt or grime to be found, and wrote a shopping list. She had the basics — bread, milk, cheese and so on — but she needed to do a proper food shop. She couldn't live off cereal, and eating every day at the Cottage Bun would bankrupt her. She sat at the kitchen table and, with it being Monday, set about making a menu for the week. Of healthy and nutritious meals. She couldn't quite believe it was February tomorrow. She would only eat healthy meals at home, would take packed lunches to work and she would most definitely cut down on her jelly baby addiction. She'd look to limit the café to three weekly visits — she could afford that. She liked Sue and the gossip that she always shared with her customers. The Cottage Bun was the sum total of her social life so there was no way she could give that up altogether.

Laura filled the kettle and dropped two teabags into the yellow teapot.

It was as she poured the boiling water into the teapot that she heard the doorbell chime.

Startled, she splashed a little of the water onto the kitchen counter. She never had visitors! She popped the lid on the teapot and threw a tea towel over the puddle of cooling water.

The only local person to have knocked on her door was Gwen on the day she'd arrived in the village. Unless, could it be Lottie? Had she missed a text message from her? She glanced at her phone on the table which was plugged in to charge, but it would still be set to silent.

She looked down at her pyjamas and tatty slippers. She couldn't answer the door looking like she'd just got out of bed. She hadn't even brushed her hair. The only saving grace was that she was clean. She went to reach for her phone to check for messages but stopped abruptly as she heard the flap of the letter box clank against the door, followed by a familiar voice.

'I know you're in there, Laura. Let me in.'

It wasn't Lottie.

It was Megan.

Laura cursed under her breath. She really didn't want to open the door. She'd planned a quiet night in. Was there time to hide? Had Megan seen her through the glass? Could she make a run for it upstairs?

'I can see you. Open the door.'

Well, that answered that question then.

Laura opened the front door. On the step stood a grinning Megan. In her hand was a bag of jelly babies.

'Hey, you,' Megan said. 'I thought I'd pop by. We haven't chatted for a while.'

Laura stepped aside to let her new friend into the small hallway. 'What a lovely surprise.'

'No, it's not. You'd rather I wasn't here so that you could sit on your couch and read a book.' Megan's grin widened when she saw the look of shock plastered on Laura's face.

Laura flashed her friend an embarrassed smile. 'Got me. I'm not very sociable at the moment, I'm afraid.'

'I know,' Megan said, losing the smile. 'That's why I brought you these.' She thrust the bag of jelly babies towards Laura, who took them with a thank you. All notions of curbing her addiction were now forgotten.

'You didn't need to buy me these just so you could call round.' Laura laughed, beckoning Megan into the kitchen. 'Want a cup of tea? Or I have a bottle of white in the fridge.'

Megan shook her head. 'No. And I needed to get in your good books because I'm taking you out.'

'What? I can't go out.' It was almost a shriek.

'Why not?' Megan asked. Laura could see she was doing her best not to scowl. 'We'll just go out to the Fox and Hound for a quick drink.'

Laura needed to think on her feet. She really didn't feel in the mood for sitting in a pub. She had planned for a quiet night in, but one look at Megan suggested that that wasn't going to happen.

'Just one drink,' Megan said pleadingly. 'I really need to talk to you about something and I'd feel more comfortable in the pub.'

Laura's resolve softened a little, helped by the fact she was far too curious. What was on Megan's mind? One drink couldn't hurt, she supposed, and she liked Megan. She'd been a good friend. Laura had been so wrapped up in her own little world that she wasn't being as kind as she should be. It was time to be less selfish.

'I'll just go and get changed,' Laura said.

Megan smiled, then placed her hands together in a sign of prayer.

* * *

The two women had chosen to sit at the table near the open fire. The fireplace had been stacked with logs and it roared with a fierce heat. It was why this particular table was usually the most popular place to sit in the pub, but tonight the Fox and Hound was suspiciously quiet. Only a few lone, elderly men lined the bar, nursing pints of bitter and chewing salted peanuts from a bowl.

'Why's it so quiet in here?' Laura asked.

'It's always like this on a Monday,' Megan said, as if the answer was obvious. 'No one comes out on a Monday night.'

'Except us.' Laura forced a smile.

Megan picked up her glass of wine and took a small sip. Her lips were stained red.

Laura noticed that Megan's hand shook slightly as she lifted the glass. Was she nervous? If so, what was she nervous about?

Laura picked up her oversized coffee cup with both hands, blew on the hot liquid then gently sipped. It was still far too hot. But deliciously bitter.

She was still amused that Bill hadn't even tried to hide his astonishment when she'd asked for a coffee. Again. He had even shaken his head in disbelief.

'You don't drink?' Megan had asked after Laura had placed her order.

Laura explained that she did like a drink, now and again, hence the white wine in her fridge at home, but she wanted to keep a clear head for work tomorrow. She also wanted to keep a clear head, to be better prepared for whatever Megan wanted to say to her — not that she voiced that. She didn't want to let her guard down. She had a sneaky feeling that it involved Richard.

Now, Megan gently placed her wine glass down on the table. Her eyes flickered upwards to meet Laura's gaze.

Laura placed her coffee cup down and relaxed back into the comfort of the old leather armchair. 'So, what do you need to tell me?'

'I just wanted to talk about Richard and Sally. What happened to them. What happened to him.' A forlorn look crossed Megan's face as she spoke.

Megan's words took Laura by surprise. She opened her mouth to speak, but Megan beat her to it, shaking her head.

'Just hear me out, okay?' Megan pleaded with her eyes.

Laura sighed and nodded, despite her better judgement.

'It's just that if you know about what happened to them, then you'll understand Richard so much more, and right now he could really do with a friend.'

For the second time that evening, Laura was taken by surprise. She felt uncomfortable with the entire situation. She knew far too much about this family. Far too much. All she had wanted to do was come here and hide away after her own family breakdown, and now she was being drawn into another family drama, one which really didn't concern her at all. And anyway, wasn't it up to her and Richard if they should be friends? Why did Megan feel the need to become involved?

Laura swallowed down her anger. She had to keep calm, find out exactly what was going on here. This family grew stranger by the minute.

She decided to be brave. She took a deep breath.

'Megan, listen, this really isn't any of my business.'

'I know, I'm sorry, it's just that . . . well, it's been so difficult for him, these past few years, after losing Sally. They'd been together since they were fifteen. Met right here in the village.'

'Really?' Laura said. 'They were childhood sweethearts?' Something softened inside her. He really had lost the love of his life. 'I just assumed they met a little later.'

'Because of Henry?' Megan asked. 'That's an easy assumption to make.' Megan sipped her wine then cleared her throat. 'It took them three rounds of IVF to make Henry and then she found out she had breast cancer.'

'Oh, Megan, I can't imagine what they must have gone through. The joy of having a baby and to then find out that you have . . .' Laura's words trailed off, at a loss of what else to say. It was all so very tragic.

'It was devastating. Richard found it hard to be happy about the pregnancy because it was endangering his wife's life. They had been told to have a termination, but Sally refused.

She said that getting rid of the baby would kill her, even if the cancer didn't.'

'She sounds like a remarkable woman,' Laura said.

'Yes, she was.'

'So she had the baby and then started treatment?' Laura said. 'That must have been incredibly draining and emotional for both of them. Poor Sally. She should have been putting her feet up and nursing her newborn. Not having chemo.'

Megan shot her a look. 'That's where you're wrong,' she said.

'What do you mean?' Laura asked. But then, she quickly put the pieces together. In a hushed voice she said, 'She never had the treatment, did she?'

Megan looked over Laura's shoulder, as if looking into the past. She shook her head. 'Sally refused to have any treatment.' Megan slammed her palm on the table as she spoke, making Laura jump. 'No, that's not fair. It wasn't as simple as that. She made an informed decision, having been given all the statistics. She weighed up the odds of surviving post-treatment. They only gave her an extra five per cent, so she refused. Sally said she would rather spend the time she had left with her baby, not trapped in some hospital bed.'

'I can understand that,' Laura said.

'So could I, but Richard couldn't. He tried to persuade her to have the treatment. That it was worth the risk, if it meant her being able to spend that little extra time with Henry. But she stood her ground. She wanted to live, and die, on her terms.'

'It would have been her last chance to have some sort of control over her life,' Laura said. 'Control had been taken away from her and it was her decision to make.'

Megan nodded. Picked up her glass and drained the remaining wine.

Laura bit her lip. All of this made her feel very uncomfortable. This was Richard's private life they were discussing, in a pub.

'Look, I know this is making you feel uncomfortable,' Megan said.

'You're right there. This is private stuff. I shouldn't be hearing any of this,' Laura said sharply.

'Yes, you should,' Megan said, now with more steel in her voice. 'You need to hear this so that you understand. So that you can help Richard when the time comes.'

'What do you mean?' Laura asked. 'When the time comes for what?'

'Gertie,' Megan whispered.

'Gertie,' Laura echoed.

And then Laura knew. She knew what this had all been about. Of course. All roads led back to Gertie.

'You know, don't you?' Laura asked cautiously. Although she had her suspicions, she didn't want to break a confidence in telling Megan. After all, Gertie could have told her something completely different.

'About the cancer? Yes, she told me. And she told me that you knew too,' Megan said.

'But Richard doesn't know, does he?' Laura said. 'I mean she told me that she didn't want Richard to know about the cancer and I have to respect that. It's her decision, but it doesn't feel right, knowing what she is going through and her own grandson being oblivious. Kept out in the cold. It just feels so very wrong.'

'I feel exactly the same way, but I, too, can't break a confidence.'

'Who else knows?' Laura asked. 'I mean, is it really only the two of us? She hasn't told Tracey?'

'Just us two,' Megan said. 'But I'm so glad that she told you, because to be honest, I don't think I could bear this secret alone.'

Laura reached out and grasped Megan's hand, giving it a gentle squeeze. 'I've only known her a very short time, but I already know that she's a very strong and special woman. And I know that she means the world to you. I'm here if you need me, and after, well, once Gertie passes, I'll be there for Richard too. Because as you say, he'll need a friend, and sometimes it's just easier to speak to someone who isn't family.'

Megan squeezed Laura's hand and then pulled away gently. She smiled a sad smile. 'Thank you. That means so much to me.'

Laura picked up her now cold cup of coffee but drank it anyway. She needed the distraction. Something to do with her hands. She drained the cup.

Something was still niggling away inside her.

She understood how Megan would want to share the burden of knowing about Gertie as Richard didn't know. It was so much for one person to keep trapped within them. So, telling Laura, sharing this terrible secret — they now had each other to talk to. Megan was no longer alone.

But . . . had Gertie told Megan about the supposed prophecy too? It was Gertie's reason for confiding in Laura so . . . Surely Megan didn't know about that? That couldn't be the real reason behind this conversation, could it? Had Gertie told Megan that she needed to put pressure on Laura?

And then Laura remembered their conversation from the park. When they had watched Henry playing. Megan had told her that Gertie had foreseen Richard meeting Sally, and Megan had said this without a trace of humour or irony. Megan had believed in the prophecy nonsense then, and if Gertie had shared this new prophecy with her, she would most probably still believe in it now.

Laura decided to bite the bullet. She needed to tell Megan that Gertie had seen her and Richard together in the future. She needed to know if she should believe what Gertie had said about her and Richard.

So Laura spoke her truth. Her voice shook slightly but she got the words out.

'Gertie has it in her head that me and Richard will be together in the future. It is her *prophecy*.' Laura made quotation marks with her fingers to highlight this irony. 'She has told me on several occasions that I will fall in love with her grandson. The whole thing is crazy, but I try to humour her even though I don't believe in it. It's complete madness . . . isn't it?'

Laura held her breath, waiting for Megan to let out a belly laugh. To tell her that she was absolutely right. She slowly counted to ten while she waited for this to happen.

Megan's face slowly turned a bright red, spreading up from her chest and neck. Her pale skin now looked a blotchy red colour.

Come on, Megan. Where's the laugh? She *needed* to be told that this was Gertie all over, that she was a matchmaker.

But Megan said none of these things.

Megan cleared her throat and spoke slowly. 'It's not madness. It's true.'

CHAPTER TWENTY-TWO

Laura woke early on Tuesday morning with an uneasy feeling in the pit of her stomach. She woke a full hour before her alarm, the sky still black. The moon shone brightly. For a split second she had the urge to take a photo, capture its beauty, but then reality gripped her. Last night's conversation played over and over in her mind.

Megan was convinced that Gertie could see into the future, and if Gertie had seen Laura and Richard living happily ever after, then that was what would happen. Laura still couldn't believe that Megan had no doubts about Gertie's so-called abilities. Megan was an educated, articulate and progressive woman, yet she chose to believe in all of this seeing-in-to-the-future nonsense.

Laura had felt a shift between them after Megan had declared the prophecy to be true. There was no middle ground to be found. No room for compromise. Laura had made her feelings perfectly clear — that she did not believe, but she would go along with things for Gertie's benefit. There was no harm in humouring the old lady.

Megan had not liked this one little bit.

She had wrongly assumed that Laura would be happy — that she would jump for joy at such a promise of a great future

— but Megan didn't know Laura's history, didn't know what had happened to her. Plus, Laura was not a romantic. She was a realist and didn't need a man in her life to make her happy, or to lead a fulfilling life. The more Laura thought about their conversation, the angrier she became. And she couldn't be angry today. She was on the early shift and she would be working on Gertie's floor. She needed to relax and focus on the day ahead.

Laura stumbled into the kitchen and turned on the radio to hear the *Today* programme from Radio Four. She found it a good way to start the day. She then unplugged her phone from the charger and switched it on. It had just gone 6 a.m. She filled the kettle to make her first cup of tea.

The ringing phone made her jump. Laura glanced at the lock screen. It was the home.

'Hello,' Laura said, wondering who would be on the other end. She really hoped that it wouldn't be Hazel, not at this early hour.

'Hi, Laura.'

Hazel.

'Hi,' Laura said, trying not to sound disappointed. She hoped that Hazel wasn't about to ask her to work a long day. She felt dog-tired and had made plans for an early night. If Hazel asked then she would say yes. That was her problem. She could never say no. She didn't want to let the residents down.

'Listen, I know it's early and that you're probably getting ready to come on shift, but could you do me a favour? Could you work the late shift instead?'

Laura hated it when this happened, but what could she say? Hazel was her boss and all the care staff worked as a team, covering shifts as and when needed.

'No problem, Hazel,' she said, trying to keep the disappointment out of her voice.

'You're a star. Thank you.' Hazel ended the call.

Laura sighed, slightly annoyed that Hazel hadn't even bothered to explain why she needed her to swap shifts.

And now, what to do with her unexpected morning off work?

Go back to bed and have a nap? No, she was up now and there was no way she could go back to sleep.

Laura placed the mobile face down on the kitchen table and decided to have that cup of tea.

Tea, then she'd figure out what to do with herself.

* * *

'Hello! It's so lovely to see you in here again. Usual, is it?' Sue asked while cleaning the counter of non-existent mess.

Laura smiled. 'Yes, I'll have a slice of the carrot cake as well, please.' All thoughts of healthy eating plans were abandoned for the day. Well, she was trying to be good. She *had* avoided the sticky toffee pudding.

'I didn't think I would see you until tomorrow.' Sue spooned ground coffee into the filter machine.

Laura sniffed, tasting the coffee on her tongue. 'I was meant to be doing the early shift, but Hazel phoned this morning and asked if I would swap, so I did.'

'Well, that's good of you at such short notice. You could have had plans,' Sue said.

Laura held her tongue, stopping herself from saying, *What plans?*

Sue turned back round to face Laura as she passed her the coffee. 'Will your sister be visiting again soon? Must be lonely for you here without family.'

Laura shook her head, thinking of the phone call she had had with her sister that morning. Lottie had phoned just as she was preparing to leave the cottage, on her way to the café.

Their conversation had been a surprisingly easy one, with Lottie chatting about the children and life back where Laura used to live. Another life. It was only as she'd been about to ring off that Lottie had asked how Laura was. Was everything okay? And that if Laura ever needed her, she would be in the car and on her way.

Laura had reassured her sister, telling her that everything was fine. She had settled into her new working life and Buttermarsh was slowly beginning to feel like home. As Laura had spoken those words, she'd known they were true. Buttermarsh and its people had gradually seeped into her bones, whether she liked it or not.

Laura had hesitated, but then proceeded to tell Lottie about Gertie and her prophecy, stating that the old woman had foreseen Laura living a happy-ever-after life with her grandson.

Lottie had belly-laughed down the phone. Laura had heard the huge gulping breaths as her sister had tried to control herself.

It had been just the tonic Laura had needed.

It was the reaction she had needed from Megan last night.

Lottie had told her that at least it was a distraction.

Laura had laughed, saying that, yes, that was one way of looking at it. They had ended their call and Laura had left for the café.

Now, Laura looked at Sue as she passed her the steaming mug of coffee. 'I'm not sure when Lottie will next be visiting, but she loves the village and especially your cakes.'

Laura was rewarded with a bashful smile. 'Oh, that's very kind of her. Tell her that when she next visits, she can have a cake on the house.'

Laura grinned. Lottie would love that. 'I'll be sure to tell her.'

'Well then, you go sit down and rest your legs and I'll be over when the soup is ready.'

Laura smiled and turned away from the counter, scanning the room for a vacant table.

Not so many people today, and her favourite window seat was vacant so she went and sat there. She picked up her coffee and slowly scanned the room over the rim of the cup, taking tentative sips of the scalding liquid.

Had she expected to find Richard? Sitting at one of the tables, eating cheese on toast? Waiting for her?

161

She shook her head. Stupid thoughts. She was letting Gertie into her head. Richard would be at school, probably in the canteen with the kids, tucking into a shepherd's pie or a cheese sandwich. His thoughts would be as far away from Laura as possible. Why would he even think about her? Other than in relation to his gran's wellbeing. Why was she even thinking about him?

Laura put her cup down and reached into her bag for her book. She began to read, but took in none of the words.

* * *

By the time Laura arrived at work she knew that she needed to nip this prophecy claptrap, as her mother would call it, in the bud. But as she made her way along the corridor for handover she was stopped in her tracks, quite literally, by Hazel's vice-like grip on her shoulder.

Laura winced, rubbed her shoulder and scowled at Hazel, forgetting for a moment that Hazel was actually her boss. 'There was no need for that.'

Hazel ignored the snipe and smirked. 'You were going the wrong way. You're on this floor today.'

'Oh, right, well. Okay, then. It's just that I was rostered to be upstairs this morning.' Laura's heart sank. She wouldn't get to talk to Gertie until the end of her shift now and most likely she'd be in bed by then. And she needed to have this out with her once and for all, albeit in a nice way. Just politely remind her that this was her life and that although she knew Gertie cared about her, and she thought a lot of Gertie, this was something that she needed to leave well alone. Things had already gone too far.

'Yes, you were,' Hazel said. 'But you are covering me this afternoon and I was rostered to work downstairs.'

'Oh,' was all that Laura could say. There was no use in waiting for an explanation of why Hazel needed to swap. The woman didn't give a damn about anyone but herself.

Laura turned around and headed back down the stairs, Hazel following in her wake.

* * *

The afternoon flashed by with the normal routine, hustle and bustle of care work. Laura enjoyed the basic nursing care that she could give to the residents. It was hard manual work, but it made her feel alive and, more importantly, valued. She missed her work on the wards, which was a different kind of busy, but what she didn't miss were the hours working short-staffed, grabbing sips of cold tea whenever she could. She didn't miss the endless note-taking and having to make up duty rotas that consisted of far too many agency staff. She missed none of that. Her work at Cedar House care home was good, honest, basic nursing care, the kind of nursing care that had been drummed into her while training, and she liked going back to the basics. This work suited her. It grounded her. It gave her a reason for getting up in the morning, when for a long time she had questioned if her life was still worth living.

Laura grabbed her bag and coat from the staffroom, said goodbye to Linda, who she had been fortunate enough to share her shift with, and headed upstairs to see if Gertie was free for a chat.

Laura tapped gently on the bedroom door and pushed it open a crack, listening as she did so.

'Come in, Laura,' Gertie said. 'I've been waiting to see you all day. I was so disappointed when I found out they'd swapped your shifts.'

Gertie said all this while beckoning Laura into the room with a wave of her hand.

'Me too,' Laura said. 'I've been wanting to talk to you all day.'

Laura perched on the side of the bed next to where Gertie was propped up with countless plumped pillows.

'Well, what I need to tell you is very important. Do me a favour and shut the door, love. Then I can tell you what I've found out today.'

Laura did as she was told and shut the door. She would listen to what Gertie had to say and then would lay her cards on the table. Tell Gertie that she would stand for no more meddling. That this was her life.

Laura took a steadying breath before making her way back to Gertie's bedside.

'What do you need to tell me, Gertie?' Whatever it was, the old lady looked ever so serious, as if she was about to discuss life-and-death issues. Laura hoped it wasn't more bad news. She reminded herself that this amazing old woman was dying and that she probably didn't have long left. Gertie really didn't deserve any more bad news.

'It's happening again,' Gertie whispered.

'What is?' Laura asked.

'Things have been moved around my room. The things I can see from here anyway. I was in the day room all morning, but when I got back here, late afternoon, things had been moved.'

'What things?'

'My books have been moved — I can tell because they've been put back in the wrong order.'

Laura glanced at the piles of books, all tottering piles. But she didn't doubt Gertie. Laura bet that Gertie knew exactly where every book should be.

'Can you open the wardrobe door for me? Check that the cardboard box is where it should be?'

Laura opened the wardrobe door wide so that Gertie could see inside.

Instead of the cardboard box being under a pile of clothes, it was now clearly visible.

'It's been moved!'

'Yes,' Laura echoed Gertie's shout. An icy chill ran up her spine.

Someone had been in Gertie's room and had rifled through her stuff. Gertie was a vulnerable woman. A dying woman. She placed her trust in these people, in Laura.

Laura's mouth went dry.

'I've heard things as well,' Gertie said. 'When I was in the day room, I overheard Harold chatting to Margaret who told him that she can't find some of her paintings. She also swears that money has been taken from her pottery pig.' Gertie's voice grew louder with the indignation.

Laura's pulse quickened. She didn't like this one little bit. 'Has anything been taken from your room?'

'I'm not completely sure,' Gertie said, 'but I don't think so. I only think that things have been moved, but there's so much stuff I might be wrong.'

Laura's head spun. What should she do? The obvious answer was to report all of this to Hazel. But, one, Hazel wouldn't take it seriously, two, Hazel would say she would do something and then do nothing, and, three, Laura suspected that Hazel was behind all of this.

'We need to catch her,' Gertie said.

Laura nodded. She knew exactly *who* Gertie was referring to. 'But *how*, Gertie? We can't do twenty-four-hour surveillance.'

Gertie grinned. 'Oh, that's where you are wrong, love. What we need is a secret camera, here in this room, and Richard can help us out with that. He told me so when he was here earlier. He was so upset about it and thought that installing a secret camera would be the best way to catch the culprit in the act. You know, like they do on those awful documentaries.'

Laura sighed. Although this was a good plan, that they could easily put a secret camera into the room, Laura wondered why every conversation ended with Richard?

'In fact, he was so preoccupied,' Gertie continued, 'that he left his phone here. I don't suppose you could give it to him?'

It was on the tip of Laura's tongue now to tell Gertie that she knew what she was up to with her matchmaking meddling.

But Gertie spoke first.

'Has he asked you out yet?'

CHAPTER TWENTY-THREE

Earlier that same day . . .

'See you tomorrow, Henry. Be a good boy for Nana.' Richard waved goodbye to his son who stood on Tracey's doorstep, clutching her hand.

'He's always a good boy. Aren't you, Henry.' Tracey looked down to ruffle his hair with her free hand. 'He'll be fine, don't worry. Give us a call in the morning if you like.'

'Will do.' Richard closed the garden gate behind him. 'Bye, Henry.' He heard the click of the front door closing.

He drew in a deep breath and pushed his hands deeper into his coat pockets. The sky was now pitch black and he could see the stars, thanks to the very few dimly lit street lights. One of the perks of living in the village.

He made his way slowly past the few scattered cottages and along the lane towards the care home. He needed to see Gertie. Check how she was doing. He wouldn't get a chance tomorrow as he was on a day trip with his Year Six kids, hence the need for Henry to stay overnight with Tracey. It was going to be a very early start and they wouldn't be getting back until eight o'clock in the evening. Richard just wanted to see his gran and make sure she was settled and comfortable.

What he secretly hoped for was that he might bump into Laura. She would tell him how things really were and if there were any problems. But another part of him, something that was buried deep within him, just wanted to see her again. Just to see her face.

What was he thinking? He was letting Gertie and her romantic notions get to him. His attention should be on his son, who he'd abandoned to the care of his mother-in-law. Now wasn't the time to be thinking about the pretty care worker who seemed to care as much about his gran as he did. But there was something about her. A deep-rooted sadness that she couldn't quite hide. He supposed that he just wanted to know more about her. She intrigued him. She was a mystery and he liked to solve mysteries.

With every step that Richard took, he felt the guilt weighing heavier on his shoulders. Henry loved to spend the night with Nana Tracey, but Richard still felt like the worst dad in the world for leaving him behind.

Sally's voice rang strong and loud in his head.

Richard, don't be too hard on yourself. You're doing the best you can. He is so loved. You shouldn't worry.

But he did. He couldn't help it. He worried all the time about letting his young son down. He worried about his emotional development, about how losing his mother so young would affect him in later life, because Richard knew that it would. He had read studies. He also knew from his own experience of losing his own parents. How he struggled with issues of guilt and identity. But then he told himself that Henry still had his father. Henry's situation was very different to his own.

He worried too much.

Richard passed the playground and the lights of Cedar House care home came into view. He stopped for a moment, taking in the sight of the home which was all warmth and comfort.

Cedar House care home had been part of his life now for many years. He had taken it for granted. How much longer would he be walking down this very same path? He began to walk again, down the path as the light sensors flickered on, lighting the way.

* * *

Richard found Gertie in her room. Cerrie was plumping the pillows and laughing at something Gertie said as she helped the old lady lie back against the pillow mountain.

'Oh, hello, Richard,' Cerrie said.

'Hello,' Richard said to both women and bent down to kiss Gertie's cheek. 'If you're busy I can wait outside.' Richard was already backing away towards the door.

'Oh, it's fine,' Cerrie said. 'I'm finished now. Just settled Gertie for the night.'

For the night? Richard stopped himself from looking at his watch. It had only just gone 8 p.m. He liked Cerrie, but she did talk to his grandmother like a child and he didn't like that. He swallowed down his sarcastic comment. She meant well and she was kind. He shouldn't complain.

'Thanks, love, and you be careful, you hear?' Gertie said with a wag of her finger. 'Don't go back to his, and make sure you stay where people can see you. You don't know this man.'

Cerrie's cheeks flushed slightly. 'It's just a quick drink, Gertie, that's all. He's really nice. Not like the others.'

'Well then, you have fun.' Gertie gave Cerrie an exaggerated wink. 'And I'll hear all about it tomorrow, won't I?'

Cerrie laughed.

Richard cleared his throat. Had they forgotten that he was in the room? It felt that way.

Cerrie left the room with a quiet laugh.

Richard sat on the side of the bed. 'So, how are you today?'

'I'm fine, love,' Gertie said quickly.

Too quickly for Richard's liking. She wanted to shrug off his concern. Richard narrowed his eyes and looked more closely at his grandmother.

'And you can stop that right there,' Gertie said. A slow scowl had formed on her face. Her eyes narrowed. 'You don't need to try to study me to see if I'm telling the truth or not. I'm fine, considering.' She cleared her throat. 'But there is something that I need to tell you.'

Richard leaned in closer. 'What?' His mind raced with unpleasant thoughts. What was she going to share with him now?

Gertie looked over to the door that Cerrie had shut behind her.

'Things have been moved in here,' Gertie said. 'Books and things have been moved. I know because everything has its place.'

Richard sat bolt upright. Someone had been in his grandmother's room and rummaged around in her stuff. How could that be allowed to happen? And he'd always trusted the staff. Well, most of them.

'And you're absolutely sure?' Richard asked. Not because he doubted her, but because he needed confirmation.

Gertie nodded. 'Yes. It's not just me either.'

'We need to report it,' Richard said. These were vulnerable people. His own grandmother. He was furious the more he thought about it. But even as the words passed his lips, he knew that reporting it was pointless. Who would they report their suspicions to? Hazel. And it was Hazel who was the main suspect here. By the looks of things, Gertie knew it too.

'That's a bad idea, isn't it?' Richard said.

Gertie nodded. 'We need a plan to catch whoever it is,' she said. 'Any ideas?'

Richard scratched his chin, deep in thought. 'We need to catch them in the act, because without that we have no proof and we need proof.'

'So, let's get it then,' Gertie said with an unmistakable twinkle in her eye.

'But how?'

Then, almost instantly, once the idea had been planted, he knew. They needed to see whoever it was and the only way to do so was by using a video camera.

'You already know, don't you?' Richard asked.

'Of course I do.' Gertie chuckled. 'I was just waiting for you to catch up.'

Richard grinned. He couldn't help it. What was happening in this home was truly awful, but it was giving his grandmother a purpose. She was fizzing with energy and ideas. She had a plan and she loved to solve puzzles.

Richard scanned the room, wondering where the best place would be to place a hidden camera. It had to be central and obviously disguised. But they came in the size of a pinhead these days.

'Are they easy to obtain? These secret camera thingies?' Gertie asked.

'Yes, I could order one online right now and I'd get it delivered tomorrow.'

Gertie cooed. 'Ooooh, the wonders of modern technology.'

Richard fished his phone out of his jacket pocket and swiped the screen to unlock it. He tapped the screen and started to type into the search engine.

The screen was instantly flooded with images and information about spy cameras. He glanced at the prices. All were fairly cheap. He carried on scanning the text. These cameras would link remotely to his phone, so he could watch in real time or go back and watch the recording. Both options were perfect.

He turned the screen around so Gertie could see. 'Take a look. Tell me what you think.'

Gertie held the phone close up to her face. 'They all look good to me.'

'Well, I'll have a closer look once I get home and I'll order one. The sooner we can put one in here, the sooner we'll catch the scumbag.'

'Thanks, love,' Gertie said. 'I don't think they've taken anything, but who knows? I'm a little worried about my first editions. I just hope they don't come back for another rummage.'

'If they do, we'll get them and there will be hell to pay,' Richard said. 'Do you want me to take the first editions? Keep them safe for you?' He knew Gertie wasn't concerned about how valuable they were, but rather the emotional connection she had to those books.

'No, they're staying here with me. This is my home,' Gertie said. 'Right, well, let's change the subject, shall we? What about you? All ready for the trip tomorrow?'

'Yes, all ready.' Richard's mind was still on what had happened in this room. It unsettled him. For the very first time he didn't want to leave her here alone.

'You mustn't worry about me, Richard. I'm fine, and whoever is responsible won't know what's hit them when we catch them in the act.'

Richard nodded, not entirely convinced. He still didn't like the idea of leaving what had happened unreported. That's when he thought of Laura. He could tell her.

'You look tired, love,' Gertie said. 'Why don't you head on home. I'll be okay.'

Richard opened his mouth to protest. To tell her that he could stay another hour, two in fact. There wasn't much to do before the trip tomorrow. But Gertie cut him off.

'That nice young man is on tonight. The one who's going to train as a nurse. So you needn't worry.'

Richard felt a little better knowing Adrian would be there, but he still wasn't happy.

'And Laura is here tomorrow,' Gertie said, as if no other explanation was needed.

This did make Richard feel better.

'Right then, I'll head off,' he said.

He bent down to plant a kiss on his grandmother's cheek. She cupped his face with one hand.

'Have a good time tomorrow with the kids and don't worry about me.'

It was only when Richard was walking past the dim lights of the playground that he realised he had forgotten his phone. He'd put his hand in his pocket to retrieve it to send Laura a text about what Gertie had told him, and it wasn't there.

171

Muttering profanities under his breath, he turned on his heel and made his way back down the path towards the home. He must have left it in Gertie's room.

Richard retraced his steps back to the home, was buzzed back through the main door and climbed the steps, back up to his grandmother's room.

He raised his hand to knock on the door, but stopped when he heard a voice he recognised.

Gertie was chatting to Laura.

He really shouldn't be eavesdropping, but he needed his phone. He raised his fist again to knock on the door before he heard anything that would embarrass him.

Too late.

Richard clearly heard Gertie's raised voice.

'Has he asked you out yet?'

Richard thumped on the door, far too loudly, but he didn't want to hear any more of that conversation.

'Come in,' Gertie shouted.

Richard pushed open the door and stepped into the room.

Laura was sitting on the bed, just as he had done not ten minutes earlier.

'Hello,' Richard said, his words aimed towards Laura. He turned his gaze towards Gertie who didn't have the grace to look embarrassed. He had noticed Laura's blush.

'Everything okay, love?' Gertie asked.

'I think I left my phone here,' he said.

'Oh, yes, you did,' Gertie said, pulling it out from underneath her pillow.

Richard scratched his head. Had he really left it on the bed? Now that he thought about it, he was sure that he had put it back in his jacket pocket.

He took the phone and shoved it safely into his pocket.

'Right then, I'd best be off,' he said. His eyes were glued to his feet. He wasn't sure why, but it felt strange to be in his grandmother's room with Laura. Almost as if he was a guest.

Laura rose quickly from the bed and picked up her bag from the floor. 'Oh, please don't leave on my account. I was about to head off home anyway.'

'Well, that's just perfect, as Richard can walk you home. He can tell you all about the secret-camera idea.'

He stared with wide, disbelieving eyes. Had Gertie orchestrated this? Had she deliberately hidden his phone, knowing that he would come back only to find Laura in the room? Surely she wasn't that manipulative? But as he stared at his grandmother, he caught the spark in her eye.

Richard turned his attention to Laura, now busy fumbling with her jacket. 'Well, I'm walking your way, so why not?'

Laura opened her mouth to reply, but Gertie cut in.

'We need to find out whoever is behind this, so you two have a good chat.'

He bent down to plant a kiss on Gertie's cheek and said, 'I love you,' before giving her a stern look as if to say *I know your game*.

'Richard,' Gertie said just as he reached the door. 'Why don't you go for a quick drink?'

He heard the hiss of breath as Laura gasped at this suggestion, but all he could do was laugh. Gertie was sitting bolt upright, grinning at him. He stepped aside to let Laura through the door and gently closed it behind them.

He shook his head and turned to face Laura. 'Do you fancy a quick drink then?'

CHAPTER TWENTY-FOUR

The Fox and Hound was hosting a bingo evening, and the warmth and chatter quickly enveloped Richard and Laura as they entered the pub. Several regulars of the establishment looked up from their bingo cards as Richard and Laura passed them by on the way to the bar. Sue from the café couldn't keep her eyes off them and Richard bristled when he saw that she nudged old Mrs Jones who was sitting next to her and who, up to that point, had seemed to be the only person in the room not to have noticed them.

Richard quickly glanced at Laura who was looking at the bar. He hoped she hadn't noticed that the entire pub was focused on them.

He forced his gaze towards the bar, too, ignoring the many pairs of eyes now burning holes in his back.

Laura placed her bag on a stool and rummaged for her purse.

Richard wondered how she could find anything in such a large bag that was crammed with so much stuff. There were several paperbacks lurking inside and he spotted a bag of jelly babies.

'I'll get these,' he said quickly. It was Gertie's fault that they had ended up in the pub. 'What would you like?'

Laura hesitated for a moment, her hand on her purse which remained in her bag. She withdrew her hand, zipped the bag shut and then replied that she'd just have a coffee.

Richard was about to say that he could stretch to a gin and tonic but thought better of it. This wasn't a date. He didn't want to come across as arrogant, as *that* kind of guy. So he simply nodded and turned to face Bill who was already filling a large mug with filter coffee.

'Usual for you, Richard?' Bill asked.

'I'll just have half, Bill. Have an early start in the morning.'

'Righto,' Bill said and placed a half-pint glass under the optic.

'Anywhere nice?' Laura asked.

'Just a Year Six trip to Liverpool World Museum. But we're leaving school at eight to get ahead of the traffic. It usually takes us a couple of hours to get there and we need to be there at ten.'

Bill passed Richard his half of bitter. 'Never been there,' he said. 'Heard it's a good day out and that the people are very friendly, though.'

'It's a wonderful museum,' Laura said, her eyes bright with love and warmth for her home city. 'The museum has changed a lot since I used to go there as a little girl. The aquarium is fantastic.'

Richard turned his full attention on her. 'You grew up in Liverpool then?' he asked, one eyebrow raised. 'But you haven't got the accent.'

Laura picked up her bag, hoisted it onto her right shoulder and lifted the huge cup of coffee with both hands. It had two handles. 'No, I lived over the water,' she said quietly. 'Shall we find a table?'

Richard nodded, wondering why she'd wanted to change the subject. But he let it go and led the way over to a free table in the corner by the fire. Everyone else had migrated over to the tables near the makeshift stage where the bingo caller was sitting next to a professional-looking bingo machine. The coloured, numbered balls whirled around inside the giant plastic vortex, the LED lights flashing around the edge of the machine.

'Here okay?' Richard asked as he approached the table.

'Perfect,' Laura said, followed by a smile.

Richard noticed that it transformed her face. She looked years younger.

'I love sitting by the fire,' Laura said, placing her huge coffee cup onto the table and popping her bag by her feet.

'If I come here with Jack he always hates sitting at this table because he gets too hot,' Richard said, now settled into the low leather armchair.

Laura nodded. 'My sister is just like that. She doesn't feel the cold, even in the depths of winter. When she was little, she would go outside in the snow without a jumper or coat. It used to drive our mum mad.'

Richard chuckled. He picked up his drink and sipped it.

Laura cleared her throat and placed her hands around the warmth of the coffee cup.

Someone shouted that they had all the numbers, and the bingo caller asked them to go to the stage. Everyone started to clap and cheer.

Laura turned around to watch what was going on. Everyone seemed to be happy, sipping drinks and getting ready for the next game. 'I've never played bingo,' she said, her eyes fixed on the tableau in front of her.

'Really? You've never played bingo?' Richard asked. 'I thought that it was compulsory training for all care-home staff?' His mouth twitched.

'Well, I've watched people play, but never had a go myself,' Laura said.

Richard nodded his head towards the bingo players. 'Do you want to have a game?'

Laura shook her head, giving him a wry smile. 'No, thanks. Anyway, don't we need to discuss Gertie's secret plan?'

'Ah, yes, the secret camera,' Richard said. He lowered his voice. 'Are you sure that you're okay with all of this?'

'Having the recording equipment in Gertie's room? Absolutely.'

'It's just that, well, I don't want you to get into trouble, that's all. This can be down to me and Gertie. You don't need to have anything to do with it, if you don't want to.'

Laura jutted out her chin and her eyes took on a determined look. 'Believe you me, I can take care of myself and I want to catch this person as much as you do. So count me in. I'll help in any way that I can.'

Richard looked more closely at this woman who had just stumbled into his and his grandmother's life. She didn't appear to be afraid of anything or anyone. Was that a good thing?

'Well, that's good to know,' Richard said. He took a refreshing gulp of his bitter. 'I just know that Gertie can be a little bit overbearing at times. She can be hard to say no to.'

Laura smiled and nodded. 'Oh, yes, that is most certainly true, but I want to help.'

It was then that Richard knew that what Laura was saying was true. He could read it in her eyes. She really did care for his grandmother and whatever doubts he had about her, about who she was and why she was really here, temporarily faded away. This was about Gertie and keeping her and the other residents of Cedar House safe.

'Right then.' Richard fished his phone out of his pocket. He swiped the screen and navigated to the page he had last been on. 'Here are some of the cameras I've found. What do you think?'

Laura took the phone from him and scrolled down the page.

She handed back the phone.

'They all look good to me. They'll all do the job of recording what goes on in the room.'

'Yep, that's true,' Richard said. 'But I think this one is best.' He angled the phone so that Laura could see the screen and enlarged the image of a particular model. 'This one works with Bluetooth and I can watch it in real time. The good news is that you can sync it to more than one phone.'

Laura shot him a look of surprise. 'You want to link it to my phone as well?' she asked.

Richard wondered if he had made a mistake. Was he asking too much? 'If you'd rather not, I understand,' he said.

'No, no, it makes perfect sense. I can keep tabs on what's going on when not on shift. But I need to check with Gertie that she's happy for me to have access to the video feed, because it's a fine line we're treading here, and just so you're fully aware, I could lose my job over this if things go wrong.'

Richard hissed in a sharp breath, rubbed a hand over his neck. 'Let's forget all about it. It's not fair—'

'No, it's fine. I want to help.' She tucked a stray strand of blonde hair which threatened to fall into her coffee behind her ear and jutted out her chin. 'I'll take the chance because I want to help.'

'Thank you,' Richard said, knowing he needed to say a lot more.

'We'll catch them, you know,' she said.

'I know.' He drained his glass.

Laura picked up her coffee cup and let out a small laugh, placing it back down on the table.

It was empty.

'Want another drink?' Richard asked, gesturing towards the cup.

'Why not?' Laura said. 'But I'll get them.'

Richard began to protest, but Laura was already up and out of her seat, on her way to the bar.

* * *

Laura returned with the drinks and sank back down into the comfy leather armchair. She could easily get used to this. A hot drink by a roaring fire in a warm and friendly pub. The company wasn't bad either.

She'd tried to steer the conversation towards Gertie and so far it was working. Gertie was a safe subject.

Richard picked up his cola. 'Cheers,' he said.

Laura clinked her coffee cup against his glass. 'Cheers.'

'Will you sleep tonight after drinking all that coffee?' Richard asked, followed by a wide grin.

Laura thought for a moment. She was now immune to the effects of caffeine. 'Yes, no problem at all. It's all my years of nursing and working night shifts on busy wards. You build up an immunity to it.'

As soon as the words were out of her mouth, she realised her mistake. She clamped her lips together to stop herself from talking. Perhaps Richard wouldn't pick up on her wording.

'So, you're a nurse then?' he asked. His brow creased, clearly confused.

Laura sipped her coffee to give her a few moments to think about how best to answer the question. She could lie and say that she was using the term *nursing* in its broadest sense to mean care work, but she had a sneaky feeling that Richard would see through that lie. Or she could tell the truth and hope that he didn't ask any questions.

She opted for option number two.

'I was a nurse for many years but needed a break. I wanted to go back to my nursing roots, to basic nursing care, and so the care home was the perfect solution for me.' Laura forced a smile. She willed Richard not to ask any more questions. Willed him to believe that she would give up a career in nursing to move to a village and work in a care home. This version of the story just didn't ring true.

He didn't smile back. His brow furrowed even more.

Laura could tell that he wanted to ask more questions. It was obvious that he didn't believe her.

'Well, I'm glad you decided to come and work here,' he finally said.

She stopped holding her breath. She needed to be more careful. She just found it so incredibly easy to talk to him and that was when those little secrets slipped out.

Richard shuffled back on his chair and cleared his throat. 'Do you think we should tell Linda about the camera? Involve her in what we're doing?'

Laura was surprised that he had changed the subject so quickly, but she was glad. She shook her head. 'No, I think it should just be the two of us. I trust Linda, but it wouldn't be fair on her.'

'I agree,' Richard said. 'Okay, we'll leave things as they are and I'll order a camera once I get in.' He looked at his watch. 'I should be making a move really.'

Laura covered her mouth to stifle a yawn. 'Me too. It's been a long day.' She bent down to pick up her bag.

That was the moment when Richard asked his question.

'What's the real reason you gave up nursing?'

The question took Laura by surprise. That, and the brisk no-nonsense manner in which he'd asked it. She was unprepared. Of course, he had seen through her lie. She straightened up in her chair, pulling her bag up onto her lap. She hugged it for protection, putting a physical barrier between herself and this man who was far too shrewd.

'I needed a change. Something happened . . .' She swallowed and took a breath. 'Something happened in my life and I needed to take a step back, that's all.'

Laura stood up.

She couldn't talk about Mark. She wouldn't talk about him. This was all getting far too complicated. If she told Richard the real reason for giving up her job and moving to Buttermarsh then she would have to talk about Mark and she wasn't prepared to do that. Not yet. It was too soon. She didn't want to see the look of pity in his eyes or what would be even worse, disgust, at the fact that she'd been complicit in her husband's death. Best to leave the past alone for now. Here, in this remote village, she was Laura the care assistant who lived a single life, and she wanted it to stay that way.

'I need to go now,' she said, without looking at Richard. 'Let me know about the camera and what I can do to help.'

All of this was said while she was slipping her arms into her coat.

Richard stood, grabbed his coat from the back of his chair and started to put it on.

'See you soon,' Laura said. She turned and strode towards the door.

All Richard could do was stand and stare as she walked away from him.

* * *

Back at Cedar House, Gertie turned off the bedside light. A slow smile crept across her face. In her mind's eye she could see the two of them sitting before a roaring fire in the local pub. Her smile grew wider. Perhaps things would work out after all.

CHAPTER TWENTY-FIVE

Richard poured honey hoops into Henry's red bowl and added a splash of milk. 'Here you go. Eat them up and I'll make you some jam on toast in a minute,' he said.

'Can I have a banana as well?' Henry asked, already scooping up hoops with his spoon.

'Sure you can,' Richard said. 'Just let me pop the coffee machine on and then I'll get you one.'

Richard busied himself with filling the filter machine, trying to keep himself focused on Henry and the busy day ahead. The trouble was that he felt dog-tired. The Year Six day trip the previous day had been longer than expected and he hadn't got back until long gone seven. But he had still picked Henry up from Tracey's so that Henry could spend the night in his own bed. One night away from home was enough.

He had managed to order the secret camera, as Gertie was now calling it, and with any luck it would arrive by the time he got back from school.

The coffee machine started to splutter and gurgle and the room began to fill with the rich, bitter aroma of Columbian coffee.

An image of Laura sprang to mind — sitting in the pub, cradling that huge cup of coffee.

He still couldn't work out why the night had ended so abruptly.

He poured his coffee and pulled out a kitchen chair so that he could sit opposite Henry who was engrossed in reading a book about a cat and a bat.

He didn't mind books at the table — that was fine — but as Henry grew older, Richard wouldn't allow screens to be at the table.

Richard picked up that morning's local paper and started to scan the headlines. Nothing of great importance met his eye. But, to be honest, he wasn't really concentrating. He had so many thoughts vying for his attention. He pushed the paper away and picked up his coffee cup.

Why had Laura wanted to leave the pub so abruptly? He closed his eyes to recall their conversation, wondering if he had managed to upset her in some way, but he didn't think that was the case. They'd just been two adults sitting in a pub having a conversation. Obviously, the reason they had been there was because of Gertie. There would have been no need for them to meet and have a chat if not for his grandmother, but once he had started chatting to Laura, he had quickly realised that she was good company.

So why had she wanted to leave him behind so quickly?

The way she had acted towards him had almost been rude.

'You okay, Daddy? Do your eyes hurt?' Henry pointed his spoon at Richard's face.

Richard's eyes snapped open to look at his son.

Henry had put his spoon down now and was staring at him with such concern that Richard wanted to hug him there and then.

'I'm fine. Daddy was just thinking.'

'What about?' Henry asked. He began to scoop his honey hoops onto his spoon, all concern now gone.

'Just stuff. Planning my day at school.'

Henry nodded and continued to eat his cereal.

'I'll make us that toast, eh?' Richard said.

He picked up his cup and carried it over to the worktop. He busied himself making toast then smearing it with butter and jam.

Sally would have told him off for the amount of jam he used.

She didn't like jam on her toast. She had preferred it plain. Henry took after his father, both of them jam monsters.

'Here you go.' Richard placed the plate of toast in front of Henry, then sat down at the table.

Henry pushed his bowl away and picked up the toast.

So, where had things gone wrong? Richard couldn't help but think that he had said or done the wrong thing, but he couldn't for the life of him work out what it was.

He ran through the end of their conversation in his mind once more. The last thing they had spoken about was the fact that she had been a nurse. And Richard knew that the reason she'd given for the change of career wasn't the whole story. He could see it in her eyes. The story about wanting to have a less hectic life, to take it slower and get back to basic nursing care to some extent rang true, but it was almost as if it was a practised response. Richard tried to put himself in her shoes. A successful nurse working on the busy wards in a city hospital — that's the impression he had grasped from their conversation — and then she had swapped that life to come to this village which nobody had ever heard of to work in a care home. People left this village never to return. They never had new people coming and staying, the odd tourist or relative, perhaps, but never anyone who actively chose to live and work here. So, what was the real story behind her decision? Why move away from her home, alone, to live and work where she didn't know a single soul?

'Daddy, can I have my 'nana, please?' Henry asked.

Richard jumped and knocked his cup, splashing coffee onto the table. He had been so deep in thought that he had forgotten that Henry was with him.

He jumped up, grabbing the tea towel to mop up the pooling coffee before it reached Henry.

Richard, really. The tea towel? Use a cloth.

'Daddy made a mess.' Henry laughed.

Richard laughed too, mopped up the coffee, then chucked the tea towel into the washing machine.

'Right, here you go.' Richard handed Henry a peeled banana. 'You then need to go and wash that jam off your face.'

Henry nodded and bit into the banana.

Richard sat back down to think.

So, there were only two possible reasons that he could think of for Laura abandoning a nursing career and moving here, although he was eternally grateful that she had made that decision.

She was either running away from *someone* or running away from *something*. Both reasons led to the same conclusion — that she was hiding away here. An unpleasant thought then entered his mind. Was her real name even Laura? If she was in hiding, then surely it would be sensible to change her name?

Richard drummed his fingers on the kitchen table, lost in thought. There was only one way to find out, but going down that path would mean there was no turning back. What if he didn't like what he found? But then there was Gertie to consider. Without realising, he'd grown closer to Laura, what with the secret camera business and the private messaging. He not only needed to protect his grandmother, but Laura, too, as she was now part of this mess. Problem was, he knew nothing about her.

He needed to know.

He waited for Henry to go to the bathroom before opening his laptop and typing her name into the search engine. The page loaded in seconds with news articles.

Richard stared in disbelief and began to read.

* **

Cedar House was slowly winding down for the evening. Residents were sitting in the lounge watching the soaps, while others preferred to be in their rooms, reading or listening to music. Gertie was one such resident, but she wasn't alone. Laura was with her, reading aloud from a copy of *Great Expectations*. Gertie sat in bed, eyes closed, listening to Laura as she told the story.

'This is far better than a talking book,' Gertie had said not long after Laura had started to read.

Laura could only agree, and she gained as much pleasure from reading as Gertie did from listening. It was also a relief to sit down and kick off her shoes — her feet were killing her. She had only been rostered on to do an early shift, but on arrival at the home, Linda had asked if she could work a long day. Linda, who was in charge that day, had been apologetic, telling her that she wouldn't normally ask a member of staff who had already covered a shift that same week, but she was finding it hard to find staff. Plus, as Laura had the following day off, Linda thought that she wouldn't mind.

Laura had agreed. Mainly because she liked Linda, but also because she couldn't leave the floor short-staffed. Once again she was covering for Hazel who was supposedly sick. This couldn't carry on for much longer. The only good thing was that there had been no further suspicious activity in Gertie's room. Was this further proof that Hazel was the culprit?

Laura finished reading the chapter and looked to Gertie to see if she wanted her to carry on reading.

'No, that's fine, love. We'll pick up the story when you next have time to sit and read to me.'

'I'm not here tomorrow, but I'm here on Saturday,' Laura said.

'Right then, I shall look forward to it,' Gertie said with a smile.

Laura couldn't help but notice that Gertie was looking tired. Even more tired than usual. She had tried to persuade the old lady to let her take her observations, but Gertie flatly refused, telling her there was no point. It wouldn't change anything, would it?

Laura could only agree, but it would have made her feel much better. As if she was doing something. She hated doing nothing.

She placed the book back on the shelf by the bed and helped Gertie to sit forward while she plumped up her pillows.

'Is that better?' Laura asked as the old lady rested back again.

She was rewarded with Gertie's deep sigh. 'Perfect, love.' The elderly woman tapped the space next to her on the bed. 'Now, sit yourself down and tell me all about your date with my grandson.'

Laura had been holding her breath, waiting for Gertie to ask this question. She was just surprised that it had taken her so long. She really wanted to say that it had just been a chat about installing the secret camera. It hadn't been a date at all, more like a business meeting, but one look at Gertie's radiant face which had suddenly come to life with the thought of Laura and Richard, halted Laura in her tracks.

She wanted to make Gertie happy.

'Well, it was just a drink in the local pub, Gertie,' Laura said, her tone light.

Not a date.

'We just chatted about the secret camera really,' she added, but then seeing Gertie's disappointed expression, she carried on. 'But your grandson is great company — a very interesting man.'

At least this was true. Richard was good company and she was sure that given time they would have interesting and lively discussions about all sorts of things, but at the moment her head just wasn't in the right place. Meeting someone new had not been a part of her plan. Getting as close as she had to Gertie and her family had not been part of her plan either, but here she was and there was nothing she could do about it.

It was too late to distance herself from Gertie. This was a bond that could not be broken.

It was Richard who was the problem.

Gertie beamed.

Laura had obviously said the right thing.

'He's perfect for you, love. It's all going to work out — I just know it.' Gertie reached over to grab Laura's hand. 'The colours are changing, you see. Not so much darkness anymore.' Gertie lowered her voice and moved her face closer to Laura's. 'But you need to be honest with him, Laura. You need to tell him why you moved here, what happened. And before you tell me that it's none of his business, it really is. It will change everything.'

Laura held Gertie's hand and nodded, but she clamped her lips together to stop her true feelings from being said.

There was no point in arguing her case. Gertie simply wouldn't listen.

Gertie squeezed Laura's hand before letting go. She took a deep breath, as if preparing herself to say more, but the knock at the door stopped those words.

'That'll be Richard,' Gertie said, and raised her voice. 'Come on in, love.'

Laura pushed herself up from the bed and straightened her dress. She quickly stepped into her shoes, not wanting to appear unprofessional in front of him.

'Hello,' Richard said to Gertie. He then turned to face Laura to say a quick hello. 'I come bearing gifts.' He opened up his laptop bag and removed a small padded envelope. 'It arrived while I was at school this morning.'

'Is that the camera?' Gertie asked, her eyes wide with disbelief. 'It's tiny.'

Richard laughed. 'It sure is. He placed his bag on the floor and sat down on the armchair in the corner of the room. He removed the secret camera from the bag. It was a piece of wire attached to a piece of metal which looked no bigger than a pinhead.

'That's the camera?' Gertie gasped. 'But when we looked online it was attached to a big boxlike thing.'

Richard nodded. 'There is a box that comes with it, but we don't need that. This simply needs to be switched on, linked to a phone and it starts recording.'

Laura watched as Richard unwound the electrical cord. She took in his long, slim fingers, and the wrists which were covered in short dark hairs that she hadn't noticed before. He turned his attention back to her. 'Where's the best place for this, do you think?' he asked.

She noticed that he didn't look directly at her.

She scanned the room as she thought about the perfect place for surveillance. 'Perhaps on the dresser with the dried flowers, so that you get a view of most of the room. The only thing it won't capture is the wardrobe. The flowers will easily hide the wire though.' Laura looked at Gertie. 'What do you think?' she asked.

'I think that's as good a place as any,' Gertie said. 'Although it's a shame it won't show the wardrobe, but there's no way round that.'

'At least we know they've looked in there already. I just wonder what they're looking for,' Richard said.

'Me too,' Gertie said.

'Right then, I'll set this up and see if we can catch them,' Richard said.

Laura moved out of the way and sat once more beside Gertie on the bed.

As she watched Richard work, her thoughts started to wander. Something didn't feel right. Richard hadn't looked directly at her since he'd stepped into the room.

It was almost as if he was ignoring her.

But something else also unsettled her. He hadn't told her that the camera had been delivered, nor that he was going to install it tonight. Both things he had promised to do.

Something had changed between them. An unseen shift that she could feel with every bone in her body. The strange thing was that this shouldn't have bothered her. Hadn't she wanted to take a step back from him? To distance herself. Laura felt as if she had lost him and that made no sense at all.

* * *

189

The humming of the refrigerator and the ticking of the wall clock were the only sounds to be heard as Richard sat at his kitchen table, eyes fixed on his laptop screen.

Once he had left the home, he had picked Henry up and treated them to fish and chips at the Fox and Hound. Gwen had been over the moon to see Henry and she had given him extra chips.

Richard had kept himself busy once home. He had showered Henry, read him a bedtime story and had then caught up with the day's marking.

It was only now, as he sat in the dim light of his kitchen, that he had time to think about what he had learned that morning.

Now, he refreshed his memory as he read again the articles that he had found online.

It had been fairly easy to find her name. Laura Lewis actually was her real name and this had given Richard some comfort. Nobody would be chasing after her.

Richard was deeply unsettled and saddened by what he had read — the tragic case involving her husband.

He had found her secret, but he so wished he hadn't.

It was all so clear to him now.

That urge to start a new life, to be anonymous where nobody knew your past, your grief. Hadn't he wanted the exact same thing after Sally had died? The only thing that had stopped him was Henry.

Richard could understand why Laura hadn't told him. She didn't need to tell him anything. She owed him nothing. He'd broken her trust and he wasn't sure if there was any way back from that.

Now he would have to keep this to himself, pretend that he didn't know.

He had made a poor job of it so far when he'd bumped into her in Gertie's room. He'd clearly seen the hurt in her eyes as she'd questioned why he hadn't told her that he'd been going to install the camera.

Pretending that everything was the same and that he didn't know her most intimate secret was going to be incredibly difficult.

Richard cursed, turned off the laptop and made his way up to bed.

CHAPTER TWENTY-SIX

Laura had started the day at 5 a.m., waking with a throbbing head and the need for cold, freshly squeezed orange juice, which she did not have. As an alternative to the orange juice, she gulped down a pint glass of tap water and popped two ibuprofen, hoping that the headache from hell would go away and that it wouldn't morph into a migraine. It had been a long time since she'd had one of those. They were usually brought on by stress and drinking far too much coffee.

No surprise she had one then.

Once showered and dressed, Laura went into the snug, switched on her phone and opened the app that Richard had installed for her — the one that linked the video footage from the secret camera in Gertie's room directly to her mobile screen. Almost instantly the familiar scene of Gertie's room appeared. It was now just gone 7 a.m. and Cerrie's bright-pink hair could be clearly seen as she stooped down to make Gertie's bed. Laura watched, completely mesmerised by what she could see happening in real time. She felt guilty, yet was captivated at the same time. The room seemed so much bigger on the small screen, and the bookcases appeared taller. It was strange for Laura to observe the comfort and familiarity of

Gertie's room in her own home. It was almost as if it wasn't real.

Laura knew she had to watch as she had promised Richard. If she saw anything suspicious, she would tell him straight away. At such an early hour he would be busy with Henry. He wouldn't have time to do surveillance, but she still felt a little uncomfortable watching her colleague. Cerrie had no idea that she was being filmed. It was an incredibly fine line that she, Richard and Gertie were treading. Laura just hoped that it all worked out and when the culprit was caught on camera, the other members of staff would understand.

If Laura was in their shoes, then she knew that she would understand the situation. But still . . .

She watched for a few more moments before closing the app. She had no concerns whatsoever about Cerrie. She trusted her and she did not want to violate that trust.

The long day now stretched ahead of her. Although she needed to keep tabs on the secret-camera footage, she had no intention of being glued to her phone screen all day.

She needed to get out, grab some fresh air while she could. Being cooped up indoors was no good for the soul. Once again Laura felt the urge to be surrounded by people, while still enjoying her own solitude.

But she needed to venture out of the house. She also needed that huge glass of freshly squeezed orange juice and she knew just the place to get it.

* * *

The Cottage Bun oozed a quiet and soothing atmosphere at seven o'clock on a Friday morning. There were only a handful of customers, most of them regulars at that time of day who had ventured in from the cold, grey drizzle to grab a quick breakfast before they set off to work. Sue was busy making cups of tea, buttering slices of toast and whipping up scrambled eggs and crispy bacon. Laura knew this was Sue's favourite time of day, as she thrived on being busy. Sue had told her that she had been asked many times why she didn't get some help in running the café, but she had always been adamant that as the café was only small and served only the local residents, even in the heart of summer, there was very little point in hiring someone to help out. They would soon get bored and yearn for something a little livelier, more challenging. Which was fine by Sue. The café suited her very nicely. It paid the bills, gave her a reason for getting up in the morning and she could chat to her friends while working. In her eyes, Sue had said, it was the perfect job.

It was shortly after seven and Sue didn't even attempt to hide her surprise at Laura's presence.

'What are you doing in here at such an early hour?' Sue waved the butter knife in mid-air.

'It's my day off,' Laura replied, not quite knowing why she had to justify a visit to the café.

'Oh, I know that.' Sue huffed, all matter-of-fact. She placed the knife down onto the breadboard, much to Laura's relief. 'What I mean is, why are you in here so early when it's your day off? Shouldn't you be having a lie-in?'

Laura shook her head. A lie-in? Not when she had a thumping headache, but she didn't want to say that, as she knew Sue would only worry and try to mother her. 'I just woke up early and fancied a bit of fresh air. I was on a long day yesterday.'

'Ah, well, yes, that makes sense.' Sue nodded in agreement. 'The home is lovely, but it isn't half warm in there. Makes my mouth feel so dry. I love visiting the Knit-and-Natter group, but, oh my, I'm gasping for ice-cold water when I step outside. That and lungfuls of fresh air.'

Laura smiled, trying to ignore the wincing pain behind her eyes.

'So, what can I get you?' Sue asked.

'Do you have any fresh orange juice?' Laura quickly scanned the menu. She couldn't see it listed.

'Yes, I do, and what about something to eat? You need a good breakfast to see you through the day.'

Now she thought about it, Laura realised that she was hungry, and as if on cue, her stomach growled in protest. 'Just some jam on toast, please.' Laura hoped Sue wouldn't try to persuade her to eat a full English breakfast. She couldn't stomach that.

Sue nodded and gave her a friendly and efficient smile. 'Go grab a table and I'll bring it over to you.'

Laura thanked her and made her way over to her favourite window table. A quiet sit-down as she watched the world pass by was just what she needed. When she got back home after a quick visit to the village shop, she'd check in again on Gertie's room. What would she see?

She spent a pleasant hour in the café and then wandered along to the village square to grab a few essentials from the village shop. She felt guilty about the two large bags of jelly babies she bought, but she was going to ration them. Once stocked up with bread, cheese, milk, coffee, tea bags, some frozen pizzas, sliced ham, a microwave lasagna and some yogurts, she returned home to catch up on laundry and housework. It was only once the chores had been done that Laura made herself a cup of tea and settled herself down at the kitchen table to check the app. As she did so, her heart was in her mouth. She wanted to catch the thief in the act, but at the same time she wished for ignorance, as seeing it would make it real. She couldn't understand how a person could work with vulnerable older people, gain their trust, their confidence, care for them, and then steal from them. It just didn't bear thinking about.

Laura picked up her tea and glanced at the screen.

Nothing to see.

The room was empty.

She clicked on the history tab and scrolled back to seven that morning. The camera hadn't picked up any movement, but she scrolled through the footage anyway just to make sure. Nope, there was no sign of their thief.

What she did notice was that Gertie had placed her hand-bag on the bed, as they had all agreed. It was in full view of the camera. If anyone was going to snoop in her room again, then the first thing they would do would be to have a look in the bag, open up her purse and take out the twenty-pound note that Richard had planted in there.

Laura sipped her tea. The seconds ticked by.

She needed a biscuit to dunk. She walked over to the worktop and took the lid off the biscuit tin. She was greeted by a selection of custard creams, Bourbon biscuits and choc-olate-chip cookies. She took one of each and told herself that once these biscuits had been eaten, she would buy no more. That healthy eating plan needed to start soon.

Laura sat back down and munched on the custard cream. Still no action. It was nearly lunchtime, so all the staff would be busy preparing meals and settling residents in the day room. It was probably the wrong time of day to do surveillance.

It was only as Laura was having this thought that she saw movement, a shadow in the corner of the screen, which indicated that the door was being opened.

Sure enough, a figure could now be seen on screen.

Laura froze. She slowly placed her cup down onto the table as she peered at the screen. At the moment she could only see the back of the person, but that and the fact that they were wearing a different uniform was enough to identify them.

It was Hazel.

Laura held her breath, safe in the knowledge that the app was recording what was happening now. Laura glanced at the time, made a mental note. She carried on watching, now unable to look away. She didn't want to miss a thing.

Perhaps Hazel was just going in to have a quick check. Laura would often go around and check each room for any washing or the odd cup and saucer. But something in Hazel's movement and the way she loitered by the bed told Laura that this wasn't the case.

Laura watched with her heart in her mouth, her cup of hot tea now growing cold, the biscuits forgotten.

Hazel turned briefly and looked at the door which Laura assumed she had closed. Laura wished she could hear what was going on.

Hazel reached over the bed and picked up the bag. Gertie's bag. Her hands worked quickly as she unzipped it and then dipped her hand inside. Within seconds, she'd taken out the purse.

Laura felt sick.

Once again Hazel glanced quickly towards the door before turning her attention back on the purse. Laura continued to watch, feeling helpless and like a voyeur who couldn't change what was unfolding on the screen, as Hazel opened the purse, pulled out the twenty-pound note and shoved it in her tunic pocket.

'Got you,' Laura mouthed.

But the violation of Gertie's room and property did not end there.

Hazel began to open drawers. She rummaged around in them, pulling out all of Gertie's personal things. Laura shouted at the screen in sheer frustration for her to stop, tears pricking at her eyes. This was just awful, disgusting. How many others had she subjected to this?

Now Laura had a dilemma. Contact the police or phone Richard? After a moment's thought, she knew what she had to do. Reluctantly, she closed the app and scrolled through her phone contacts. She quickly located Richard's number and hit the call button.

It was nearly lunchtime. She hoped the odds were in her favour and that he'd be able to take the call.

The phone rang once, twice, three times.

Laura waited.

On the sixth ring, just as Laura was about to lose hope, he answered.

'Hi, Laura,' he said. His words came out rushed, as if he was walking somewhere in a hurry. 'I've just seen the footage. Is that why you're phoning?'

'Yes,' Laura said. 'I thought I'd phone you and then if I couldn't get hold of you, I was going to phone the police.'

'Thanks, I appreciate that, Laura. I can't believe what she did. Listen, I'm in a rush. I'm heading to the home now.'

'Okay,' Laura said. 'I'll let you go. I'm just glad that we caught her.'

'Me too,' Richard said quickly, before adding, 'and thanks again.'

Laura stared at her phone and wondered what would happen next? What would happen to Hazel now?

Then Laura realised it was absolutely none of her business. The only thing that mattered was that Hazel had been caught and that she wouldn't be able to hurt anyone else again in Cedar House, and hopefully any other care home.

* * *

Laura spent the remainder of her day pottering around the house. She read for a while, then she tidied the kitchen while she listened to the afternoon play on Radio Four. Before she knew it, it had grown dark and her thoughts turned to what to cook for tea. It was a choice between the frozen lasagna or pizza, so she opted for the lasagna, thinking that at least it had been made with more vegetables.

Laura had loved to cook. Mark had disliked cooking, always preferring to grab a takeaway or warm up some beans. It had been left to Laura to cook the meals, even batch-baking and freezing them so that Mark would have something to eat when she worked lates or nights. That had been before the relationship had turned sour. Before he'd started to look at other women and had then been unfaithful. There'd been no more batch-cooking and freezing of meals after that.

Laura sighed as she placed the slab of frozen lasagna into the microwave. What had happened to her? Why had she let things slide so badly? She really did need to take better care of herself.

She set the timer and sat down at the kitchen table with her book for company.

She was so engrossed in the story that when her mobile rang and vibrated along the table, she physically jumped. Her heartbeat quickened, pulsing in her chest. It was so quiet in Church View Cottage.

Laura glanced at the screen and was surprised to see her mum's name displayed alongside her smiling profile image. For a fraction of a second she considered not answering the call, letting it go to voicemail, but then she felt guilty. She would have to talk to her mum eventually.

'Hello, Mum,' Laura said, trying to make herself sound happy and relaxed. Her mum always picked up on her tone and could tell if she was feeling tired, sad or simply fed up. Her mother had a sixth sense.

'Hello, love . . .' There was a pause and Laura could hear her breath down the line. 'Listen, I know I said I wouldn't phone until you phoned me, but I was worried. And even though Lottie has told me that you're okay and are making friends, I just . . . well, I just wanted to hear your voice.'

'Oh, Mum,' Laura said, her words sounding strangled as her throat thickened with tears. It seemed such a long time ago that she had heard her mum's voice. What had she been thinking? Trying to shut everyone out of her life? Especially her mum? 'I'm so sorry.'

'Sorry? What for? You haven't done anything wrong. There's no need for any of that.'

Laura gulped back the tears. She couldn't cry as that would really upset her mother and she would be on the next train and bus. Nothing would stop her. So, Laura moved the phone away from her mouth, took a deep and steadying breath, and then slowly exhaled. 'I'm sorry I haven't called,' she eventually said. There was so much else she needed to say sorry for, but doing so would set her off.

'Don't be daft. Anyway, we're talking now. So, how are you?'

'I'm good,' Laura said, realising that she actually meant it. 'I'm busy at work and as Lottie has probably told you, I've made some friends. It's harder than you think trying to isolate yourself in a small village.'

Maureen huffed down the phone. 'Well, I did tell you that.'

'Yes, you did, but I'm still glad I moved here.' It was true. Laura had been given the chance to take a step back, to breathe, to think about what had happened. This wouldn't have happened if she'd stayed in her little flat, doing the same job, surrounded by the same people. The people who also knew Mark. And she wouldn't have met Gertie, and she knew deep down that she had needed to meet someone like her, to make her look at her life in a different way. Gertie understood her.

'Well, I'm happy as long as you're happy, and that's all that matters,' Maureen said.

'Thanks, Mum.'

The microwave pinged three times, signalling that the lasagna was ready.

'Is that the microwave I can hear?' Maureen asked, the indignation clear in her voice.

'Yes, I'm having lasagna.'

'From the microwave?' Now she seemed even more shocked.

Laura couldn't help but laugh. Her mother never cooked anything in the microwave. Everything was cooked from scratch. Come to think of it, her mother didn't even own a microwave.

'It's a one-off, Mum. I usually cook on the Aga.'

'Laura, don't lie to me,' Maureen said, but Laura could detect the humour and the fact that her mum was trying not to laugh. 'Listen, I'll let you go.' Laura could hear the hesitation in her mum's voice before she spoke again. 'But, remember, I'm always here, whenever you need to chat.'

'I know,' Laura said. It was just that, sometimes, it was the hardest thing in the world to talk honestly and openly with those you loved the most.

* * *

Laura was washing up when the doorbell rang. It had just turned eight o'clock, but even so it was unusual to have visitors, unless it was Megan? Laura hadn't spoken to her since they'd had that awkward conversation in the pub. She really needed to give her a call.

She opened the door, not even thinking to ask who it was. Which was why she was startled to see Richard standing on the doorstep holding a huge bouquet of flowers in front of him. They obscured half his face.

'Hi,' he said.

When Laura had closed her mouth, she said, 'Hi.'

'I just wanted to say thank you for your help with this whole secret-camera business,' Richard said. He thrust the flowers towards her and Laura grabbed them awkwardly, hugging them to her chest.

'Thank you,' she said.

The two of them stood there for several moments until Laura remembered her manners. 'Come on in. I'll make us a cup of tea if you like?'

For a moment it looked as if Richard was about to decline the offer. He had stepped away from the door, placing his hands in his pockets. But to Laura's surprise, he nodded and followed her down the hallway.

Once in the kitchen, Laura placed the flowers in the sink which she then filled with cold water. She popped the kettle on, while Richard stood by the Aga.

As Laura busied herself making the tea, Richard informed her that Hazel had been suspended.

'She'll be charged, no doubt,' he said.

'Yes, and hopefully she'll never be allowed to work with elderly or vulnerable people again.'

Richard nodded in agreement and wrapped his hands around the hot mug of tea she passed to him as they sat at the kitchen table.

'I've removed the secret camera,' he said. 'Just in case you were wondering.'

'I thought you would, now that it's no longer needed.' Laura wondered why Richard was talking to his cup and not to her face. He hadn't looked at her once since setting foot in the cottage.

'Right then. Well, erm, I'd better be off. I've left Tracey looking after Henry.' Richard stood, scraping the chair's legs on the flagstones.

'Okay,' Laura said, surprised. He hadn't touched his tea.

She followed him back down the hallway and opened the front door, standing aside to let him pass.

It wasn't until he reached the gate that he turned to face her.

'Thanks again, and, Laura . . .' He hesitated, looked down at his shoes and then his gaze fell on her face.

'Yes?'

Richard looked down at his shoes once more. Shook his head. 'It was nothing, never mind. See you at the home.'

And with that, he turned and strode down the narrow lane, back to his house.

Laura stood on the doorstep and wondered what the hell had just happened.

CHAPTER TWENTY-SEVEN

Richard received the phone call at eight in the morning. He had just made Henry his toast and poured himself his second cup of coffee in an hour. Henry had woken late, his hair tousled but his stomach growling for food. So, when the phone rang, Richard had been tempted to ignore it. Probably cold callers. When it rang the second time, he had a horrible feeling in the pit of his stomach that the news he would receive would be anything but good.

Now, Richard found himself sprinting down the lane towards the home, fearing the absolute worst. Linda had been calm on the phone and had done her best to reassure him that Gertie was stable and alert, but that it looked as if she had taken a turn for the worse and that it may be good for him to come in and visit her. Richard had cut her off mid-sentence. He needed to get to the home.

As Richard turned the corner of the playground, the home came into focus. He strode down the path, forcing himself not to run, and pressed the intercom. The door lock clicked open within seconds and Richard pushed himself in, and upwards towards Gertie's room.

Should he have brought Henry with him? He had asked Linda this question and she had told him that it was his decision, that he knew Henry best. But Richard didn't want to upset the little guy He had no idea what state he would find his grandmother in, and what Henry saw would stay with him for ever. Richard told himself that he would gauge the situation and then decide what to do with Henry. Luckily, Megan had answered her phone when he'd called, and had readily agreed to watch Henry. As soon as she had stepped through the door, Richard had left. He needed to see his grandmother. His stomach clenched at the thought of her being in pain or being weak. He ran up the stairs to her room, arms pumping, face pinched with fear for what scene was about to greet him.

Without thinking, he pushed open the door and lurched into the room.

'Oh, hello, love,' Gertie said from her bed. 'Everything okay? You look like you've been running.'

Richard stood panting in the middle of the room. He hunched forward, hands on knees, both in relief and exhaustion.

Linda burst into the room. She looked at Gertie and then swivelled on the spot to face Richard. Her face was bright crimson.

'I'm so sorry,' she mouthed.

Richard looked from Linda back to his grandmother, wondering what was going on here. He had expected to find Gertie on her deathbed, not sitting up and talking.

Linda wouldn't look at him.

How had she got the situation so wrong?

'Whatever's up?' Gertie asked.

'Nothing, nothing at all,' Linda said quickly.

Gertie was not easily fooled and clearly knew that something was wrong.

Richard straightened himself up and took several deep breaths before he spoke. 'I was just a little worried about you, that was all. I had a phone call this morning from . . .' He paused, looked sideways at Linda and thought better of saying her name. 'Well, I had a phone call to say that you weren't feeling so good, so I came to see you.'

Gertie sighed and shot Linda a cutting look.

Linda blushed an even deeper red.

'I'm fine, love. No real change with me. Just felt a bit off this morning, that's all. A good rest is all I need.'

'I'll leave you to it,' Linda said, backing out of the room.

'See you later, Linda,' Gertie said.

Linda shut the door.

Richard sighed once more. Poor Linda, she must have been worried to have phoned him. He pulled the chair from the corner of the room, placed it at the side of the bed and sat down.

He looked more closely at his grandmother, paying attention to her pallor, the lines on her face and the fact that there was an untouched cup of tea on her bedside table.

Gertie was good at covering her tracks, but she couldn't completely fool him. She now appeared to be smaller, more shrunken in on herself. A spark had gone from her eyes. That mischievous twinkle had dimmed. Was it because they had solved the mystery of the intruder in her room? That she no longer had something to occupy her mind? But as these thoughts raced through Richard's brain in quick succession, he knew that this was only part of the answer. His grandmother was seriously ill, he knew that, although he didn't know her condition. She was deteriorating slowly before his eyes.

'Tell me what Laura thought about those flowers,' she said.

Gertie waited for Richard to answer the question.

Her grandson sat with his open mouth forming a perfect O.

'Flowers,' Richard said. 'How do you know about the flowers?'

Gertie shook her head and tutted. 'The question should be, how wouldn't I know?' She chuckled.

Richard continued to gawp. As if he had no idea what to say. Eventually he said, 'I never mentioned anything about flowers.'

'I never said you did,' Gertie said, touching the side of her nose. 'Anyway, how was she last night?'

Richard scratched his head. 'Hang on a minute. I never said that I was going to see Laura last night.'

'Yes, you did,' Gertie said.

'No, I didn't.'

'Yes, you did.'

'No, I didn't,' Richard said.

'I know, and it doesn't matter how I know, does it!' Gertie had raised her voice.

Richard said nothing.

'So, what happened then?' she asked. 'Did she love the flowers? Did you ask her out on a proper date?'

Richard leaned forward in his chair and held his head in his hands. 'What do you mean what happened?' he asked, his own voice now rising — in exasperation.

'Oh, you're just full of questions this morning, aren't you,' Gertie said.

'*Nothing* happened. I went round to the cottage with a bunch of flowers and thanked her for helping us. That was all.'

Gertie nodded, knowing that there was more to this story. She just needed to wheedle it out of him.

'How was Laura? Did she tell you anything?'

'Like what?'

'Oh, I don't know,' Gertie said. 'You know, just stuff.'

'I just went round with flowers to say thank you. That's all there is to it.'

'But flowers always mean something.' Gertie knew this to be true. There was no such thing as innocent flowers.

'They don't have to mean anything at all,' Richard said, jaw clenched

Gertie knew that she was now annoying him, but she was enjoying this game far too much and she needed to learn the truth. 'A woman always thinks flowers mean something and a man only gives flowers when he wants to say sorry or I love you. So which is it?'

206

'Neither,' Richard said slowly. 'I went to say thank you.' He pushed himself up and out of the chair. He strolled over to the bookcase and pulled out a random book from the shelf. He gazed at the cover. He wouldn't look at her.

Gertie had hit the nail on the head. He had gone round to say sorry.

'You are so stubborn, just like your father,' Gertie said gently.

Richard turned to face her. 'Well, I wouldn't know, would I?' he said, but his tone was gentle. A statement, not a criticism. 'Let's talk about something else, eh?'

Gertie nodded.

Richard sat back down.

'Do you have any more news on Hazel?' he asked.

'All I know is that she's gone,' Gertie said. 'Good riddance to bad rubbish, I say.'

* * *

Laura woke with a fuzzy head and a bad feeling in her tummy. She hadn't slept well. She felt groggy from the lack of sleep and a long day stretched ahead, again.

When she entered the kitchen, she was bombarded by the scent of freesias and lilies. it was a smell she would usually love, but which now only made her feel desperately sad.

The flowers had been moved from the sink to a bucket. She didn't own a vase.

Why had he brought her flowers? Why such a big bunch tied up in a pink ribbon? A bunch of daffs would have sufficed.

He hadn't seemed happy to see her. In fact, he had seemed rather sad. More to the point, why was she making such a big deal about this? All he had wanted to say was thank you with flowers. But he hadn't even looked at her. He hadn't wanted to be anywhere near her. That much had been obvious. And that had felt like a slap in the face. Laura had thought they were friends.

Why had he looked so uncomfortable? Awkward? Like a caged animal that wanted to bolt.

What should she do with the flowers? Looking at them made her feel so unhappy. But she couldn't bring herself to throw them in the bin, so instead she picked up the bucket and carried it down the hallway. She'd put them in the front garden.

With the bucket of flowers balanced on her hip, she flung open the door and the bucket very nearly slipped from her fingers.

Megan squeaked and jumped backwards.

Laura grabbed the bucket with both hands before it could topple to the floor and caught her breath.

'My God, you nearly gave me a heart attack.' Megan shrieked with laughter, her hand covering her mouth. 'I hadn't even rung the bell.'

Laura clutched the bucket to her chest. 'I was just putting these outside,' she said.

Megan stared at the flowers, still wrapped in cellophane and tied with the pretty pink bow. 'But why are you putting them outside?'

'I don't want them in the house,' Laura said, all matter-of-fact.

Megan reached forward to touch the petals and inhaled the floral scent. 'Oh, they're too pretty to put outside,' she said. 'Here, give them to me and I'll take them home.'

Laura gave her the bucket. Why was Megan on her door-step at this early hour on a Saturday morning?

Megan placed the bucket by the step. 'I'll leave them here and pick them up when I leave.' She tilted her head to one side. 'I didn't realise you were allergic to flowers.'

Laura simply nodded. She'd let Megan think that she was. Far easier to say that she wanted rid of the flowers because they made her sneeze, as opposed to not being reminded of Richard's sad face and obvious disdain for her. 'Do you want a cup of tea, then?' Laura asked.

Megan smiled and nodded. 'That would be lovely.'

Laura made the tea and Megan chatted. She spoke about her work, in that she had a lot of writing projects on the go at the moment. She spoke about how she and Jack were planning to go to Italy for the first time this summer, and she spoke about Gertie. It was only a matter of time.

'I'm so glad you helped Richard and that you caught that awful woman in the act. I'm glad I didn't catch her as I would have killed her,' Megan said. A dark look crossed her face.

Laura had no doubt that Megan had a temper.

'Well, she's gone now,' Laura said, trying to change the subject. Talk of Gertie always led to Richard.

'Who's the manager now, then?' Megan picked up her cup of tea.

'Linda, for the time being, but I know she doesn't want the role on a permanent basis. They'll probably advertise for it next week sometime.'

'You should go for it,' Megan said.

'What, me?' Laura was shocked at the thought. 'No, I haven't been there long enough.'

'Oh, well,' Megan said. 'It was just a thought.'

Laura picked up her tea and gulped a few mouthfuls.

Megan put her cup down on the table. She reached over and touched Laura's hand. 'We are still friends, aren't we?' she asked quickly. 'It's just the other night I know I offended you with all that Gertie prophecy talk and I didn't mean to. I really didn't.'

'I know you didn't.' Laura gave her hand a reassuring squeeze. 'It's just that I'm capable of meeting people myself and making my own decisions in life. I don't believe in psychics, or fate, or any of that nonsense. But Gertie does and that's fine by me.'

Megan nodded, saying nothing. She sipped her tea.

'I really didn't mean to offend you either. I know you care about Gertie and Richard, and so do I,' Laura told her gently.

Megan looked up, expectation written all over her face.

'Which is why I'm going along with all of this,' Laura added. 'Making Gertie happy — there's no harm in it, I suppose. But it's far too soon for me to get involved with any man. I like Richard, but all we can be at the moment is friends, and, to be honest, I really don't think he likes me that much.'

'What?' Megan's face was a picture of shock. She shook her head. 'No, you've got the wrong impression of him. I have no idea why you would think that.'

Laura thought about how she could explain what had happened without getting Megan's hopes up. If she knew about the flowers . . .

'Hang on a minute — he sent you those flowers, didn't he.' It wasn't a question.

'Yes,' was all Laura could say. How was she going to get out of this one?

'And you wanted to throw them the *bin*?'

Oh no. Megan looked really upset. This was bad.

'No, no, you've got it all wrong.' Laura had to keep calm. She needed to explain. 'I wasn't going to put them in the bin. Just outside the door, that's all. Just so that I wouldn't see them in the house.'

'Why were you throwing them out?' Megan asked eventually.

Laura took a deep breath. 'He came around last night to say thank you and he brought me those flowers. Which are beautiful. But it was also as if he was saying goodbye with them, not thank you. He wouldn't look at me. He wouldn't drink his tea and he left within about five minutes of sitting down exactly where you are now.' She could see Megan's expression had softened. 'He looked so sad, Megan. And awkward. And looking at those flowers makes me feel so sad, too, because I don't honestly know why he gave them to me. I'm more confused than ever.'

Megan nodded. 'Well, that makes two of us. Do you know the last time he bought anyone flowers, other than Gertie?'

Laura shook her head.

'No one, that's who.' Megan sighed, then shrugged. 'Perhaps he's worried about Gertie, has other stuff on his mind?'

But Laura didn't think it was that at all. She thought that he had realised he had made a massive mistake getting to know her and that he no longer wanted to have anything to do with her.

* * *

Laura wrapped up well for her walk to the home for her afternoon shift. She had been rostered to work on Gertie's floor, alongside Adrian, so the afternoon would pass by in a blur.

A persistent drizzle followed her as she walked through the village, past the shop then onwards towards the playground. Her pink woolly hat was pulled down low over her ears and a scarf wound tightly around her neck. She picked up her pace, not wanting to be late.

As she approached the playground, her breath caught in her throat.

She stopped and looked at the scene in front of her.

Hazel was standing by the gate that led into the playground. Laura had to walk past her. There was no other route that she could take. She thrust her fists into her coat pockets, lifted her head, jutted out her chin and strode forward with purpose.

She had done nothing wrong.

The person who should be feeling guilty was Hazel. Not her.

Laura's heart hammered in her chest. She would not let this woman intimidate her.

Just as Laura was about to walk past, Hazel flung her arm out, blocking the path.

Laura had no choice but to stop.

She would be brave. She would speak her truth.

'I've been sacked because of you and that bloody man.' Hazel spat the words out like venom.

Laura folded her arms across her chest. She looked directly at her. 'You got sacked because you stole from old and vulnerable people.'

211

You stupid woman.

'It's your fault. I know your type, with your bloody airs and graces. You swan in here from the city thinking you're so much better than us country bumpkins.' Hazel pointed her finger at Laura's chest, stabbing at her with every word.

Laura tried to control her breathing. *In and out. In and out.* She did not want, nor have the time, to have an argument.

'I'm late for work, Hazel. Just let me pass.'

'Oh, you're late for work, are you?' Hazel's voice dripped with sarcasm, her face now inches from Laura's. 'Well, at least you have work, you stuck-up cow. I am a single mum. How am I going to feed the kids now? Pay the rent, the bills? Afford the bloody school uniform and shoes? You have no idea what it's like for me. No bloody idea at all.'

Hazel's words struck Laura like a blow to the chest. She was a single mum? What would happen to the kids now that she'd lost her job? What if she lost her home? Laura felt sick to her stomach.

'I'm sorry,' she said. 'I'm sorry you thought you had to steal to make ends meet.' She meant every word, she *was* sorry, but that didn't change what had happened or that Hazel shouldn't be punished for her actions. But still, the kids . . . 'Is there anyone who can help you? Family, friends—'

'I have no one,' Hazel spat back.

But Laura saw a weakening in the woman's defences. A vulnerability that hadn't been there before. 'I can help—'

'I don't need your help,' Hazel said, but her words lacked conviction.

Laura opened her mouth to offer help once more but Hazel cut her off.

'I checked your references, you know. I wondered why a trained nurse would choose to work in the middle of nowhere as a care assistant. What exactly are you hiding?'

'Nothing, nothing at all,' Laura said quietly to herself before walking away. *You wouldn't understand.*

CHAPTER TWENTY-EIGHT

The residents of Cedar House care home were fast asleep. Well, all but one. Gertie sighed one of those deep sighs of the utterly exhausted who simply could not rest. She opened her eyes and looked at the bedside clock. 2.15 a.m.

It was the pain that had woken her from a restless sleep. She pushed herself up the bed as best as she could and rested her head against the headboard. She forced herself to lean over the bedside table and switched on the bedside light. She needed a distraction. Something to take her mind off the searing pain that was slowly working its way up her spine and twisting around her middle, her gut. It was no good calling the carers to come and take a look. There was nothing they could do. Painkillers wouldn't touch this pain. She really needed morphine, but that was a downhill slope and she knew that she would end up in hospital. So, she squeezed her eyes tightly shut, and inhaled and exhaled deeply through the pain.

One, two, three in . . . One, two, three out . . .

It would pass. It always did. Only then would she press the buzzer for a cup of tea.

She picked up the book from the top of the pile on her bedside table. The battered old copy of *Great Expectations*. She found the page where Laura had inserted the bookmark.

If Pip and Estelle couldn't take her mind off the pain, then nothing would.

It would soon fade.

Then time for tea . . .

* * *

'Come here, Henry,' Gertie said, giving her grandson a big, gentle cuddle from the safety of her bed.

Henry wrapped his arms around her and rested his head on her shoulder.

She planted a kiss on top of his curls. 'Oh, I've missed you, my lovely boy.'

'Can I have a biscuit?' Henry asked.

'Course you can, love. Go and get two from the biscuit tin.'

Henry jumped off the bed in one quick leap and swiftly located the biscuit tin.

'Tell you what, Henry, would you like to go and play in the day room? I'll have a quick chat with Daddy. Would you like that?' Gertie suggested this with a smile.

Henry's eyes lit up. He loved the toy basket in the day room. He liked the cars best.

Richard peered at his grandmother. This was so unlike her. She usually didn't want to let Henry out of her sight. He studied her more closely. He noted the pinched look of her face. The black circles under her eyes. She hadn't slept well.

'I'll ask Adrian to stay with him for half an hour — he won't mind,' Gertie said.

Now Richard was really worried. This was so unlike her.

'I'll take Henry with me and go and find him,' Richard said, his throat tight. He found it hard to get the words out. He needed to sound normal. He didn't want to sound panicked. Gertie would hear it in his voice.

Twenty minutes later, Henry was settled in the day room with his cars and juice. Richard sat in the chair by the side of Gertie's bed with a cup of tea that warmed his hands. Gertie's cup of tea was sitting on the bedside table, untouched.

'She is such a clever girl,' Gertie said with a faraway look in her eyes.

Richard wondered who she was talking about, but he didn't ask. He would simply let her talk. Gertie's voice lacked its usual strength and clarity. Her words seemed strained to him. As if she was using a great deal of effort to speak to him.

'That girl is such a good judge of character. She knew it was Hazel straight away, you know, and she helped us, and now look what's happened.' Gertie tutted, a scowl forming on her face.

Laura? She must be talking about Laura. Richard wondered what had happened?

'She hasn't told you, has she?' Gertie said.

'I-I haven't seen Laura since I gave her the flowers.' His heart raced and he felt a cold chill run down his spine. Had Hazel hurt Laura in some way? 'What happened to Laura?'

Gertie cleared her throat. 'Can you pass me my cup, love?'

Richard handed her the cup so she could have a sip of tea, then put it back on the bedside table.

'Hazel stopped Laura outside here yesterday. Well, not exactly outside the home, but in the playground. She obviously didn't want anyone to see her. The coward.' Gertie hissed the words.

Richard placed his own cup down. He hunched forward on his seat and nodded in encouragement. 'What happened to Laura?'

'Well, Hazel started shouting, telling Laura that it was all her fault. Oh, and apparently it was yours too. Silly woman.'

Richard raised his eyebrows. 'Really, she said that? That Laura and I were to blame for what happened to her? She actually believed that?'

'Yes, she did,' Gertie said. 'Told Laura that she was a struggling single parent and what was she going to do now that she had lost her job.'

Gertie leaned back on the pillow and sucked in a deep breath.

'You okay?' Richard asked, worry making him frown. This was all too much. She needed to rest. Take it easy.

'I'm fine, love. Just a stitch.' Gertie offered him a wobbly smile.

'Should I call someone? So they can give you your pain medication?' He could see that she was in pain but knew she wouldn't admit it with him in the room.

'No, no, I'm fine. Stop fussing.' She batted him away with a flutter of her hands. 'Now, where was I? Oh, that's right. Laura. Well, she felt guilty then, about the kids, because what will happen now that Hazel doesn't have a job?'

'I had no idea she was a single parent, that she was struggling,' Richard said. The last thing he wanted was for the kids to suffer. 'Do you know if she has any family who can help her out?'

'Laura asked just that and Hazel said no.'

Richard knew all too well the realities of being a single parent, but he had the safety net of family surrounding him, and it appeared Hazel had no one.

'I know that look,' Gertie said with a knowing smile.

'You do?' Richard asked.

'You want to help her, don't you?'

Richard nodded. 'But only because of the kids, and maybe if we help her, then maybe she can get back on track and help herself.' He shrugged. 'It's not fair on the kids otherwise,' he added.

'I agree,' Gertie said, before adding, 'I'm going to drop all charges.'

'Wh-what?' Richard asked, thinking he'd misheard.

'I don't want her to go to prison. All I wanted was to catch the thief and I did that.'

'But what about her punishment?'

'I think losing her job and the entire village knowing what she did is punishment enough, don't you?'

Richard wasn't entirely sure about that, but it wasn't his call to make.

'I think she needs people around her, supporting her, and as a village, we're good at that,' Gertie said.

He couldn't disagree with that. 'I'll have a think, see what I can do. Maybe we could do a collection or something? I'll chat to Tracey. Laura too.'

'She's such a lovely girl,' Gertie said after a few quiet moments.

Richard nodded. He knew where this was going.

'You know what happened to her, don't you?' Gertie asked.

'Know about what?' Richard asked, confused at the change of topic.

'What happened to her husband, of course.'

How did she know about Laura's husband? Laura must have chatted to her about it. but how did Gertie know that *he* knew?

'How? How do you know?' Richard asked against his better judgement.

'She told me, of course,' Gertie said with a shake of her head. 'But what I really want to know is how *you* found out? I know that she didn't tell you.'

'I . . . Well, she did tell me,' Richard said.

'Oh, Richard, don't lie to me. I can always see right through you. Ever since you were a little boy. So, tell me the truth. How did *you* find out?'

'I googled her,' Richard admitted, his face hot with shame.

Gertie shook her head. 'You really shouldn't have done that. You shouldn't have been snooping on her. It's never a good idea, love.'

'I know,' Richard said. 'I wish I hadn't now. I don't know how . . .' He paused, not sure if he should say aloud what was on his mind. 'I'm not sure how I should act around her now. I feel awkward, knowing her secret.'

'Whatever do you mean?' Gertie asked. 'You just need to be yourself. And, anyway, you only know half the story — the sensationalist rot that the papers print. You haven't heard Laura's story. Her version of events. About what really happened.'

Richard knew that his grandmother was talking sense. He did only know half the story, but this still made being around her incredibly difficult.

'I feel ashamed, knowing what I know about her. I can't *un*know it. Go back to how things were. It's not that easy.'

'Well, I'm not sure, love. Maybe you just need to tell her.'

Richard spluttered. 'Tell her?' No, he couldn't tell her that he had done an internet search to find out who she really was. She'd never forgive him, and who would blame her? Even if he told her he'd done it with the best of intentions, that he'd been worried about her safety, there was still no excuse for what he'd done when he could have simply asked her.

'I just mean that you could tell her that you found a newspaper article or something,' Gertie said. 'That you found out by accident.'

'They're not easily found, Gran, those articles,' Richard said. 'You have to dig deep to find them and have a reason to do some digging. As you said, she's clever. She'd see right through that excuse.'

Gertie pondered this for a moment. 'You're right. You'll just have to keep this from her then and hope that she tells you about it in her own good time, just as she told me.'

Richard nodded, but he doubted that Laura would want to share something so intimate with him.

'You could always talk to her about Sally. Open up about what happened after she died. Perhaps she would open up to you?' Gertie said gently.

Richard froze. No, he wasn't ready for that. Very few people knew what had happened to him after Sally's death.

That he had fallen, crumbled, and that he had never quite become whole again.

He shook his head.

'Oh, this should all be so simple,' Gertie said.

'What should be so simple?' Richard asked with a sigh. Nothing in his life was simple.

'You and Laura,' Gertie said, as if the answer was so obvious. 'Oh, Richard, just ask her out, before it's too late.'

* * *

'Laura, come and grab this cup of tea, before it grows cold,' Linda shouted across the day room, the cup held aloft in the air like a prize.

Laura pushed herself up from the floor where she'd been sorting through the contents of the bookshelf, thinking there really should be a better selection of books. Gertie had a better range of books in her room. She stood up, placed her hands on her hips and arched her back. She had been crouched on the floor for far too long, absorbed in her task of sorting out the various paperbacks. It had been fairly quiet after lunch, with many of the residents snoozing, so she had grabbed the chance to do a bit of tidying. She had been meaning to do it for weeks now.

'Thanks,' Laura said, taking the cup from Linda.

It had been hours since she'd had a cup of tea, but her shift was nearly over and she planned to go home, heat up a microwave meal and get stuck into a good book.

The two women stood in the doorway and sipped their tea.

'So, what are you up to this afternoon, then?' Laura asked. She knew that Linda usually spent Sundays with the grandchildren. She still couldn't get over the fact that Linda was old enough to have grandchildren.

'Milly is calling around with the kids for a late Sunday lunch and then I think I'll put my feet up.' Linda laughed. 'What about you? Anything nice planned?'

Laura appreciated that Linda was asking her about her plans, but she always gave the same answer. 'Just a quiet afternoon in the house.' Laura followed her words with a shrug.

'Well, that's nice. Always good to have a rest.'

But Laura could easily read Linda's expression. The way in which she looked at her said the exact opposite. What Laura saw was pity. 'I'm fine. Honestly, I am. I'm happy at home by myself.'

Linda lowered her cup and touched Laura's arm. 'Listen, if you ever need a bit of company, you can always pop to mine. I always have enough food to feed a small army. It would never be a problem. In fact, it would be lovely to see you outside of work.'

Laura sipped her tea. 'Thank you.'

Linda smiled and lifted her own cup. 'Right then, we'll finish our drinks and do our usual end-of-shift checks, eh?'

Laura nodded, her throat too tight to speak.

* * *

Laura had just shrugged her coat on by the front door and was about step outside into the much-needed fresh air when she heard a man's voice shout her name.

She spun around to see Richard running towards her.

As usual, his satchel was slung across his shoulder and his black curls were sticking up, as if he had just raked his hand through them, either from worry or sheer frustration, she couldn't quite tell.

He stopped in front of her. 'I'm so glad I caught you before you left,' he said, taking a few deep breaths.

Laura stood there, open-mouthed. She couldn't make this man out. The other day he could barely look at her, and now he was running after her, obviously desperate to talk to her about something.

Time stood still. It must be Gertie. Her hand flew to her mouth.

'What's happened? Is Gertie okay?' Laura asked.

'Gertie? Oh, she's fine. I just left her.'

'Oh, that's good to hear,' Laura said, relief washing over her. Her heartbeat slowed. 'Oh, I thought something had happened to her and that's why you were running after me.'

Richard shook his head and muttered his apology. 'I'm so sorry. I didn't think and didn't mean to startle you.'

Laura smiled. She noticed the worry lines on his forehead and the way in which his eyes crinkled as he spoke. 'No problem,' she said. 'I popped up to see her before I started my shift, but she was asleep.'

Richard shifted from foot to foot before he spoke. 'Well, I just wondered, as it's Sunday, if you wanted to come to mine for Sunday lunch?' His words came out rushed, all in the one breath.

The question came as such a surprise that Laura couldn't quite hide her reaction of pure shock. Why was he inviting her to his home?

'I'm, well, I'm not so sure. I think perhaps that . . .' Laura's words died on her tongue as she saw his expression change from expectation to disappointment.

His eyes lost their crinkle and he looked away from her as he fiddled with the strap on his bag. 'That's fine. Don't worry.' He turned to walk away.

'Richard,' Laura said to his retreating back. 'Wait.'

Richard turned around to face her.

'Are you cooking?' she asked.

'Good heavens, no,' Richard said. 'I wouldn't subject you to *that*.' His mouth twitched trying not to laugh. 'Tracey is cooking, and Jack and Megan will be there. Henry, too. He's with Adrian at the moment and I need to go get him.'

Laura pondered this for a moment. What harm would it do? She still thought that Richard was acting strangely towards her, but it was only Sunday lunch after all.

'If you're at all worried, then I have to tell you that it's not a date,' he said.

Laura's face grew hot. 'Oh, I know that.'

'So, is it a yes, then?' Richard's voice shook ever so slightly. Laura wondered if he was nervous.

'It's just that I promised Gertie I would invite you to lunch.'

There it was. The truth. Of course, this was Gertie's doing.

Laura sighed. 'Well, it has to be a yes, then, doesn't it. I don't want to let Gertie down.'

CHAPTER TWENTY-NINE

'Come and sit down, Henry.' Richard hollered to his son from the kitchen where he was busy spooning potatoes into a serving dish. Tracey carved pieces of chicken and placed them onto a serving plate, while Jack drained the carrots. It was like a well-oiled production line. Everyone had their job.

'I want to sit next to Laura,' Henry demanded from where he sat on the couch. Then, without waiting for an answer, he grabbed Laura by the hand, pulled her up from the couch and led her over to the dining table which had been pulled out into the middle of the room so that everyone could comfortably sit around it.

'I'll sit next to you too,' Megan offered with a smile as she made her way to the table. 'So I can keep an eye on this little monkey.'

Laura laughed. She liked this little boy, with his no-nonsense way of speaking. Children were like an open book. They simply said what was on their mind. No messing. You knew where you were with kids.

As Laura moved across the room, she glanced at her surroundings. The decor was modern and bright, and very much what Laura would choose for her own home. But was it Richard's taste or his late wife's? Something told her that Sally had chosen the wallpaper, the soft furnishings and over-all colour scheme, not Richard. But perhaps they had chosen it together? Her eyes loitered on the floor-to-ceiling bookcases that lined the walls of the dining room. Richard had an eclectic taste in books. Had he got this passion for reading from Gertie? Probably.

'It was so kind of Richard to invite me to Sunday lunch,' Laura said to Megan as they sat down on either side of Henry. 'I hope I'm not imposing.'

'Oh, you're not imposing,' Tracey said. She'd just appeared in the room carrying the tray of carved chicken. 'It's always a pleasure to have one of Richard's friends to Sunday lunch.' She leaned forward a little and lowered her voice. 'It's been a long time since he's invited anyone around for Sunday lunch with the family.'

Laura felt her face grow hot. She lowered her eyes and avoided looking at Richard who had just entered the room carrying a huge serving bowl of new potatoes.

This was going to be so much harder than she'd first thought. She also didn't like the way that Tracey was talking about Richard. This was his home. He'd invited Tracey and Jack and Megan, and he had chosen to invite her too. That had nothing to do with Tracey. So she shot Tracey a defiant look and a forced smile.

Richard cleared his throat and placed the serving dish on the table.

Laura couldn't believe the effort he had gone to, just for Sunday lunch. The table groaned with food. Plus there was a bottle of sparkling wine alongside a jug of water. Did they do this every Sunday? Surely not.

Remembering her manners, Laura turned her attention back to Tracey who had just sat down opposite her. 'This is lovely, Tracey. You've gone to so much effort. I really appreciate it. It's been a while since I've had a home-cooked meal.'

A deathly hush descended around the table.

All eyes were on Richard.

Had she said something wrong? Laura, too, looked at Richard, whose face was slowly turning a crimson colour. He wouldn't meet anyone's gaze as he looked down at his empty plate.

'Richard is the cook,' Tracey explained, breaking the silence. 'He always cooks us Sunday lunch, and usually we all get together at least once a month.'

'Oh,' Laura said. Had she misheard Richard? No, she had distinctively heard him say that he wouldn't subject her to his cooking and that Tracey was the cook. Why would he lie? Surely he wouldn't be embarrassed about the fact that he could cook? He had a small child to take care of. He needed to cook. It was a good thing that he could. And then it struck her. He hadn't wanted her to know, because then it would look like he was making too much of an effort. Like it was a sort of date. He had wanted to appear casual, as if it was a throwaway invite, but that didn't even make sense as this whole idea had apparently been Gertie's. And then the truth hit her like a thunderbolt. This hadn't been Gertie's idea at all. Inviting her along to Sunday lunch to meet his family had been all his own doing.

The chicken stuck in her throat.

'Oh, I'm so s-sorry.' She stuttered in her attempt to say something, anything. 'I just assumed . . .' She picked up her water glass and gulped down a mouthful of water. He had added lime.

'Don't worry about it,' Tracey said. She shot Richard a look, as if silently willing him to say something.

Richard looked up and smiled sheepishly at everyone. 'Right, well, here's to friendship. Old and new.' He raised his water glass and everyone held their glasses aloft in a silent toast. He looked over at his son who was sitting opposite him. 'You hungry, Henry?'

'Yep,' Henry said. 'But I do not want to eat my carrots.'

'What a surprise! But you have to eat at least one carrot. That's the rule.' Richard tried to hide his smile.

Henry pulled a face but nodded in agreement.

225

Laura leaned over towards Henry and whispered in his ear. 'I don't like carrots either, so I'll do you a deal. If you eat a carrot, so will I.'

Henry studied her for a moment, as if pondering this deal and wondering if it was a good one, before breaking out into a huge grin. He thrust out his hand. 'Deal. Let's shake on it.'

His face looked so serious that Laura had to clamp her mouth shut so as not to laugh. She shook his hand.

Out of the corner of Laura's eye, she saw Tracey smile as she looked pointedly towards Richard.

Laura helped herself to more chicken and tried to forget what she had just seen.

* * *

'That was lovely, thank you,' Laura said, pushing her empty plate away. She couldn't eat another thing.

'No problem,' Richard said. 'Glad you could make it.' His eyes widened and he flashed her a quick smile.

It was the first time he had directly addressed her during the meal. His attention had been on Henry, or he had chatted to Jack. Laura had talked to Megan, who had tried to bring Richard into their conversation without success.

'Right, I'll go and make us some coffee then,' Richard said.

'It'll go nicely with the chocolate cake I bought,' Tracey said.

Henry's ears pricked up at the words *chocolate cake*. He turned to Laura and touched her on the arm. 'I love chocolate cake.'

'Me too,' Laura said with a grin.

Henry grinned back, and Laura was taken aback by how similar he looked to his father when he smiled. Richard should smile more.

Tracey stood up and began to gather plates. All efficiency. She made Laura nervous.

'Here, let me help you,' Laura said, taking Henry's plate.

'No, you're fine. You sit there and have a rest. You've been working all morning,' Tracey said.

Laura lowered herself back into her seat. She wasn't comfortable not doing anything. She preferred to be busy.

Richard retreated into the kitchen. 'I'll make that coffee.'

Laura watched Richard go and couldn't help but feel that he was escaping from her. Why invite her around if he wasn't prepared to talk to her?

Henry jumped up and followed his dad, probably in search of the chocolate cake.

Megan took this as her opportunity to scoot along the table to be next to Laura. 'You okay?' she asked. 'You're being very quiet.'

'I'm fine,' Laura said. She wished that Megan wasn't quite so astute. 'Just tired.' She shrugged. 'It's been a long week.'

'Yeah, I heard about what happened with Hazel. Are you okay?'

Laura blinked, Megan's question taking her by surprise. 'I'm fine.'

'Richard wants the community to rally around the kids,' Megan said.

'Oh, I need to talk to him about that,' Laura said. 'I was thinking pretty much the same thing. He's a good man, isn't he?'

'He sure is,' Megan said, before adding, 'This is such a big thing for Richard. You know, inviting you here for lunch with all of us.'

This revelation didn't make Laura feel any better. In fact, it did the exact opposite. After coffee, she would make her excuses and leave. She craved the quiet solitude of the cottage. She felt the sudden urge to weep and she didn't know why.

'You do like him, though, don't you?' Megan kept talking. 'I know he is just as important to you, as you are to him.'

Laura pushed herself away from the table, away from Megan's intense stare. She couldn't have this conversation.

Not with Megan. Not with anyone. Not now. In her haste, she bumped the table. Jack looked up from his phone. Megan stared, open-mouthed.

'I'll just see if they need a hand,' Laura quickly said, rushing from the dining room into the kitchen.

She found Richard filling the coffee maker with water from a jug, while Tracey washed up. Henry was by her side, perched on a step stool.

What was she doing here? Laura didn't belong in this family. They just felt sorry for her because she lived alone. She didn't need their pity. Could she grab her coat and make a quick exit before anyone realised? Maybe she could if she was quiet enough.

Henry jumped down from the stool.

Too late.

He ran over towards her, arms outstretched.

'Laura, I'm washing up,' he said, the washing-up bubbles still visible on his thin arms. Some were in his black curls.

'What a good boy you are, Henry,' Laura said. 'It must be fun helping Nana.'

'Come here, Henry, and dry your arms for me.' Tracey held out a clean tea towel. It was decorated with colourful cartoon dinosaurs.

Henry took it and wiped at his arms.

'Can I help with anything?' Laura asked. She couldn't escape now so she might as well help. She didn't want to go back into the dining room and make small talk with Megan.

Richard placed the empty water jug down on the counter and rested his hands on his hips. 'No, it's fine. There's nothing to do.'

Henry wailed. 'Daddy, I've done a wee-wee in my pants.'

Richard sighed and forced a smile. 'Let's sort you out then, little man. Don't worry.'

Tracey pulled her rubber gloves off with lightning speed and threw them next to the washing-up bowl. 'Oh, let me,' she said, rushing to Henry's side and clasping his hand, no doubt before he could protest that he wanted Daddy, not Nana. 'Come on, let's get you some clean pants.'

They left the room.

Laura wondered if she should stay or follow them.

Richard grinned and shook his head. 'Subtlety is not one of her finer points.' He chuckled.

Smiling, Laura walked over to the sink. She pulled on the rubber gloves.

Richard protested. 'Oh, you don't need to wash up.'

'I don't mind,' Laura said. The truth was that she felt more comfortable doing something. It would be easier to speak to him if she was busy washing up, standing side by side.

'I'll dry then,' Richard said. He picked up the tea towel and began to dry the plates.

'Megan told me that you want to help Hazel and the kids,' Laura said, drying her hands on the tea towel.'

'Yeah, I wanted to talk to you about that, about how we could help.'

'I'll have a think. To be honest, I just think she could do with a friend.'

'You're not wrong there,' Richard said. 'Are you working tomorrow?' He put away the last glass into the overhead cupboard.

Laura shook her head.

'Anything nice planned?' he asked.

'Not really. Housework and washing, I think.'

'Right, well, yes, that is important.' What was happening to him? Why did he lose the power of articulate conversation when with this woman? She must think him a complete idiot. He had invited her around for lunch and so far he had hardly said a word to her.

The truth was that he was no good at this sort of thing. He had no idea how to talk to a woman he liked. He had never really had to do this sort of thing before. He and Sally had met when they were both so young. They'd grown up together. This was a completely new situation for him. He was out of his depth and comfort zone. Then, on top of all of that, he was worried about Gertie. He should really phone the home this evening, check in on her.

Richard looked up to find Laura staring at him.

'So, I might call in tomorrow anyway,' she said.

Richard nodded. What was she on about?

'You didn't hear what I said then, did you?' Laura asked with a smile.

'No, sorry. I was thinking about Gertie.'

Laura pulled off the rubber gloves and placed them over the mixer tap. 'I was just asking you about Gertie. How she seemed today. I told you I'd popped up first thing to see her, but she was asleep, and I didn't want to disturb her.'

'She did seem tired when I visited,' Richard said. 'And not her usual self. I'll be honest with you, I'm worried, but at the same time I know there's nothing I can do, so . . .'

'She's well looked after, you know. There is always some-one there that she can call on if she needs anything.'

Richard nodded. He knew this to be true of course. He didn't mean to sound ungrateful. He knew that the care staff were doing their utmost to care for his gran. 'I appreciate all that you are doing, and what the other staff are doing to help her. It's just that, sometimes . . .' Richard's words trailed off as he searched for the right words.

Laura stood silently, waiting for him to find those words.

'It's just that I feel a little useless,' he eventually said, his voice soft, eyes lowered to the floor. 'It's almost as if I'm power-less to do anything.'

'That's not true,' Laura said. 'When you visit Gertie, it gives her strength. She really does look forward to your visits. She can't stop talking about you and Henry.'

'Well, she does adore Henry. She dotes on him.'

'And you too,' Laura said. 'Listen, just by being there for her, as you have for all these years, is enough for her. She knows that she's loved. You can't ask for more than that.'

Richard absorbed her wise words. She was right, of course. But he still felt helpless. He just wished that he could do something.

'Anyway, enough about me,' he said, turning his attention to the coffee machine, which had stopped spluttering the last drops of coffee into the jug on the warming plate. 'How are you? Do you feel that Buttermarsh could be your home now?'

Laura didn't respond for a few seconds and Richard thought that perhaps he had said the wrong thing.

'I wasn't sure how I would settle in here,' she said, 'but actually, it is starting to feel a lot like home. Like I could belong here. Which is strange, as I haven't been here for very long.'

Richard spoke as he poured coffee into the cups on the tray. 'That's so good to hear, that you feel happy and settled here.' He cleared his throat and continued to pour the coffee. 'Especially after what happened to you.'

He realised his mistake far too late. The words had slipped out subconsciously. He placed the coffee pot back on the warmer, then turned around slowly to look at Laura. She'd backed up against the counter and her face was ashen.

'What do you mean? After what happened to me?'

Her words came out so quietly that Richard could barely hear them.

Lie or tell the truth? What should he do?

'Richard, what do you mean?' Laura said. Her voice had grown louder.

'I just mean after what happened to your husband,' Richard said. He forced himself to look at her. He owed her that much.

Laura stood, open-mouthed. Eventually she spoke. 'I can't believe that she told you,' she said, her voice breaking. 'I thought we were friends. I trusted her.' She turned away from Richard, to flee.

Richard rushed over to where she was standing and reached out to touch her arm.

Laura spun around and he stepped back so that there was space once again between them. 'Don't blame Gertie. She didn't tell me anything. She would never break a confidence,' he said.

'What do you mean, Gertie never told you? Of course she did. Don't lie to me, Richard.'

She was shouting and Richard hoped that Tracey and the others couldn't hear them. He didn't want them to get involved in this mess. He had to tell Laura the truth. Gertie couldn't get the blame. 'I found out. Okay. Just don't blame Gertie,' he said. His eyes pleaded with her to not ask *how* he had found out.

But of course she did.

'How, Richard?'

Richard closed his eyes. Shame burned at his soul. 'I googled your name and read newspaper articles associated with your husband's death,' he said quickly.

Laura shrieked, no longer able to hide her disgust. 'You *googled* me?'

'I'm so sorry. It's just that I wanted to make sure you were safe. I wasn't sure if someone was messing with you. I mean, I knew nothing about you and you were involved in catching the thief.' He took a ragged breath. I just wanted you and my gran to be safe.'

'What?' Her voice came out in a croak. 'You thought I was a danger to your gran?'

Richard clenched his jaw and looked up at the ceiling. He was making matters worse. 'Of course not. I trust you. I was worried for you, and for my gran.' He needed to stop talking.

'You are unbelievable, you know that! I am not a danger to your gran. The woman who *was* a danger has now been arrested and you know what, I helped to get her caught.' Laura had taken several steps towards him and was jabbing her finger towards his chest, eyes ablaze and fire in her belly. 'My husband took his own life. He chose to do that, and that is something that I have to live with every day for the rest of my

232

life. I came here for a fresh start. To start again, and I thought that I could. But you know what, I'll never be able to outrun what happened to me. Because people like *you* have to keep on digging and digging and then drag everything out into the open once again. Stuff that needs to be kept buried.' Laura took a step closer until her face was inches from his. Their eyes locked. She spat her words at him. 'But do you know the worst thing? That you don't trust me. You say you do, but you searched for me on the internet, and that's the opposite of trusting someone. And you know what? I would have told you. Gertie told me to tell you and I wanted to, but it would have been in my own time. I was getting there, healing. But now that wound has burst right open and you've ruined everything. I'll never forgive you, Richard. *Never.* Because without trust you have nothing.'

Laura turned and fled from the room.

Richard stood rooted to the spot. Unable to move or speak.

Moments later, Megan appeared. She propped herself up against the doorway, arms folded. 'What on earth have you gone and done?'

CHAPTER THIRTY

The evening stretched ahead for Laura who felt trapped within the thick stone walls of Church View Cottage. She had stomped along the narrow lanes back home, having made her excuses to Tracey. Her eyes stung with unshed tears and her throat felt thick and swollen. She had practically run home in an attempt to shed the rage building up within her. That and the burning shame she still felt for what had happened.

The bottle of white wine she had taken from the fridge now stood unopened on the kitchen table. Droplets of condensation ran down the outside and smeared the wooden table top.

She had wanted a drink so badly but had refused to open the bottle. One glass would lead to another, and before she knew it the bottle would be empty. So she picked it up and placed it back in the fridge. A reminder that she didn't want or need it.

There was a restless fizzing inside her. She needed to do something, but she didn't know what. She dared not step outside for fear of who she might bump into.

She needed to think. She needed to plan her next step.

Richard knew about her past and he would never look at her in the same way again. She had seen the look of pity on his face, but she had ignored it, not suspecting for a minute that he knew about Mark and her reasons for moving to Buttermarsh. How stupid she had been.

Richard knew, and that meant that so did Megan and Jack and Traccy.

What must they think of her?

She hadn't set out to live a lie. All she had wanted was a fresh start. But now, not revealing her past might just jeopardise her future here. Then what? Where could she go? She couldn't go back home with her tail between her legs. Although they wouldn't tell her outright, she knew what her mother and sister would be thinking.

We told you so.

Laura steadied her breathing and sank down onto the kitchen chair. She forced herself to think like a rational person.

She had been under no obligation to tell anyone about her past. It was her right to live a secluded and private life. She had done nothing wrong. If Richard hadn't played private investigator then no one would be any the wiser.

No harm done.

But they did know. So what should she do?

She could ignore Richard. But the problem was that the village was only small and the likelihood was that she would bump into him at some point. She could choose not to stop and talk to him, but he visited the home to see Gertie. She couldn't avoid him there. The only way to deal with that problem was to act in her usual professional manner, or to request that she didn't work on Gertie's floor. But she loved Gertie, so that wouldn't be fair on either of them.

Laura buried her face in her hands. The situation was hopeless. A complete mess.

She would just have to face it head-on. Be strong. She didn't have to explain her actions. She hadn't lied. She had just omitted the truth. She was still Laura and she was still working in the caring profession. She had blown this up out of all proportion.

The one thing that she could not do was forgive Richard for his lack of trust. The fact that he hadn't trusted her was what hurt the most.

She swallowed down the urge to cry because of what had happened with Richard.

She glanced at her phone which she'd placed on the table, wondering if she should give Lottie a call. Talk through what had happened this afternoon.

Laura sighed. It was only eight o'clock. Far too early to go to bed. She just wanted to bury herself under the duvet and forget the whole day. Moving here was meant to be a new start, but Laura had found herself coming full circle. Everything began and ended with Mark.

She was just contemplating going up to bed with a cup of tea and a book when the doorbell rang.

There was another thing she had wanted when she'd planned her move to Buttermarsh. A quiet hideaway where she knew nobody and would have no visitors. It hadn't quite worked out that way.

She didn't have to answer the door. She could hide in the kitchen until whoever it was gave up and went away.

She sat on the wooden kitchen chair and held her breath. Quite why she didn't know.

The doorbell rang again.

Please go away, whoever you are. I'm not in the mood.

Laura strained her ears for the retreating footsteps.

Nothing. Please go away.

The sound of knocking on the door.

Laura jumped, her heart pounding in her chest.

The letter-box flap was pulled open.

'Please, Laura, let me in. I just want to have a quick chat. I don't want an argument. Honest. I just think you need a friend.'

Megan, not Richard.

Laura knew she wouldn't go away. Reluctantly, she opened the door. She said nothing as she allowed Megan to follow her down the hallway into the kitchen.

Laura sat down. Megan mirrored her, sitting on the opposite chair.

'So, now you know,' Laura said, offering Megan a defiant look. She would not make herself look weak. She would not apologise for hiding her past. It was her business. Nobody else's. Let them think the worst of her.

'I'm glad we know,' Megan said. 'About Mark and what happened to him. Why you moved here. We wish you could have told us. I can't imagine what you've been though.'

'I needed—'

Megan cut her off with a wave of her hand. 'You don't need to tell me anything, Laura. I'm mad at Richard, and I told him so. I'm not mad at you. Why would I be? You did nothing wrong.'

The tears that had been threatening to flow all afternoon suddenly burst free. Laura couldn't stop them.

'Oh, Laura,' Megan said, jumping up from her chair and placing a comforting arm around her shoulder.

It had been such a long time since Laura had been held, and it felt both alien and comforting at the same time.

'I'm sorry,' Laura said between sobs. 'Sorry for getting upset.'

'Oh, don't be daft,' Megan said soothingly as she rubbed Laura's back. 'Listen, why don't you go and sort yourself out, and I'll make us a cup of tea, eh?'

Laura tried to smile and did as she was told.

* * *

In the end, Megan stayed for over an hour and Laura had been sad to let her go, But Megan had an early start in the morning. She was off to London for a conference. Laura had waved her off and had then made herself another cup of tea. She took her cup, book and phone into the snug with her. As she sipped her tea, she mulled over Megan's words — *You did nothing wrong.*

The bleak truth was that Laura could no longer trust him. Whatever had been growing between them, and she still didn't know quite what that was, had disappeared in a puff of smoke. He had gone behind her back and that stung. His actions had completely jeopardised her future in Buttermarsh.

Laura's head hurt. She didn't need this drama. She was going around in circles.

She needed Lottie.

Scrolling through her contacts, she found Lottie's number and hit the call button.

Lottie answered on the second ring.

'Hi, you okay, Laura?' Laura could hear that she was out of breath. Had she run to pick up the phone?

'Hi, I'm fine. Just thought I'd give you a call,' Laura said.

There was a pause before Lottie spoke. 'Laura, I know you too well. What's happened?'

So, Laura told her sister what had happened, the words tumbling out in a wonderful release.

* * *

'It'll all work out, mate, don't worry,' Jack said, as he handed Richard a cup of coffee.

The two men were alone in the sitting room. Tracey had gone back home and Megan had popped out to the shop, or so she had said.

Henry had been tucked up in bed.

The house was quiet. All that could be heard was the rolling news on the television, set at a low volume.

'I should never have done that internet search,' Richard said. 'What must she think of me? Going behind her back like that.'

Jack balanced his cup on his knee. Then he appeared to measure his words. 'I can't believe you did that. It's so out of character.'

'Tell me about it. I'm regretting it now,' Richard said. He put his cup down on the coffee table and hunched forward, elbows on knees.

Jack placed a hand on Richard's shoulder. 'Listen, what's done is done. You can't change that. Do you want my advice?'

Richard nodded. He needed all the help he could get right now.

'I know that you have feelings for this woman—'

Richard made a noise of protest, but Jack carried on. 'You do, I can tell, and although you may not admit this to yourself, it's obvious to me. If you want Laura to still be a part of your life, then what you need to do is very simple.'

Richard sat up straighter. He was all ears.

'Give her time and hope that she forgives you.'

* * *

'Laura, I can't believe he did that!' Lottie said, followed by a sigh. 'No wonder you're so upset.'

'I'm okay.'

'No, you're not and it's okay to feel that way. Richard digging up information about you must have brought up feelings about Mark, feelings you're still trying to process.'

'I still blame myself,' Laura said, not quite believing she'd said those words out loud. But it was true. Mark's mother blamed her, and a part of Laura's soul still felt guilty.

'You can stop right there. What happened to Mark was not your fault. It just happened. And what Richard did, again, that's not on you. That's on him. You have every right to keep your life private.'

'I know you're right, but sometimes it's hard when you feel the world's against you.'

'Oh honey, the world's not against you. It just feels that way sometimes, and anyway, I've always got your back.'

Laura smiled, her heart lifting a little at her sister's kind words.

'It's okay to be happy. You know that, right?' Lottie said.

'Yeah, yeah, I know.'

'I'm being serious, because I really think you need to know that and believe it, and I don't mean with a man. Be happy with yourself first and then, if you think Richard deserves your forgiveness, then maybe with him. But you deserve to be happy, for you.'

'Thank you.' Laura tried not to cry past the burning in her throat.

'Can I just say one more thing?'

Laura nodded, then laughed quietly as her sister couldn't see her. 'Sure.'

'I think you need to put yourself in his shoes,' Lottie said. 'Just for a moment. His grandmother is ill. As you know, she is dying. He doesn't know this, but he knows she probably doesn't have long left. She brought him up, was a mother to him. He lost his wife to cancer and is bringing up his son on his own while working full time.'

'You do listen to what I tell you,' Laura said, her tone light.

'Ha ha, very funny. Anyway, he has all of this stuff going on in his life and then you come along and turn his ordered world upside down.'

'I wouldn't put it quite like that,' Laura said.

'You came along and shook things up. Breathed new life into the home. Gertie befriends you, trusts you, yet he knows nothing about you. Just think about it. You're a single woman who moved from the city to a tiny village in the middle of nowhere to work at a care home, when you are a trained nurse. He knows nothing about your past, your history. What would you think?'

Laura muttered under her breath. Damn her sister. Why did she always have to be right about these things?

She said nothing.

'I know that you care about him,' Lottie said, her voice low and gentle, trying to coax the truth from her.

'No, I don't.'

'Laura, of course you do, otherwise you wouldn't be so upset.'

Laura squeezed her eyes shut and pinched the bridge of her nose. Lottie was meant to make things simpler, not confuse the situation even more.

'Just pick up the phone and talk to him. Life is too short, Laura. Surely you know that.'

It was true, life was short. Could she forgive him and move on? The answer was so simple. She would have to forgive him, for Gertie's sake.

Laura said her goodbyes and stared at her phone screen. She would phone him now. While she had the courage to do so. It would be easier than talking to him face to face.

But as she started to scroll for his number, her mobile rang.

It was Richard.

She took a deep breath and answered the call.

* * *

Gertie rested her head back on the pillow and closed her eyes. A feeling of great calm washed over her. She had been worried for a little while, she didn't mind admitting that, but everything now seemed to be resolved and back on track.

The pair of them could be so stubborn. They needed their heads bashing together. But all was coming good.

It would all work out in the end.

She could see the future so clearly in her mind.

He would no longer be alone, or unhappy, or feel that he had failed Henry in some way.

He now had someone to share that future with.

A weight had been lifted.

It was time.

CHAPTER THIRTY-ONE

Richard rubbed his eyes and stared at his reflection in the bathroom mirror. What greeted him was a man with red-rimmed eyes and pale, blotchy skin. He barely recognised himself. He hadn't slept well. He'd tossed and turned all night, and at just before five he had woken from a vivid dream which had made his heart stutter and his palms sweat. Gertie had appeared in the bedroom, had sat on the edge of his bed. She had touched his cheek and then whispered in his ear. Her words had been crystal clear.

Don't be sad, my love. I've had a good life. Now it's time to live yours again.

Richard had sat bolt upright. Eyes wide, convinced that Gertie was in the room. It had taken him a minute or so to realise that he had been dreaming. But the experience had rattled him and so he had shuffled quietly out of bed and gone downstairs for coffee.

Now it was nearly six, so he grabbed a quick shower before making his way to Henry's room. Henry needed at least twenty minutes to fully wake up and it took him half an hour to eat his breakfast and get dressed, ready for his day at nursery.

Richard was about to open Henry's bedroom door when he heard his mobile ringing downstairs. He had left it on the kitchen table.

His heart thudded against his ribcage as he ran down the stairs two at a time.

He grabbed the phone, answered the call. It was the home.

'Hello, Richard.'

It was Linda.

His throat was dry and he swallowed. 'Hello.'

'I'm sorry to call so early,' she said. 'Listen, are you sitting down?'

He closed his eyes and grabbed the back of the kitchen chair to steady himself. He could hear a faint buzzing noise in his ears. 'Yes,' he said, lying.

'Richard, I am so sorry, love. We have just done our usual morning checks and when we checked on Gertie . . . I'm so sorry, but she passed away in her sleep. When we checked in on her at four a.m., she was fast asleep.'

Richard gripped the phone tighter, pulled the chair out and lowered himself down. Linda's voice faded away.

All he could think about was the dream and that Gertie was gone.

'Do you want to come and see her? We'll give her a little wash, change her clothes.'

Richard concentrated on his breathing, sucking in the air. He felt sick.

'Yes, I'll be there as soon as I can. I just need to . . .' He paused. What was he going to say? Henry. What would he do about Henry? 'I'll need to sort out Henry.'

'There's no rush. Just give me a buzz when you're on your way and I'll look out for you.'

He ended the call.

He shivered. The room suddenly felt cold. He rubbed his face. He needed to phone Tracey, ask if she could come over and watch Henry. He'd need to phone school.

He squeezed his eyes shut and resting his head on the kitchen table, he wept. His heart was breaking all over again.

* * *

Tracey arrived twenty minutes later. She radiated efficiency and structure, telling Richard what to do. She woke Henry and sorted him out with breakfast. She sat next to Richard while he told his son that Nana Gertie had died. He used the word *died*. He knew the importance of saying the right words, that he needed to be clear from the very beginning. His voice cracked as he spoke.

Henry stared at him, confusion in his eyes. 'Where is Nana Gertie?' he asked. 'Is she in heaven?' His face crumpled and he started to cry.

Richard swallowed, pulled Henry towards him and enveloped him in a hug.

'Yes, mate. She's in heaven now.'

Richard had made a snap decision before Henry woke up. He would not let his son see Gertie. Not in the home. He wouldn't understand. He would assume that she was asleep, and he knew that seeing her would only confuse him.

Tracey had agreed with him.

Richard wanted Henry to remember his nana as a woman who had been full of love and life. The nana who had given him biscuits and cuddles and told him stories of boys who had wonderful adventures.

He didn't want his son to remember his nana as she was now — still and lifeless.

Richard hugged Henry tighter to his chest. Kissed the top of his head. 'Listen, I need to go to the home and sort out a few things. So Nana Tracey is going to look after you. That okay?' Richard asked, his face buried in his son's hair.

Henry nodded. 'Can I stay at home?' he asked.

Richard sat up and looked over at Tracey, perched on the edge of the armchair. She nodded, then mouthed, 'I'll stay here with him.'

'Yes, mate, you can have the day off nursery,' Richard said.

'Will I get into trouble?' Henry asked.

Richard shook his head and ruffled Henry's hair. 'No, you won't get into trouble. It's a sad day, isn't it?'

Henry looked down at his feet swinging in mid-air. 'I am sad, Daddy.'

'Me too,' Richard said. 'Me too.'

* * *

Laura received the phone call at 6.15 a.m. Linda apologised profusely for calling her at such an early hour on her day off, but she thought that Laura should know what had happened.

Laura asked how Linda was feeling. The woman had cared for Gertie for years.

'I'm fine. You know how it is — you just cope, don't you? But I feel so sad that she died all alone. We did our usual checks at two and four, and she was fast asleep. So she must have died some time between four and when we checked in on her at six.'

All Laura could see in her mind's eye was Gertie, all alone in her room. Had she been frightened? Had it been a peaceful death? God, Laura hoped so. She couldn't bear the thought of Gertie being in pain. Why hadn't she been there for Gertie? She should have been there. Gertie should have been surrounded by those who loved her.

'You okay, love?' Linda asked gently.

'I'm fine.' Laura forced the words out. 'Just thinking of her all alone.'

'I know, but maybe it's what she wanted,' Linda said. 'She didn't want a fuss. Didn't want anyone to see her in pain.'

Laura hadn't thought of that. Perhaps Linda was right. That Gertie had wanted to go quietly from the world. But it still made her feel sad. No one should die alone. 'I take it you've phoned Richard?'

'Yes, just got off the phone to him. Poor man. He's already been through enough. First his wife, and now Gertie.'

'Was he okay?' Laura asked. Her heart ached for him, for his loss, despite how angry she still felt. She'd deal with her anger later.

'He was cut up. I could hear it in his voice. He'll be calling in soon, once he's sorted out childcare for Henry.'

Henry. Laura had forgotten about him and about how Gertie's death would affect the bright little boy.

'Listen, I shouldn't really be asking you this, but there was another reason why I called,' Linda said.

'You want me to come in and work an extra shift?' Laura asked, already wondering if she had an ironed uniform at hand.

'No, we're fine. We're not short-staffed,' Linda said. 'You enjoy your day off.

'Thanks for letting me know,' Laura said, before ending the call. She thought about what was happening right now in Richard's home. Was he making Henry breakfast? Had he called Tracey, or Megan to look after Henry? Or, would he take Henry to the home with him? Laura didn't think that he would.

She stared at the clock. It was only twenty past six. So much had already happened and the day had only just begun. She willed herself to be brave. She wasn't sure if she would ever forgive Richard for going behind her back, but right now she needed to do the right thing and help him any way she could. She picked up the phone.

* * *

As promised, Richard phoned Linda when he set off on the short walk to the home. He could have taken the car, but he needed to clear his head, and, if he was being truly honest, he needed a little more time. He had seen dead bodies before, the last being Sally. Although she had looked peaceful and no longer in pain, the woman who he'd seen laid out in the hospital bed had no longer been his wife. He had touched her skin. It had been so cold. Sally had hated the cold and he had wanted to put an extra blanket over her, to keep her warm. That image had lingered in his memory for a long time and it still woke him up in the middle of the night.

He was scared of what would greet him. He wasn't scared of death itself, or of dying, but he was scared of what was left behind. Of what you left behind.

He was so preoccupied with his thoughts that he had forgotten all about Laura, who was walking alongside him, until she spoke.

'How are you?' she asked. 'Sorry, that's a stupid question,' she said with an apologetic shrug. 'You don't need to talk.'

Richard shook his head. 'Sorry, miles away. Just thinking, you know.'

'I know,' Laura replied as she looked ahead and matched his step.

Richard was glad that she wasn't trying to make small talk with him. To fill the silence with endless chatter.

They carried on their way, side by side in silence.

* * *

Linda greeted them at the door with a hug for both of them. Without a word she led them up the stairs towards Gertie's room.

Richard climbed the steps, legs like lead, his heart heavy with unshed grief.

Laura followed, her footsteps echoing on each step.

Richard's heart thumped against his ribcage as he attempted to control his rising anxiety. He'd be okay. It would all be okay. She was at peace now. She'd had a good life. *Just think of that.*

Linda reached the door and paused for a moment, waiting for him to catch up with them. She stepped to one side to allow Richard to enter the room.

He cleared his throat and reached out to touch the handle of the door, the same way he had done hundreds of times before. But his hand shook. He couldn't do it.

'Do you want me to go in first, Richard?' Laura asked, her voice gentle, radiating calm.

He nodded and moved away from the door.

Laura pushed open the door and he followed her in.

'I'll be outside if you need anything,' Linda said.

But Richard didn't hear her. His gaze, his entire focus, was on the woman who lay motionless on the bed.

He could smell death in the room. That smell that cannot be described, that doesn't really have an odour, but a heavy presence that fills the empty space.

He stopped by the end of the bed.

Gertie looked as if she was asleep.

He told himself that she was asleep.

She looked at peace.

He took another step towards the bed. And then another.

Laura had moved over to the corner to sit on the chair.

Another chair had been placed by the side of the bed. Linda most probably had put it there. She was thoughtful like that.

Richard crumpled onto the chair and stared at his gran. The woman who had brought him up, who had never complained, who had taught him to be a man. To be kind and thoughtful and creative and loving.

He wanted to reach out and touch her, but he was scared. Her skin would be cold and he wanted her to be warm.

He took a deep breath and reached out to hold her hand.

He felt the shock in his core that her fingers did not grasp his.

He choked on his tears, bent his head and cried.

He wasn't sure how long he sat and wept. Seconds and minutes passed by, but for him time stood still. He was no longer afraid. He wasn't alone in the room.

Laura sat silently in her chair.

Richard thought of all the good times he'd had with his gran. She would not want him to wallow in grief. If she saw him now, she would be telling him off.

What are you doing, Richard? Why aren't you asking Laura to join you for a coffee?

The thought made him smile. That's what Gertie would want for him.

It was with a heavy heart that he stood and planted a kiss on her forehead. 'I love you, Gran,' he said.

Richard stood and surveyed the room. He would have to arrange to come back and sort out her things. Her books. But that could wait. For now, it didn't matter.

His eyes lingered on the chest of drawers where he spotted a small cardboard box. He didn't recognise it. In fact, he was sure he'd never seen it before.

Laura noticed what he was looking at and went over to it.

On top of the box was a handwritten letter. Gertie's handwriting, which simply said: *Laura, keep his memory alive.*

Richard raised an eyebrow at her. 'What's in the box?' he asked.

Laura hesitated before she answered. Her fingers touched the box gently, stroking the lid.

'They are letters,' Laura said slowly. 'Letters that she wanted me to keep for her. I hope that's okay and—'

Richard cut her off with a shake of his head. 'If it's what she wanted then that's fine with me,' he said. 'We all have our secrets, don't we.'

Laura opened her mouth to say something but closed it again.

Richard could see two envelopes sticking out from under the box. He pulled them free and looked at the writing.

'This one's for you,' he said, handing over the one with *Laura* printed on it.

She took it without a word and shoved it in her bag.

Richard slipped the letter that was addressed to him into his jacket pocket to read when he was alone. 'I'm ready now,' he said. 'To go.'

Laura went to pick up the cardboard box. 'Okay.'

'Please, let me,' Richard said.

She moved aside and he lifted up the box. It was heavier than it looked.

He stood by the end of the bed and looked at his gran once more. A feeling of comfort swept over him and he wasn't sure why.

'I saw her,' he said. His words were directed towards Laura, although he didn't look at her.

'Saw who?' she asked.

'Gertie,' he said. 'Listen, can we talk once we get outside?'

Laura looked at him with a strange expression on her face, but she nodded and followed him out of the room.

CHAPTER THIRTY-TWO

They made it as far as the playground when Richard suggested that they sit down. Laura said it was a good idea that they rest for a while on the bench opposite the swings, and so Richard placed the heavy cardboard box of letters at one end of the bench and they sat down next to each other, both of them staring into the distance, lost in thought.

Laura waited for Richard to speak. He obviously wanted to talk about Gertie, but his body language, and the fact that he wouldn't look at her, suggested that he was finding it hard to formulate the words.

So, she waited.

Eventually, he spoke. His words came out disjointed and he spoke so quietly that she could barely hear him. 'I saw her. I saw Gertie in my room last night. I thought it was a dream, but now . . .'

Laura gasped. What was he saying? That he had seen Gertie's ghost? She didn't believe in ghosts. Once you were gone, you were gone. Ghosts were only for stories. Ghosts could not harm you. Only the living could do that.

'I know what you're thinking,' he said with a shake of his head. 'That I'm mad, that it was only a dream, but it was real.

She was real. She spoke to me.' Richard caught his breath and his next words came out in one great gush. 'She spoke to me and what she said was something that only she would say. It was her. It was real.'

'I don't think you're mad,' Laura told him gently. 'Why would I think that?' she asked. He was a man in the midst of grief. Of intense and raw pain. All she could do was listen to him. Be there for him. Allow him to talk and get those feelings out in the open. Off his chest.

Richard shook his head. 'Because I'm telling you that my gran, who died—' he stopped for a moment and rubbed his neck — 'who died in the early hours of the morning, visited me at gone five this morning. She sat on the edge of my bed and I could see her as clearly as I can see you now, and she told me . . . well, it doesn't matter what she told me. She told me something and then she kissed me, and then she was gone.'

'Oh, Richard,' Laura said. She stopped herself from reaching out to him. Stopped herself from placing a comforting hand on his, or touching his shoulder. Some people didn't like to be touched. She didn't know him well enough. She placed her hands over her bag which was on her lap. 'I just think that must be so comforting for you. That you saw her.'

Richard turned to face her. 'Really? You believe that?'

Laura nodded and shifted closer to him on the bench. 'If you saw her and it gives you comfort, then that's a good thing, isn't it? That's all that matters.'

Richard stared at her for a moment, as if trying to read her mind, before he looked away and shrugged. 'Yes, I suppose you're right. It doesn't matter if it was real or not. All that matters is that it was real to me, that she was there and told me . . .' His words trailed off.

Laura hoped that whatever Gertie had told him would bring him much comfort in the weeks and months to come.

Richard turned his attention to the box at the end of the bench. He stared at it for several seconds before he spoke. 'Do you mind me asking who the letters are from?'

She looked at the box.

'Are they letters from my grandfather? I never met him, but she spoke about Robbie a lot.'

Laura stared at the cardboard box and bit her tongue. She couldn't tell him the whole truth. Gertie had confided in her. Had trusted her. This was Gertie's story to tell, not hers, and she didn't have her permission. So, she chose her words carefully, only telling him a half truth. She told herself she wasn't lying.

'There *are* letters from your grandfather,' she said slowly, before adding, 'but there are other letters. Private letters that she wanted me to have for safekeeping. I'm not sure if she would want you to read them.' Laura opened her bag and pulled out the letter that Gertie had left in the bedroom. 'I'll read this and then maybe I'll know more, but I'll read it when I get home. If that's all right with you.'

'Of course,' Richard said. 'I don't want to make you feel uncomfortable and for what it's worth, I'm very sorry about my behaviour yesterday.'

Laura's smile was tinged with sadness. 'I don't think any of that matters now, do you?'

'Yes,' Richard said. 'It does matter. I should never have gone behind your back. I don't usually act in that way—'

'Richard, let's forget about it, move on.' Laura needed that more than anything. She'd been dwelling in the past for far too long. Her conversation with Lottie had opened the floodgates, made her confront her past in a way she'd never done before. 'It's what Gertie would have wanted,' she added.

He coughed and stretched his long legs out in front of him. 'Thank you,' he said, 'and for this. For being with me. It helps.'

'I'm glad it helps. To be honest, you're helping me too. I know I've only been here a short time, but I really felt like I knew her. She was more of a friend to me than many of my old friends back home.'

Richard turned his full attention on her and nodded. 'She had that effect on people. She put you at your ease and was easy to talk to. She was so clever, so bloody clever, but she never made anyone feel stupid. She treated everyone as an equal.'

'She did.' Laura nodded. 'She was a wonderful woman.'

The quiet of the moment was disturbed by the squealing of excitement coming from a toddler running into the playground, followed by his young mother, yelling at him to slow down.

The boy ran over to the little climbing frame and began to slowly and tentatively climb, even though it was only three rungs high.

The mother stopped dead still at the sight of Richard and Laura. Her face was an expression of pure confusion at seeing the local teacher sitting in a playground with a strange woman, a cardboard box, and without any children. Her expression of confusion slowly turned to one of embarrassment as she realised she had been blatantly staring at them.

Richard nodded in acknowledgement. Laura smiled.

The mother looked away.

'Do you know her?' Laura asked.

'Yes, her eldest son is in my class. She is probably wondering why I am here when I should be at school.'

'Do you want to go?' Laura asked.

'Yes,' he said. He stood and picked up the cardboard box.

* * *

Laura made them each a cup of tea which she placed on the kitchen table along with the biscuit tin. She knew that neither the tea, nor the biscuits, would be touched, but she went through the ritual anyway. It made her feel calm and in control while giving Richard that sense of normality and the time he needed to process what had happened. Sometimes the simple things helped in getting through the hardest of times.

Laura sat down and placed her hands around the mug.

'I won't stop long. I need to get back to Henry,' he said.

'I know,' she said. But she wanted to give him the chance to breathe, to have a moment before he ventured back home to noise and movement and doing things. He needed this little bit of time. 'Thank you for carrying the box for me.'

'No problem. It was the least I could do.'

'Listen, I know it's early days, but if you need any help with the funeral, just ask. It's no bother,' Laura said, hoping that she hadn't offended him. He had Tracey and Megan who would help him, but she felt the need to also offer her help.

'Thank you, that's kind, but I'll be okay.'

Richard continued to stare at his tea, making no attempt to pick it up.

Laura thought about putting the radio on for a bit of background noise, but thought better of it. It would come across as insensitive.

'Things will be different now, won't they?' Richard said, looking up from the table.

Laura wondered what he was referring to but nodded in agreement anyway. Did he mean life without Gertie in it? Not going to the home?

'Life will be so strange without her. She was the only mother I knew. She brought me up, asked for nothing in return.' He stopped to wipe his eyes with the back of his sleeve, turning his face so that Laura wouldn't see him.

She got up and pulled a sheet of kitchen roll from the dispenser, silently passing it to him.

He took it and thanked her.

Laura sat back down. She wanted to give him a hug. This big man was breaking before her and she didn't know what to do.

'I'm sorry,' he mumbled as he shoved the kitchen roll into his pocket. 'I think I should go. I need to be with Henry.'

'Of course,' she said, standing up.

She followed him to the front door.

'Please let me know if I can do anything. If you need help in sorting out her things, then just ask.'

'Thank you. That would be a huge help.' He smiled and touched her on the arm. 'Thank you again.'

'No problem.' Laura hesitated for a fraction of a second, before leaning forward and kissing him on the cheek.

If Richard was surprised, he didn't show it. His jaw remained clenched and he smiled his lop-sided smile. He studied her face for a few seconds, as if weighing up if he should say out loud what was on his mind. 'So, I won't be seeing as much of you now, as I won't be visiting the home.'

Laura swallowed and fought back her own tears. She forced a smile. 'You can always call round here for a chat or a cup of tea. Anytime. I'm a good listener.'

'I might well do that,' Richard said before opening the door. He stepped outside and without looking back he walked down the path.

Laura slowly closed the door behind him and rested her forehead against it. She would miss him. She needed to see him again. And it had nothing to do with the promise she had made to Gertie.

* * *

Later that night, Laura sat in bed with Gertie's note clutched in her hand. She had summoned up the courage to open the envelope, but she now needed more courage to read the contents. This would be their last connection. Once read, she could never go back and read it for the first time again.

She took a deep breath and unfurled the pages, smoothing them out on her lap. She began to read.

To my Laura,

From the very first day you walked into the day room and into my life, I knew that you were special and that you would change my and Richard's life. I wasn't wrong, was I? When I told you that I had seen the future, and that you would be with Richard, I could tell that you didn't believe me and that you still don't, but that doesn't matter now, love. Just look after yourself. Remember you are young, you are loved,

you're worth it. Be happy, live your life to the absolute fullest,
and know that my grandson will always be there for you, as
you will always be there for him.
   Your friend,
   Gertie.

The tears came then. Laura let them fall as she wept for her friend and the grandmother she never had.

* * *

On the other side of the village, Richard sat alone in his living room. Henry was safely tucked up in bed. Tracey and Megan and Jack had all offered to stay with him, telling him that he shouldn't be alone at a time like this, but he had told them that he was fine. That he preferred to be alone and that if he needed anything, he would call.

Tracey had taken the most persuading and in the end Richard nearly had to push her out the door, but she had gone with the promise that she would be round first thing in the morning to help Henry get ready for preschool. Richard didn't have any fight left in him to protest, so he simply agreed. But he didn't need any help. The school had given him two weeks' leave and more if he needed it. So all he had to do in the morning was focus on Henry, and that's what he needed. A reason for getting up and getting on with things. As the saying went, *life goes on*, and Gertie would want him to carry on. She had told him as much, hadn't she?

The Tupperware dish that contained chicken curry was in the microwave, where he had heated it up half an hour earlier. Now the smell of curry filled the whole room, but Richard had no appetite to eat. So, he left it cooling. He would put it back in the fridge for tomorrow.

Richard hadn't bothered to turn on any lamps, so now he sat in the dark. The only light in the room came drifting in from the lone street light outside. He couldn't even face watching the rolling news, which was how he spent most nights. What was the point? He couldn't concentrate on anything.

Tracey had tried to strike up a conversation with him on his return from Laura's, but had quickly given up due to his monosyllabic responses. Instead, she had ushered him into the living room to sit with Megan and Henry while she made endless cups of tea.

He had never quite worked out the link between tea and bad news. That somehow tea could solve everything. If only.

So he had spent most of his day making small talk and keeping Henry entertained. It had been draining, and now, as he sat on his recliner in the dark, he knew that sleep would not come, despite feeling tired to the bone.

His chest ached, that visceral all-consuming pain in his bones and muscles and heart. That ache, which made it hard to breathe. That's what he felt right now. The physical pain of losing Gertie, the only mother he had known, and he didn't know what to do with that pain.

If he was being honest with himself, it took him right back to losing Sally. The pain he felt now mingled with the pain of the past and intensified it somehow.

Breathe. Just breathe and you will get through this.

He had to get through this pain. He had Henry. He had responsibilities. He had done it before and he would do it again.

He needed to focus on the positives. He needed to think about only the good things. The full life she had lived. The fun times they had spent together when he was a little boy. Her laughter, her warmth, her smile, her courage, her love.

All now gone.

This was no good. He shouldn't be sitting here in the dark. Wallowing. No good would come of that.

It was then that Richard remembered the letter, the one he had found in Gertie's room under the cardboard box. The one which he had shoved into his jacket pocket. He pushed himself up and out of the chair, and went to retrieve it from where he had hung his jacket on the hook in the hall.

Richard paused at the bottom of the stairs. He listened for signs of life upstairs. All was quiet. Henry had quickly settled, but he would go and check on him again in a little bit. Make sure he was still asleep. He still wasn't sure how Henry would cope with Gertie's death. He had been quiet all day. How did any child cope? All Richard could compare it to was losing his own mum and dad, but he had been so young and he couldn't remember them. It would be different for Henry. He would remember his gran, and Richard wanted those memories to help his son. He needed to find photographs of the two of them: Gertie and Henry on a day trip to the farm, celebrating Christmas, reading a story together, when Gertie had come to Sunday lunch. They were all images that he had posted online. He would print them all off. Make an album for his son to keep for ever. Richard wanted these memories to stay fresh for his little boy, as he did for himself.

He made his way back to the living room and flicked on the table lamp. He lowered himself down onto the recliner.

What have you got to tell me, Gertie?

He opened the envelope, pulled out the letter and blinked in surprise, his heart hammering in his chest. There was another letter, one she'd left for safekeeping in the care home's safe. A letter, she told him, that would explain everything.

CHAPTER THIRTY-THREE

Life carried on as normal in Buttermarsh. The seconds, minutes and days passed by. Laura had worked every day since the news of Gertie's death and she was glad of that. She needed to be busy, to care for others so that she had no time to think about herself. Every day she had arrived at work early and stayed long after her shift had ended. When she eventually made it home, she was so exhausted that she didn't even bother to eat. Just a quick shower and straight to bed.

Gertie's death had stirred up emotions in her that she'd thought had long been buried deep. Feelings of guilt, inadequacy and the feeling that she should have done more. Listened more. Every time she passed the closed door of Gertie's room she stopped for a moment, placed her palm on the smooth wood and said goodbye to her. Her hand touching the very spot where Gertie's photograph had been, the photograph Richard now carried in his wallet. she told her that she would keep her promise. On one occasion, Cerrie had been passing by and had stopped to watch what she was doing. Laura had just shrugged, said nothing, and to her relief Cerrie hadn't probed any further. Perhaps she'd understood.

Laura made her way to the staffroom for her mid-morning break. She normally wouldn't have bothered to go to the staffroom, preferring instead to spend the time with Gertie over a cup of tea and a packet of custard creams. But Gertie was no longer here.

Laura pushed open the staffroom door and was greeted by the smell of fresh coffee and burnt toast. Linda was buttering two slices of thick toast but turned around when she heard the creak of the door.

'Hello, Laura. Do you want me to pop some toast on for you?'

'No, don't worry. You sit down.' She walked over to join Linda by the toaster. 'I'll make some toast.'

Linda smiled, picked up her plate and cup of coffee, and sat down on one of the fabric-covered armchairs that had seen better days.

'How are you getting on? Is everything okay?' Linda asked.

Laura didn't turn around. She dropped the bread into the toaster and then poured herself a cup of coffee as she spoke.

'I'm fine, you know. It's just a bit strange without Gertie here.' She turned around to look at Linda. 'It must be very strange for you too. You knew her such a long time.'

'I did, and Richard, too, of course, and Henry. It'll be strange without them, but we carry on, don't we?'

Laura nodded, turning back around to check on the progress of her toast. It would be strange without Richard. She'd miss seeing him. Did miss him. He stirred up feelings in her she hadn't felt in a very long time and she wasn't quite sure if she wanted to acknowledge them. She shoved the thought aside. 'What about you?' she asked Linda. 'How are you coping?'

Linda had been working as stand-in manager since Hazel had been dismissed, and Laura knew that Linda really didn't want the role. She had only taken it as she had the most experience and was the longest-serving member of staff. Plus, she didn't have a choice.

Linda offered Laura a wry smile. 'Actually, that's what I need to chat to you about.'

Laura was in the middle of buttering her toast but stopped, spinning around to face Linda. 'What do you mean?'

'Bring your coffee and toast over here, and I'll tell you.' Linda patted the chair next to her. When Laura had sat down, Linda removed an envelope from her tunic pocket. 'I've been meaning to give this to you, but I was waiting for the right moment,' she said. 'Now seems like the right time.'

Laura froze. This was what you got for not being honest with people. She shouldn't have tried to hide her past work experience and qualifications. It had obviously backfired on her and this was her notice. What was she going to do now? She had a bit of money saved, but she couldn't stay in Buttermarsh if she had no job.

Linda smiled and waved the envelope at her. 'Well, aren't you going to take it?'

Laura just stared at the envelope. Surely Linda wouldn't taunt her like this if she was about to sack her?

Linda thrust the envelope towards her. Laura took it with trembling hands. She slowly opened it . . . and read the words.

'Well, what do you say?' Linda asked.

Laura had to read the letter twice, making sure that she hadn't misunderstood what it was telling her. The manager's role was hers if she wanted it. She couldn't believe it. 'I don't understand . . .'

'What do you mean? There's nothing to understand. If you want the manager's job, then it's yours.'

'You don't want it?'

'You know I don't,' Linda said, with a sad smile. 'If I was twenty years younger then maybe, but not now. I want to spend more time with the grandkids, and anyway, in less than a year I'll be heading for retirement. It needs to go to someone younger. Someone who is passionate about caring for elderly people. Someone who has vision and can lead. And that person is you.'

'I don't know what to say,' Laura said. She tried to hide her blush. This was all such a shock. 'I haven't been here that long. It doesn't seem fair.'

'Listen,' Linda said with a wag of her finger. 'It doesn't matter how long you have been here. All that matters is that you're the best person for the job. And to be honest, we're all rooting for you.'

Everyone was rooting for her? 'Really?' Laura said, unable to hide her shock. 'You think I should accept?'

'Of course you should!' Linda said, patting her on the hand. 'Whyever not? But you need to think about it. Take your time and let me know. The big boss said you can have a week to let me know your decision.'

Laura nodded and slipped the letter into her tunic pocket. She had moved to Buttermarsh to escape the past, to create a new life, and she had managed to do that in such a short amount of time. Work was good. She enjoyed working at Cedar House. So why not be the manager? What was there to stop her? She could do the job with her eyes closed. But she didn't want to rush into anything. She needed to think carefully about this. Taking the job would mean that Buttermarsh would become her permanent home, not just the village she had escaped to. So, she would need to think about it. She told Linda that she would let her know by early next week.

Linda smiled and sipped her coffee.

* * *

Linda had left the staffroom to take care of some phone calls, leaving Laura alone with her thoughts. Not for the first time that week, she couldn't help but think that she had let Gertie down. She had hardly spoken to Richard, apart from the two times he had called her for a quick chat on the phone. Their conversations had been professional, about matters to do with the home. As Laura took a final bite of her toast and washed it down with the cold dregs of coffee, she knew in her heart

263

that she hadn't been a good friend to him. She needed to try harder. To make more of an effort. She liked Richard and it was only now that Gertie wasn't around that she realised how much she missed him. He had slowly become a part of her life, so slowly in fact that she hadn't realised how important he would be until he was gone.

Sitting alone in the staffroom, Laura had the sudden urge to phone him. To tell him that she had been offered the job, to share her news with him. To hear his voice. He would be at home as he was still on bereavement leave, so he would be able to take the call.

Laura jumped up and went over to the staff lockers to retrieve her mobile. She quickly scrolled to his number and pressed call before she could change her mind.

'Hello.' Richard answered the call after only one ring.

'Hi, Richard, it's Laura.'

'Oh, hello. Everything okay?'

Laura could hear music in the background — it sounded like the theme tune from a children's programme. Henry must be at home.

'One minute,' Richard said.

She heard footsteps and the closing of a door. The music faded away.

'Sorry about that. Henry is with me today.'

'Oh, I'm sorry to bother you.' She shouldn't have phoned him. He was obviously busy.

'It's no bother. It's actually nice to hear another adult voice.' Richard laughed. 'Did you want to ask me something? Is it about Gertie's room? I can pop in tomorrow and sort out the room if you like? It's just that . . .' He paused and cleared his throat. 'Are you in work tomorrow? It's just that I wondered if you might not mind giving me a hand?'

Laura felt a pang of sympathy. She was sad that he felt so awkward about having to ask her. 'Of course, I'll help you. I'm actually off tomorrow, but I don't mind.'

'Oh, I can't ask you to help me on your day off.'

'No, it's no problem at all. Probably easier when I'm not on shift, to be honest. It'll give me more time.'

Richard hesitated before he finally spoke. 'Well, as long as you're sure.'

'I am,' Laura said. 'I hope you don't mind, but I wanted to sort through her books. I was wondering about setting up a library in Gertie's honour, what with her love of reading. She has a lot of books and I was wondering . . .' She cleared her throat, unsure if she was making a mistake. 'Well, if you would donate some of her books?'

Richard's reply came quick and fast. She heard his smile. 'I love that idea. It's what she would have wanted.'

'I'm so glad you like the idea,' Laura said with a sigh of relief. 'But actually, that's not why I phoned you.'

'Oh, I'm sorry. I just assumed.'

Laura laughed. 'Don't worry. It's just that I wanted to share some good news with you. Well, I think it's good news. I 've been offered the position of Manager and I think I'll take it.'

'That's absolutely brilliant, Laura. I can't think of anyone better for the job.'

Richard sounded genuinely pleased for her.

'But why do you need to think about it?' he asked gently. 'Surely you'll accept?'

'I think I will, but I just need time to process it. It's come as a bit of a shock,' she said.

'Well, I'm happy for you, and I think that the residents of Cedar House will be happy for you too,' he said.

'Anyway, enough about me, how are you?' Laura asked. She expected the standard, *I'm fine*, so was surprised when Richard spoke slowly and with honesty.

'I'm coping, but it is so very odd with her not in my life. It takes time, doesn't it?'

'Yes, it does,' she said. 'Time is the great healer, so they say, but I don't think that is true.'

'Me neither,' Richard said.

'Anyway, I'd better go. My break's nearly over.' Laura stood up to rub the small of her back.

'Okay, I won't keep you,' Richard said. 'Oh, before I forget, the undertakers called me earlier and the funeral will take place next Friday, so if you want to, well, you know . . .'

'I'll be there, Richard. Of course I will. If you need anything you know you just need to ask.'

'I know,' he said softly.

Laura listened to his breathing down the phone, wishing she could see him, give him a friendly hug. Tell him it would all be all right. It was all so difficult when on the phone.

'I'll see you tomorrow then,' he said.

For a moment Laura had forgotten that they had arranged to sort out Gertie's room. 'Oh, yes, I'll meet you here. What time is good for you?'

'Would ten o'clock be okay?'

'Perfect. See you then.'

'Yes, see you tomorrow.'

'Bye,' Laura said, and ended the call.

* * *

Laura followed Linda to the home's front door as they finished their shifts and both waved goodbye to Adrian who was in charge of the night shift.

Linda shoved her hat on. 'Any problems you can give me a call, okay? You can phone me any time.'

'Will do,' Adrian said. 'But I think we'll be okay.'

'I'm sure you will,' Linda said. They walked out of the door into the cold night air.

'Right, well, I'm off home for a spag bol and a soak in the bath,' Linda said.

'Sounds like a plan.' Laura wondered what she was going to do with the rest of her evening.

Linda said goodbye and was about to step away when she stopped. 'Ooh, look who it is,' she said.

Laura turned in Linda's direction and saw Richard striding towards them, hands shoved deep into his pockets, a scarf wound around his neck. His dark curls were poking out of his hat.

Laura's breath caught in her throat.

'I'll leave you to it. See you tomorrow,' Linda said. Richard was closer now. 'Hello, Richard. I'm in a rush, but I'll see you tomorrow,' she said, stepping past him on her way down the path.

Richard wished her goodnight and turned his full attention on Laura. She'd folded her arms across her chest, resisting the urge to reach out and hug him. What was he doing here?

'Everything okay?' she asked. Perhaps he wanted to make a start on Gertie's room? She didn't mind helping him if he did.

Richard smiled. He looked down at his feet before looking back at her, taking a deep breath and thrusting his hands deeper into his pockets. When he spoke, his voice shook with nerves.

'Do you want to go for that drink?'

CHAPTER THIRTY-FOUR

Six months later

August soon came around and Buttermarsh looked completely different in the summer months. The lanes were now full of wildlife, with colourful butterflies fluttering in and out of the hedgerows, followed by the fluffy, buzzing bumblebees. Locals enjoyed a potter around the lanes and a trip to the Cottage Bun before heading back to their homes. The children played in the safety of the playground, and the rose garden in Cedar House care home was full of red, yellow and pink roses, surrounded by wild lavender. The air smelled sweet, people were happy and the sun shone. It was like a scene from a country-life magazine.

Laura still couldn't believe how lucky she was to live and work in this friendly, close-knit community, where everyone looked out for each other. Hazel was now part of that community. Sue had given her a job at the Cottage Bun and she made a surprisingly good latte. Given time, Laura hoped they could be friends. If someone had told her six months ago that she would still be working at the home, and that she would be the manager of that home, and that she was surrounded by people who loved and cared for her, then she would have laughed at them and told them they were mad.

But that was her reality now.

She had been incredibly lucky. *Was* incredibly lucky.

She had been able to extend the six-month lease on the cottage, with the owner only too happy to rent it out on a long-term basis to a local, and a nurse at that. Laura had grown to love Church View Cottage and now really did consider it home.

Lottie and her kids visited her regularly and enjoyed the odd weekend with her. Laura's mother had also visited for a long weekend and had been delighted to see her daughter finally settled and living life. When Laura had taken Maureen to the Cottage Bun, Sue had been so happy to see mother and daughter reunited that she'd given them a huge box of cakes to take home in celebration.

So Laura spent her days at the home and her days off catching up with her chores and reading. Nothing much had changed in that respect, but she now had friends. She also had Richard in her life.

* * *

Laura was determined to keep her promise to Gertie. In the quiet hours she'd sit and read Gertie's letters, the ones from Jim. She hadn't read them all yet, but she would, just as she'd honour her promise to keep Jim's memory alive. She wouldn't forget what this man had meant to Gertie, just as she would never forget Mark. He'd been a huge part of her life, but a new chapter was beginning. A new life and she was more than ready to move on and live it.

Life was good.

During the long summer evenings, Richard told her and Henry stories about Gertie and her past. They both wanted Henry to remember his gran. Richard told his son the stories she used to tell him as a little boy, about her love of books and life. Henry would listen, mesmerised, soaking up the words, as if saving them to memory.

Laura and Richard decided to take things slowly. Partly for Henry's sake, but also because they were both in counselling. They needed to heal themselves before they could think of any future together. But Laura knew that it would only be a matter of time.

It would happen.

* * *

Richard kissed Henry goodnight and padded back downstairs to the warmth of the kitchen where Laura was sitting, a paperback open on the kitchen table next to a cup of coffee and photographs of Gertie when she was younger. He sat down next to her and picked up the nearest photo.

The photo had been taken in the back garden of the house he had grown up in. The house he was in now. He couldn't remember who had taken the photograph, but he remembered that day as if it had been yesterday. They had spent the afternoon in the garden, sprawled out on blankets, reading and drinking ice-cold lemonade. In the photograph, Gertie had her arm around his narrow shoulders. He must have only been about six or seven. Her face was pressed close to his. Both of them were smiling at the camera. She looked so young, was Richard's first thought. So young and happy, as if she didn't have a care in the world. But she had lost her son and daughter-in-law in the most tragic of circumstances. Yet she had carried on. Kept smiling. She had been a remarkable woman.

'A penny for them,' Laura said gently, as she placed her hand on his.

Richard squeezed her fingers. Smiling, he shook his head. 'Just thinking.'

'You know,' Laura said, 'if it wasn't for her, then we would never have met. Isn't that strange?'

Richard smiled at her and winked. 'Oh, I don't know. If Gertie was here now, then she would tell us that fate always finds a way.'

Laura nodded. 'Yes, I suppose that's true,' she said with a smile. 'Fate always finds a way.'

Richard thought about the note that was burning a hole in his wallet. The one he'd found in the safe. He would carry it with him always, wherever he went. The note written by Gertie that told him he would meet Laura, a young woman from the city, who wore bright-yellow wellies, loved jelly babies and who had lost her husband in tragic circumstances. A woman who was a nurse. A woman who needed him, just as much as he would need her. In the note, Gertie told him to be patient — that they would both need time to heal — but that second chances of happiness did happen and that Laura was his second chance, as he was hers.

The letter had been written two years ago. Gertie had dated it, sealed it with a wax seal and had put it in the care home's safe for safekeeping. It hadn't been touched since. Linda had verified this. She had been the signed witness and had placed it in there, alongside letters for Henry as he grew, for when Nana Gertie was no longer around.

He had yet to tell Laura of the letter's existence. He wasn't sure if he ever would.

He looked at Laura and felt the love in his heart. He smiled around the lump forming in his throat and thought, *Yes, Gran. Fate found a way.*

THE END

ACKNOWLEDGEMENTS

Once again, thank you dear reader for taking a chance on this book. I do hope you enjoyed Laura and Richard's story. As ever, this still feels like a dream come true, that I get to write stories while sitting in my kitchen drinking coffee.

Thank you to my lovely editor, Sarah Pursey, who just gets me and brings out the best in me. I loved working with you and hope we will work together again.

Thank you to the Choc Lit/Joffe team, and in particular Jasmine Callaghan for her help and understanding this year after the passing of my stepdad, Scotty. Her kindness and understanding made all the difference.

Thank you to the very talented cover designer.

Thank you to the Tasting Panel for giving the thumbs-up and for their constructive feedback. As ever it is much appreciated and valued.

I wouldn't be able to write without music. During the writing of this book I listened mainly to Taylor Swift and James Taylor on repeat.

Finally, thank you Andrew, especially for not saying anything when the kitchen island becomes my writing desk. I love you.

THE CHOC LIT STORY

Established in 2009, Choc Lit is an independent, award-winning publisher dedicated to creating a delicious selection of quality women's fiction.

We have won 18 awards, including Publisher of the Year and the Romantic Novel of the Year, and have been shortlisted for countless others. In 2023, we were shortlisted for Publisher of the Year by the Romantic Novelists' Association.

All our novels are selected by genuine readers. We are proud to publish talented first-time authors, as well as established writers whose books we love introducing to a new generation of readers.

In 2023, we became a Joffe Books company. Best known for publishing a wide range of commercial fiction, Joffe Books has its roots in women's fiction. Today it is one of the largest independent publishers in the UK.

We love to hear from you, so please email us about absolutely anything bookish at choc-lit@joffebooks.com

If you want to hear about all our bargain new releases, join our mailing list: www.choc-lit.com/contact